Acclaim for Joshua Furst's

The Sabotage Café

A *Chicago Tribune* and *Rocky Mountain News* Best Book of the Year

"*The Sabotage Café* is hard-core—tough, uncompromising, and utterly brilliant." —*The Buffalo News*

"The gritty world of riot, rebellion, alienation, and despair is perfectly rendered." —*The Boston Globe*

"Julia's struggle to do the right thing in spite of illness and in spite of— and sometimes with—her husband's help is utterly captivating." —*Rocky Mountain News*

"Furst understands the frustrations and fears of furious, confused teens; Cheryl's insecurity and moodiness feel familiar to anyone who has ever been a teenage girl." —*Chicago Tribune*

"At once poignant and dreamlike." —*Time Out New York*

"Original. . . . [Furst] is able to capture distraught teens and confused parents in an affecting and unaffected way." —*Blueprint* magazine

Joshua Furst

The Sabotage Café

Joshua Furst is a graduate of the Iowa Writers'
Workshop and has been the recipient of a
Michener Fellowship, the *Chicago Tribune*'s
Nelson Algren Award, and fellowships from
The MacDowell Colony and Ledig House. He
lives in New York City.

ALSO BY JOSHUA FURST

Short People

The Sabotage Café

The Sabotage Café

JOSHUA FURST

Vintage Contemporaries
Vintage Books
A Division of Random House, Inc.
New York

FIRST VINTAGE CONTEMPORARIES EDITION, JULY 2008

All rights reserved. Published in the United States by Vintage Books, a division of
Random House, Inc., New York, and in Canada by Random House of Canada
Limited, Toronto. Originally published in hardcover in the United States by
Alfred A. Knopf, a division of Random House, Inc., New York, in 2007.

Vintage and colophon are registered trademarks and
Vintage Contemporaries is a trademark of Random House, Inc.

The Library of Congress has cataloged the Knopf edition as follows:
Furst, Joshua.
The sabotage café / Joshua Furst.—1st ed.
p. cm.
1. Mothers and daughters—Fiction. 2. Minneapolis (Minn.)—Fiction. I. Title.
PS3606.U78S24 2007
813'.6—dc22 2007009775

Vintage ISBN: 978-0-375-71408-5

Book design by Wesley Gott

www.vintagebooks.com

Printed in the United States of America
10 9 8 7 6 5 4 3 2 1

For Janet, again

I'm a blank spot in a hectic civilization. I'm a dark smudge in the air that dissipates without notice. I feel like a window, maybe a broken window. I am a glass human. I am a glass human disappearing in rain. I am standing among you waving my invisible arms and hands. I am shouting my invisible words. I am growing weary. I am growing tired. I am waving to you from here. I am crawling around looking for the aperture of complete and final emptiness. I am vibrating in isolation among you. I am screaming but it comes out like pieces of clear ice. I am signaling that the volume of all this is too high. I am waving. I am waving my hands. I am disappearing. I am disappearing but not fast enough.

—DAVID WOJNAROWICZ

The passion for destruction is a creative passion too.

—MIKHAIL BAKUNIN

I

See Ya

One

THESE THINGS ARE HARD TO SAY. I'm not sure what's true and what isn't. My experiences don't even make sense to me, so I can't imagine they'll make sense to anyone else. What I can promise is that I'll be sincere.

Here's what I know:

On May 24, 2004, my daughter, Cheryl, locked her bedroom door and blasted the angriest, most frantic hardcore she owned. She changed out of her little pink and green bikini into a pair of black cutoff cargoes and a t-shirt she'd worn so hard that the fabric had begun to disintegrate and the Tori Amos tour dates on the back had cracked and flaked into a ruin of crusty nubs. Then she stuffed a pair of jeans, two more ratty t-shirts, a red hooded sweatshirt, a bra and a handful of panties into her backpack. She zipped her Discman—that embarrassing outdated device which we'd refused to upgrade to an iPod—into the pack's front pocket, grabbed a case of CDs off the dresser and scanned the room, wondering what else she'd regret leaving behind.

If she'd glanced out the window, she would have seen me, still in my bathing suit, sitting in the Adirondack chair on the deck Robert had built around the pool. The glass of Crystal Light was still cradled in my lap, but I hadn't sipped from it since she'd run inside. My eyes were closed to help me concentrate. If she'd bothered to look, she would have seen that I'd managed to remain calm despite her tantrum.

She didn't look, though. She fished a half-empty bottle of spring water out from under her bed, dropped her cell phone in the pocket of her shorts and balled the cord into her backpack, then laced up the Doc Martens she'd spent so many hours defacing with Wite-Out and silver paint. She pounded the off button on the clock radio, grabbed the Camel Lights she thought I didn't know about and left.

On her way down the hall, she ducked into the bathroom to grab a handful of tampons. Then, pausing in the kitchen, she stood like a ghost at the sliding door, one hand lightly pressed against the fluttering screen, her fingers curling slowly in on themselves.

What she was doing was cursing my existence.

When I opened my eyes and peeked toward the house, I saw her in the living room walking away from me. Her shoulders were hunched, her pack covered in graffiti and safety-pin starbursts. The fuzzy scruff of her hair glowed white as the glass door hissed shut behind her.

"Where you off to?" I called. "Cheryl?"

By the time I'd made it to the front yard behind her, she was clomping down the middle of the street, nearing the corner where Jonquil Court opens onto Jonquil Way, angling south, headed toward East Fish Lake Road. She wasn't running. She wasn't even walking all that quickly.

"Wait a sec, Cheryl. When will you be home?"

As she hit the far curb, she picked up her pace.

"Cheryl!"

My weight is a problem. I walk slow. I get tired. But I tried to follow as best I could.

Our neighborhood only has so many streets and all of them loop around to Hemlock Lane, the road no one lives on, the one that links our cell to the rest of Plymouth and connects us to the highways and superstores. Pausing there to catch my breath, I leaned on a tree, barely more than a sapling, held upright by wooden rods and wires. It gave slightly under me but didn't fall.

"As your mother, I'm saying stop. Now, stop. I can't go any further."

And she did. She stopped. She turned and glared at me. "Then quit following me, Mom. Jesus!"

A gray sedan, its headlights on despite the sun, slowed and turned the corner. The driver was a woman I knew from the neighborhood. Mrs. Konrad. She dressed her dachshund in stupid little sweaters and when she was out walking with it in the morning, she'd peer around haughtily, making sure everyone saw her from their windows and understood what an exemplary citizen she was. We avoided each other. She wasn't my people.

"You know?" Cheryl said, once the car was gone. She held an emptiness between her open palms, and when I didn't answer, she shoved it toward me like I was supposed to know how to catch it. Then she turned her back on me.

All I could do was watch her recede, running now, her backpack bouncing against her shoulder, her shorts slipping in increments down her hips. She was pulling away, willing herself toward a place—any place—where I'd no longer be able to infect her. She dipped into the ditch along the edge of the road and all I could see was her shoulders, her head. Then she was up again, crunching through gravel, running with traffic, pacing herself to veer and lunge through it. Across six lanes and she was still running, slower now, jogging. She landed wrong on her heel, almost collapsed. Her knee buckled, and then snapped back into place, but she shook it off, kept going, ran toward the highway, raced across intersection after inter-section, not looking, not caring if she got hit. At the cloverleaf she turned down under the entrance ramp and disappeared into the shadows below I-169.

From there she forged through the waist-high crabgrass and leapt into the dry culvert where her skater friends hung out, followed it, not really sure where she was going, away from me, further away from me. Names had been sprayed across the culvert's rough surface, crude hearts and curses and dripping phalluses. She took a swig of water and slowed her pace.

First standing, then leaning against the green power box jammed into the edge of the block, I waited on the corner and gazed off at the place she no longer was, past this place, trying, still, struggling to keep up.

She walked through the trash, through bleached chip bags and ziplocks and faded beer cans, hunks of pink deteriorating Styrofoam, shards of glass and scraps of colorful plastic, twisted rags, broken mops, petrified children's briefs. She walked through tunnels that took her under access roads, then up, eventually, miles from home. She followed a chain-link fence past loading docks, past the whitewashed backsides of unfriendly box stores, Family Dollar, Kmart, Menards, Staples, an AMC 16 Multiplex. And when Plymouth finally bled into New Hope and the fence veered north, she pulled herself over it and dropped the twelve feet to the other side. She needed to hew east. Away from the sun.

Padding through the New Hope Village Green Golf Course, she nabbed a ball she found submerged in the rough. A lawn mower had sliced a smile in its casing. Taking a running start, she whipped it sidearm at the clubhouse up the hill in hopes of breaking a window. The ball didn't even make it to the next hole. She found another one and tried again. Then, laughing, she gave up. There'd be things to break later.

Back on the corner, I continued my vigil. I lowered myself to the ground and sat, my legs out straight in front of me on the grass. I waited.

Rush hour had finally trickled out to us. I could just imagine what my neighbors streaming past must have been thinking: *That freaky fat woman's on the loose again and this time she's wearing a swimsuit.* It probably pleased them to see me like this, confirmed their beliefs, gave them more evidence against me. One of the cars would eventually be Robert, and when it was, he'd stop and he'd take me home. I'd have to come up with something to tell him then. Right now, though, he was still at the office, working late—or more likely, staying late, trolling Westlaw for reasons to stay later. I couldn't rely on him for a thing.

As the sun set and the shadows compounded, I kept thinking I saw her coming back to me. But no. Each time, it was a squirrel, a crow, a shift in the darkness brought on by a turning car. It was always something else, never her.

Around ten thirty, the temperature dropped and I started to shiver and my bones began to bounce. There was nothing else I could do. I hobbled home.

And Cheryl kept moving. Every step she took was one more away from me, but however far she walked, she couldn't escape. I lived inside her, just as she lives inside me. In the distance, she could make out downtown Minneapolis: skyscrapers, looming pink; the silence of city lights. As good a place as any to try to become lost.

Plus, she already sort of knew her way around.

Two

I SHOULD EXPLAIN what Cheryl was like before she left, and how we ended up living in Plymouth. To do that, I have to go back to Willmar, the town out in Middle-of-Nowhere, Minnesota, where I was born and where I grew up. I have to talk about my sister, Sarah, who died in 1980.

She'd been up in Little Falls, two hours' drive away, taking pictures of the Willmar High hockey team in action against their rivals, the Flyers. Though she wasn't a fan—she hated aggression—hockey was the huge sport at Willmar and she worked for the yearbook; they wanted a picture, so there she was. She'd driven up alone in her green Ford Fiesta in order to avoid riding on the bus with her classmates, most of whom traveled with hidden liquor stashes—Slurpees spiked with vodka, whiskey-filled Pepsi cans—and by the trip home would be violent and cruel. During the game, a blizzard had swirled in.

This is all part of the public record. The next day, the snowplows found her car half submerged in a snowbank out on State Highway 23. It had a broken fan belt and a blown gasket. She wasn't in it. Five weeks later, during the brief January thaw, her body was discovered in a cornfield three miles away. The cause of death was determined to be hypothermia, but internal cuts and bruises implied she'd been raped. No semen was recovered; there was no sign of struggle. The Stearns County sheriffs investigated the case for a year, unsuccessfully, and then they moved on.

Her death became one of those reference points that high schools keep alive through cycles of students, those stories of incomprehensible tragedy that small communities use to scare their children and inspire them into submissiveness, convincing them to cleave close to home and fortify themselves in simple small-town life.

Sarah—especially receptive to the world as she found it—would have been disappointed by this. She had none of the filters most people use to color and distort their sense of others, to stop themselves from recognizing the beauty in eccentricity. And maybe in the long run this was a detriment, maybe this was why she'd gotten in trouble. Our father thought so: what I call faith, he called gullibility; what I call love, he called naiveté. She believed people were either open or closed, that everyone started out open but gradually most of us got scared and closed down. And often, when people saw her sensitivity, they revealed their shrouded selves to her. She was special. It wasn't just me who thought so. At school, she was the star of all the musicals—*Babes in Arms, Guys and Dolls, South Pacific*—and the photo editor of both the yearbook and the *Willmar Tattler*.

Unlike her, I was a melancholy kid, shy and uncertain, ostracized. I had an unconventional mind. What to others was simple common sense was complicated, often unsettling, to me. I seemed to always ask the wrong questions. And when I felt odd and haunted, when no one else would tolerate me, I knew, if I slipped into her room and sat on the little white stool in the corner, she'd take what I had to say seriously. "You know," she'd say, "everybody has different gifts. Some people are good at doing math, some are good at playing softball. But you, Julia, you're good at turning the world upside down and showing us all a new way of seeing it. That's one of the greatest gifts there is."

The reason for her death didn't puzzle me at all. Her car had broken down and she'd set the safety flares like our father had taught her. Two young men—friendly, probably farm boys, though they could just as easily not have been—stopped to help her, or that's what she'd thought as she opened the hood for them. Looking over the engine, they teased her: "Yeah, we know how to fix this. We can have this back and running in a jiffy, but first, let's talk. Let's make a deal. You're pretty cute. Come on, let's work something out." She knew what they meant. It's not like she was stupid. Blushing, she wagged a finger at them. "You guys," she said. She believed men were harmless if you didn't fear them, if you just kept yourself open. They told her they needed parts. They made her climb into their truck. The snow pushing past in the headlights was a universe of stars with no beginning and no end. Only as they turned into the field where she died did she suspect maybe she'd made a mistake, that people weren't quite as benevolent as she'd hoped. And when she felt herself beginning to close, she couldn't bear the thought of living in a world set up to shatter things like love and joy and faith. She made a choice. She left before her goodness could be taken from her.

I can't explain how I knew this. I just did. She'd shown me. And she wanted me to join her—she'd shown me that too. Which was how, in the summer between freshman and sophomore years, I ended up spending twenty days in Woodland Centers, talking to shrinks about whether or not life was worth the effort.

To pass the time until I got out, I drew pictures of dogs and cats and rainbows and storm clouds, all sorts of inscrutable pretty things. I made sure to put Sarah in every one, sketched her in white crayon on the white background so nobody but me would know she was there. My plan was to douse the pictures with watercolors when I was released and watch her rise up, glowing, out of all that blank space, but I never did. I decided it was better to keep her floating there, hidden.

Two years later, during Baby Week at Willmar High, I, along with all the other junior girls, learned how to be a mother. For seven days, we nurtured and protected raw eggs, an exercise that was meant to help us appreciate how difficult it was to pay attention to something, anything, other than ourselves. If our eggs cracked, we'd be doused in yolk, and we'd understand, suddenly, that life was fragile.

I named mine Sarah and the first thing I did with it was cart it to the cemetery for my sister's blessing. At school, I positioned the milk-carton crib I'd made on the corner of my desk and carried on long, silent conversations with the egg, tuning out Mrs. Blau's Carl Sandburg or Mr. Loeb's trapezoids or whatever it was, Mr. Anderson's corny filmstrips explaining how atoms move in liquids and gases, all of which, that week, seemed much less important than my silly dreams of domesticity.

Getting our eggs through the day required cunning and vigilance. Dean Swanson and Tim Schreiber—both of whom had made first team All-State in hockey—together with the thuggish boys who emulated them, patrolled the halls on a mission to destroy. They'd steal our eggs during the break between classes and pelt them at the scrawny kids on the forensics team. They'd drop-kick them across the cafeteria and grind the shells under their heels. Poking through those treacherous corridors, we had to be ready at any moment to dodge away, the eggs rattling in Kleenex-lined ziplocks, hidden in our purses or cradled on one arm, just like real babies, while we juggled our Trapper Keepers and everything else, our textbooks, our science projects in the other. And because Sarah was watching over it, my egg survived the week intact, protected from all those bad boys.

Baby Week did just what it was supposed to. It got me longing for a real child to raise, believing, at least for a couple years, that aspiring to anything else was a sacrilege, that there was no higher goal than to marry and have children, bring them up in Willmar and teach them to fear.

The problem was, because I was so freaky, one of the things everyone else feared was me.

As soon as I graduated, I fled to the Twin Cities and started taking classes at the U of M.

When I met Robert, I was surprised by his patience. We got married. I was twenty-one and I didn't have many other options at the time. I wanted a daughter. I wanted Sarah back. Not long after I discovered I was pregnant, I told Robert we should name our child after her.

"I don't think that's such a hot idea," he said.

Months later, as I lay on the couch, my water-swollen feet propped up on pillows, he knelt like a penitent near my head and floated baby names from a book past me. Alcea. Camillia. Dalia. Holly. He liked the ones that had been derived from flowers. "Here's one," he said. "Roselani—it means heavenly rose."

"What's wrong with Sarah?"

Stroking his beard, he gave me a second to register the scope of his disappointment. "Don't you think we can do better?"

"No," I said. "I do *not* think we can do better."

He'd spent the last three years perfecting his lawyerly demeanor, and when he argued, he did so defensively, waiting and listening and taking mental notes, preparing himself for the crucial moment when, in a fit of uncontrolled emotion, I gave him the evidence he needed to show me how I'd defeated myself.

"You know what I found out from Debbie Stone?" I said. "The reason to name your children after the dead is so they'll have someone to guard over them throughout their lives. That's why the Jews do it. They've got a rule."

"We're not Jews," he said. Then, as an afterthought, "And a lot of good it did them."

"Don't be obnoxious. You know what I'm saying. A lot of other cultures do it too."

"We don't even know if it's going to be a girl." Locking his index finger around mine, he gave a little tug. He was trying to be cute, to convince me to drop it.

"Don't touch me." I yanked my hand away. "She *will* be a girl and she wants to be called Sarah."

He rubbed his right eye, where his headaches often started. "How 'bout we explore all our options first? That way we'll know we've made the right choice."

Already, then, he treated me like a child. He's a very linear thinker, pragmatic, practical. In his quiet way, he brooks no argument once he decides something.

"How 'bout we don't," I said. "Because she's already told me. She wants to be Sarah."

"Stop that." He was scared now, his tone tentative. He had that look on his face that said, Don't do this, don't spin away from me, please. But he was angry too, violently angry. "Listen to me," he said. "I will absolutely not allow you to name this child Sarah. I won't. I'm not going to let her spend the rest of her life trying to live up to your myth of that woman. My daughter deserves to be her own person."

The loathing that lunged out when he said *that woman* shocked us both, but he didn't apologize. Giving me one more sad, lingering look, he reeled from the room. He went to his parents' house in Duluth and didn't come back for three days.

When he returned, he was tearful and contrite, but no more compromising than he'd been before. He wrapped an arm around my waist and showed me a daguerreotype his mother had given him. A barrel-chested woman wearing a black gown, a starched frilly bib snapped tight around her neck, stared out from the weathered cardboard. She looked coarse and rugged and very frontier. Cold. I didn't like her—or, more to the point, I could tell she wouldn't have liked me.

"What's this?" I asked.

"Cheryl Sturm. My great-great-grandmother. The one who came over in the covered wagon. She was tough. She hid Indians in her potato cellar and taught in a one-room schoolhouse out in Sheldon. She'll be a good protector."

I'd pushed the subject as far as I could. "Sure," I said. "Fine."

But, secretly, I continued to think of Cheryl as Sarah. I was convinced some part of my sister would reemerge. My daughter would be open, not like this ancestor of Robert's. She'd be somebody I could talk to and trust. I just hoped Sarah would be waiting to watch over her when she learned how closed the world could be.

For Cheryl's sake, I tried to convince myself life was simple: you built your nest and performed your function, continuing the generations-old cycle, fortified by the knowledge that your husband loved you, that he would provide as long as you nurtured and whatever sacrifice you might think you were making was, in the long view, less important than the gift of seeing your child grow up in your image. If you found yourself experiencing a momentary crisis of faith, you could always slip next door and visit with a neighbor who'd remind you that you were part of a community, that we were all the same, that the humble walked hand in hand with God. Sometimes I believed it and sometimes I didn't. What I knew was that the other way hadn't worked for me.

We lived in a starter home in a neighborhood of small drab houses, burrowed like ticks inside the northeastern edge of St. Paul. The children here, Cheryl included, wandered free. They played hopscotch. They jumped rope. They told each other secrets and invented worlds. As long as they stayed within the four square blocks of row houses, they didn't need adult supervision. Everyone knew everyone else and someone was always watching through the window; if there was an accident or an unforeseen crisis, rescue was always a few steps away.

By the time she was six, it was obvious that Cheryl's body was developing not into the willowy mold of Sarah's but into the stocky, broad-shouldered dimensions of the women on Robert's side of the family. She was growing into her name. But like the pictures I'd drawn while locked up in Woodlawn, she contained hidden traces of Sarah. She grinned a lot and she'd walk up to anyone, whether she knew the person or not, engage them in fantastic stories about the ladybugs that lived in the flowers and the machinery they controlled there, cords to open the petals, buttons that triggered spritzing mechanisms, brightly colored levers that, when pulled, produced a variety of scents. She was open.

I didn't point this out to Robert. He would have misunderstood. He'd have worried about me, and I worried enough about myself. Control it. Contain it. That was my credo. Mask all signs of difference. Make yourself disappear. It was like living in Willmar but with less privacy.

People liked me this way. They told me their secrets. I knew who was being beaten by her husband, who'd had an affair with the dentist and why. I knew who was addicted to sleeping pills, and who was addicted to crank. Every anorexic and manic depressive around made it into my living room at some point. They didn't even have to come to me in person. I could hear them through the walls, sobbing and shouting and throwing coffee mugs, threatening to kill each other or themselves. Their voices climbed in my windows at sunrise, shook me awake. When I tried to shut them out, they became angry. They filled me up and took over my days and stole the little bits of me I had left.

Once upon a time, I would have told Sarah. She would have listened without talking back. Now the only person I had was Robert, and I worried that if I let him in on what was happening, his concern for me would subsume my needs. He'd try to console me, but in the end I'd be the one consoling him.

So when the voices grew so loud and constant that they made me nauseous and wouldn't let me sleep, it was to Debbie Stone that I risked exposing myself. She was a transplant from the suburbs of New York and we shared the same relatively esoteric interests. When the big Broadway musicals came through town and I took Cheryl to see them, Debbie and her son, Daniel, were our dates. On the way home, we'd stop at Chi-Chi's for Mexican hot chocolate and fried ice cream. She'd introduced me to bagels and lox when these foods were still novelties in St. Paul. We liked each other in a cordial, tentative way.

Plopping into a chair in her immaculate kitchen, I threw my arms across the table with what I hoped was ironic flair. "I think I'm losing it," I said. She was busy with her cleaning, fidgeting with a wire brush over the caulking around the tiles of her counter. "Well, maybe not losing it, but . . ." I took a sip of the iced tea she'd poured me when I'd arrived. "It's frustrating, you know?"

"What is?"

"Do you ever—"

"Damn it," she said, turning toward me, shaking her fingers out. She wanted to listen, I knew that she did, but now that I had her momentary attention, I wasn't sure what to do with it. Clicking her tongue against the roof of her mouth, she said, "Bleach. That's the only way," and started digging in the cabinet under the sink. "Do I ever what?" she said over her back.

"I guess nothing. It was just a thought."

She pulled out a jumbo-sized bottle of Clorox and started filling a bucket with steaming water. Rapping her fingernails against the counter, checking every second or two on the grime, she hardly noticed me. I was just a chattering voice in the background, like the radio, a sound passing through her day. And this was my best, my only, friend. As she resumed her attack on the counter, she hummed to herself—a song with no melody.

For a long time, I just watched her. The differences between us were suddenly excruciatingly apparent. She was at war with the material world, defending herself and her family from entropy, and I knew if I told her my secrets, she'd feel the need to scrub me away too. When I finally did speak, these words croaked out: "I miss my sister. I wish Sarah was here."

Debbie dropped her scrub brush into the bucket and leaned against the counter to watch me cry. I felt like a specimen, a mutant in a lab. She seemed afraid to reach out and comfort me.

"I have to go," I said.

She didn't stop me.

Later, when she called to see if I was okay, I got Robert to tell her I couldn't come to the phone.

After that, everything was cursory between us. Which isn't to say I wasn't sad to lose my friend. I missed the social things I'd done with Debbie. It's just, we'd reached the end. People arrive in your life and then disappear, and with every leaving, a little bit more of you goes away with them.

Okay. I'll say it. In 1986, a couple months after I met Robert, I was hospitalized again, this time for nine weeks at St. Paul–Ramsey. The doctor there, Sanjit Rahajafeeli, diagnosed me with Schizotypal Personality Disorder and told me things would always be difficult for me, that I'd have to take medication forever if I wanted to function in anything close to a normal way. His voice was upbeat, as though he was telling me I'd just won a prize, and he'd taken off his glasses, a gesture meant to soothe me and gain my trust but that instead confirmed my suspicions about him. He believed all the things he'd read in his books, and with enough observation and cross-referencing, he could label and delimit any amount of chaos. The possibility that I'd merely been through some nasty things, that I'd broken down, and was now getting better—there wasn't room in his verdict for this.

He put me on Thorazine and set me free. I took it for a while. I tried. I did. But its most salient effect was to make me constantly want to kill myself. It hollowed me out and gave me the shakes and swallowed my personality whole.

Robert cared that I lived. When I told him I couldn't, not and take the drugs, his face furrowed into a tight fearful smile. "We'll work together," he told me then. He promised we'd learn to recognize the warning signs, and if we were vigilant, faithful and courageous, if I checked my reality sometimes against his, we'd figure out how to reconstruct my world in a way that allowed me to experience it. "We'll manage," he said. I loved him for this.

I got better.

For ten years, I held on to myself, and throughout Cheryl's life, I'd always been normal.

But now I had to admit this wasn't true. I wasn't normal. I wasn't better. And having failed with Debbie, the only person I could tell was Robert.

"I know they're not there," I said. "I know they're not there. But I hear them. They seem so real. And every time I leave the house to escape them, I see these people and they look so suspicious and they start saying things that make no sense to me. Like they know and they're mocking me in some kind of code. And then their voices mix with the other ones and stick in my head all day. It's—I don't understand what I did to these people. I didn't do anything. I'm a good girl."

Robert held himself very still. He listened closely, nodded along. Solemn. When I ran out of words, he tapped his lip and held me gently with his eyes. "Well," he said, "what do you think we should do about it?" He took great care to show he wasn't daunted.

"Leave," I said. "I can't stand it here."

And to my surprise, he said, "Okay. Then we'll leave."

My panic began to recede just like that. Six months later, we were in Plymouth and it was gone completely. I started a garden and a compost heap. Instead of using the dryer, I hung the clothes outside on a line. I taught myself how to bake bread and cookies and stripped the complicating factors—other people—out of my life. The houses here were spaced far apart and everyone minded their own business.

Cheryl loved it; all that space—two acres of land, with our own private aboveground swimming pool. And the birds: robins, barn swallows, goldfinches, cardinals, even the crows were exciting to watch. Deer sometimes tramped through. She chased bunnies and poked sticks at turtles and frogs. After we saved Gremlin, our ancient, arthritic cat, from the Humane Society, she'd follow him as he stalked through the backyard haplessly searching for gophers.

In the summers, we sped through the chores, skipped dusting and vacuuming, cleaning up only the most glaring messes. Then we'd laze around the pool all afternoon, keeping each other company. I'd tell her stories—first about a brave Indian princess, then, when Cheryl reached the age where the hold princesses had on her imagination became embarrassing, I switched to stories about my sister and, sometimes, myself.

She was my best friend. She listened, and like Sarah, she believed I had something of value to give the world. "Mom," she once told me, "I want to be just like you when I grow up."

She was happy. Believe me. Happy and loved.

And some of the other Cheryl—the one in the photograph Robert had held out in front of me that day—was lodged in her too, like buckshot. She was passionate, fiery and, I hoped, much tougher than me.

Three

I SAT ON THE BACK DECK in the Adirondack chair, listening to the darkness and holding my body absolutely still so the motion detector wouldn't register me. The air was chilly, but I'd changed into a sweater and jeans and draped an afghan over my shoulders. Crickets churned on the lawn like a sea of high-wattage electrical current. The toads were bellowing down near the stream—their voices had a texture like mourning.

A couple years before Cheryl left, she and I found a dead timber wolf down there. She'd been going through her photography phase and she made me wait while she took pictures. One of them still hangs framed on the family-room wall, the wolf dusted with frost, its tongue frozen and twisted out of its gaping mouth. I was thinking about that day, about how excited Cheryl had become and how unperturbed she'd been by the sight of death.

When Robert pulled into the driveway, it was almost twelve. The house lights were all off, and I listened silently as he tromped from room to room turning them on, calling out, "Julia? Cheryl? Hello-hello?" In the kitchen, he saw me through the sliding door and asked, "What are you doing out there in the dark?"

"Don't move. The light will come on," I said, but it was too late. He was standing behind me, his hands on my shoulders, and the sensor popped, the flat blue-white bulb washing out the darkness.

"Where's Cheryl?"

I shrugged. He'd arrived so late that whatever need I'd had for his comfort had dissipated in the lethargy brought on by my Risperdal. "She's at Jessie's house. They're having a sleepover."

"Jessie?"

"Jessie . . . Clowen, I think?"

If he'd considered for two seconds what I'd said, he would have realized I was making it up. Cheryl hadn't been friends with Jessie Clowen since ninth grade, when Jessie had started fawning all over some slack-jawed baseball player out to borrow her homework, the kind of guy born with a smirk on his face. Cheryl's recent friends had been artsy, sickly types, either that or boys with skateboards.

Robert looked me up and down like he was taking inventory. "You gonna stay out here all night?"

"Maybe."

He lingered for a moment, suspicous.

"Do me a favor and turn the lights back off," I said.

Once it was dark again, I shut my eyes and sat as straight as I could in the chair, praying or meditating or what you will. I was hearing things, fragments and whispers and curses and sobs. They all had the hoarse texture of Cheryl's voice, and though they were faint, I understood them. I was seeing things too: where she was, what she was doing.

She'd refilled her water bottle from a backyard hose. It was empty again now and she was thirsty. She hadn't eaten since cutting through the Four Seasons Mall, where she'd picked up a chili dog and an Auntie Anne's pretzel, a meal that had cost her almost seven dollars, leaving her with three and change in her pocket. Running in a panic to an ATM, she'd gutted her bank account, and since then, the five twenties she'd shoved into her sock had grown damp and begun to itch at her heel, reminding her with each step how little she had.

The list of things she never wanted to go back to kept growing.

There was me. There was Robert. That had been it at first. But we lived in a cushy suburban locale, organized around keeping children safe. She was sick of safe. There was no such thing as safe. The security Plymouth offered was as plastic and hollow as a straw; the fantasy it peddled couldn't protect you from a father who saw his wife as a problem and who didn't see you at all. Plymouth couldn't protect you from a mother who, when you said anything, the slightest, small thing, began crying and ranting incoherently about people she'd known way back in the eighties, who took whatever you said and made it hers, as though your only role in life was to affirm her. Plymouth couldn't protect you from anything, not from the shiny, smiley idiots at Armstrong in their Lucky jeans and their Abercrombie and Fitch, who swallowed everything the advertisers told them and couldn't imagine a better life than this, nor from their parents, whose moral codes were built on real estate.

She hated all of it and she hated that she was complicit in all of it, that through no fault of her own she'd been given things, a nice house, years' worth of useless music lessons, as many CDs as she could think to buy, and before that, enough toys to dam the Mississippi. None of these things had ever been enough. Why did she care so much whether she had a Discman or an iPod? What did it matter? When she was in middle school, she'd thought the road to happiness led through the shopping mall, through buying more and better things than her friends, but she'd figured out quickly the way this game worked: there was always a bigger mall somewhere down the road and she'd always know someone who shopped at that one, and this person's happiness came not from owning whatever stupid thing it was she owned but from seeing the jealousy on Cheryl's face as she realized she'd never have baubles that big. Even understanding this, she couldn't stop herself from resenting the limits we set. She'd rather have nothing now. Nothing is what she believed she deserved.

Throughout the evening, she'd trespassed on various types of private property, the groomed grounds of corporate headquarters, industrial parking lots, one-family homes and apartment complexes. When she needed to pee, she squatted behind a bush in someone's yard or held it until she found a Caribou Coffee. Public space was nonexistent. Everything was owned and freedom was a lie. This pissed her off too, and outrage spurred her on, spiked through her veins and nullified her fear.

Eventually, her knees burning from the miles she'd clocked and a blister starting to swell where the twenties had continually jabbed at her ankle, she found a spot to collapse behind a string of retail stores. She built a little fort out of some cardboard boxes that had been piled next to MusicWorld's back door and climbed in. It was like playing make-believe, pretending to be homeless, except the terror of being discovered, of being disturbed and roughed up and knifed, was real.

She peeled off her socks and hooked them into a flap on one of the boxes, hoping they'd dry by morning. Stretching out was impossible, but she was eventually able to fix herself into an awkward horizontal position. Her blister demanded to be squeezed and prodded; to resist required all her self-control. A marbled pattern of dirt had ground into her socks, and as she lay there, she stared up at them, hanging like banners above her, and studied the glowing swirls where the cotton was still white. She smelled something funky, rotting vegetables and rancid meat—it was coming from some dumpster down the strip—but after a while she got used to the scent, started almost to like it, could almost see herself stumbling toward it in search of sustenance.

Through a slit in the cardboard, she spied on the alley outside. A chain-link fence was secured to a concrete barrier, about two feet high, and beyond that was a wide expanse of blacktop. A few scattered poles arched up in the distance, each ending in a bulb projecting a cone of light, each light illuminating nothing; they reminded her of those deep-sea creatures that dangled flashlights in front of their faces as they swam. Everything alive had been bulldozed away, and off in the distance, a swath of sky—not all of it, just one large localized section—radiated with a weathered cast of red; this was the Twin Cities, reflected in the clouds. A desolate, spooky view, but it thrilled her somehow.

When morning came, she tumbled out of her fort into the bleached daylight. She pulled her socks back on—they were stiff and scratchy now—and positioned the bills in the other ankle. Then she laced up her boots and continued to dig toward the city center. The yards got smaller. The grass faded to a pale yellow-brown and leafy creepers strangled rotting fences and rusted, sinking swing sets. Ranch homes and split-levels were replaced by duplexes with shingled siding, and eventually these disappeared as well. Housing complexes eight, twelve stories high with heavy metal doors and doomed atmospheres clustered together under names like Grover Cleveland and Chester Arthur, and Cheryl stopped seeing white people on sidewalks.

I spent the day sitting in her bedroom. Every once in a while—okay, more than that, every ten, fifteen minutes—I tried calling her. I left messages.

She'd haphazardly mounted posters of rock bands across the walls of the room. The musicians didn't look much different from those I had worshipped when I was around her age. They had the same anti-hairstyles, the same rotting clothes, but hers all looked haggard in a calculated way. The lifestyle they were peddling had been codified years before they were born; it stood for things our culture no longer believed in.

I couldn't stop calling her. It was a compulsion. I wished she had at least let me pack a lunch.

Finally, around three that afternoon, she returned my calls.

"Mom?"

"Cheryl!"

"Quit calling me!"

"I—"

"Leave me alone!"

She hung up on me.

I've never been good at recognizing the boundaries between myself and the people I love. My body responds viscerally to her emotions. My cells break apart. I turn into something liquid and throbbing. For the rest of the day, though, I stayed away from the phone. We had other ways of keeping in touch.

Robert came home late like he had the day before. He found me on Cheryl's bed, wide awake, Gremlin curled in behind my knees. Inspecting the room with deliberate, evidence-collecting eyes, he said, "Where is she?"

Though I knew the answer I refused to speak.

Since calling me, she'd traced the northwestern slums and followed Hennepin south, hoping to avoid the dangers of downtown. She was lodged now on a concrete ledge under Highway 52, burrowed in, cold, wishing she'd brought along a coat or cadged a bottle of something or other from the liquor cabinet Robert and I never opened. Her roof shook with each car that passed overhead and below her on Highway 12 semis rolled past like searchlights.

"She didn't go to Jessie whatever's house last night, did she?" Robert said.

He'd pulled the stiff kitchen chair Cheryl used at her desk into the center of the room and straddled it, leaning over it, pressing toward me. I was looking past him, watching the shadows under that highway.

"Where is she?"

Sometime earlier, Cheryl had grabbed a paper clip out of a gutter. She'd toyed with it all afternoon, bending it back and forth, wrapping it around her fingers, twisting it into the shapes of barking dogs. Since installing herself on the ledge in the underpass, she'd been grinding one end of it against the concrete, not really thinking about what she was doing, just doing something for something to do.

"Julia, I need you to communicate with me." Suddenly, Robert was standing. "Answer my question." He whipped the chair out from under himself and slammed it against the floor. "Now!"

Gremlin leapt from the bed and dashed out of the room.

Recoiling, clutching a pillow to my chest, I watched Cheryl scrape her name in the concrete, adding it to the names already there— Sal P. and Kilroy and Fuckhead and Tralala and so many others too worn away to read. Some were ornate, scrawled in marker-paint, and some had been gouged out with bonded-steel blades. Some were lightly etched surface scratches. Cheryl carved hers with care in capital letters; she went over them time and time and time again, thickening the lines, deepening the grooves, smoothing out the flaws, wearing her paper clip to a fine sharp point.

Wondering what Robert and I were up to, she tested it on her fingertip. She hoped, in a vague way, that we were crying, finally thinking about her for a change—not that she wanted us to search for her. Leaving hadn't been a cry for attention or any of that sappy TV movie shit. It was more of a mandate, a decree: *I'm Mine!* Now, for the first time since she'd left, she felt lonely. Shivering under a bridge had turned out to be much less romantic than she'd been prepared for. She longed for a group to attach herself to, a scene that would think for her and keep her warm.

Robert stomped off, down the hall, to the kitchen, slamming cupboard doors like a petulant child. When I heard him pound into the garage and start his car, I scrambled after him, but I was too late. He roared away before I could intercept him.

Cheryl flicked the paper clip across her forearm, quick, thoughtless slashes, then, because it was interesting the way her skin turned white, more-considered cuts. She carved a straight line, then went over it again. And again. And again, until she drew blood. She examined the wound. It hurt less than her blister, which had been stinging since she'd weakened and popped it that afternoon. An SUV sped past below her on the highway, and she realized how thin the ledge really was. What would happen if she rolled off while she slept? She might break a leg, two. Then she'd be stuck there in the middle of the road. A semi would hit her. She'd be pulverized. She didn't particularly want to die, but thinking this way gave her a weird feeling of satisfaction. Back at her arm, she started flicking again, moving the paper clip up and down this time instead of back and forth. She began a third line, which, along with the others, created the letter F. Then she carved a V, and next to this, she made what looked like a diamond, except that the diagonals on the right side didn't quite intersect. She'd discovered that her skin caught under the point of her paper clip, making it impossible for her to draw curves, so the diamond was a C and the V was a U. She added a K and she followed this up with a Y and an O and a final second U.

I wondered why she was so hell-bent on hurting me.

Three hours later, when Robert got home, I asked him what he'd discovered.

"What do you think?" he said, plopping down next to me on the front stoop—I had to scoot over so we wouldn't touch. He pushed at his eyes like there was smoke in them. "Jesus, I'm exhausted."

"Where'd you go?"

"Just . . . around. I got on 698 for a while, but then . . . So I went to the station and filed a missing persons report."

"I wish you hadn't done that. She's gonna come back."

"That's what the guy said, the officer. I gave him her school picture from my wallet. He's gonna stop by the house tomor—"

I suddenly snapped at him. "No, Robert, no, I won't. I'm not going to talk to any police."

For a moment, he stared at me in frustration. Then he relented. "I'm taking the day off. It's just pro forma anyway. He made it pretty

clear, they never find these kids. I'll keep him away from you. Okay?"
I knew what I was doing to him wasn't fair, but I had to protect my
daughter. "Okay?" he said again. He took my hand and squeezed it to
reinforce his words.

I nodded sheepishly.

"You know," I said, "she called me this afternoon."

He shook his head like he didn't want to hear. "This is just hopeless." Then he looked at me. "And?"

"And she didn't really say much of anything."

"She must have said something."

"When she's figured things out—"

"What things?" His voice cracked. "What happened between you
two?" With a jerk of his body, he propelled himself to a standing
position and paced out toward the Japanese maple. He tapped his lip
in time to his thoughts, a rapid nervous drumming. By the time he
turned back to me, he was calm enough to hold his voice steady.
"What the hell's wrong with you, Julia?" he said. Then he raced
toward the stoop in a panic and wrapped his arms around me. "No.
I'm sorry. Julia, I'm sorry. I know what's wrong, I know." His chest
quaked for a moment before the sobs came. "It just . . . there's . . ." He
pressed his forehead to mine and let me go, walking out blearily into
the street.

"She knows where we live," I called. "You'll see. She'll come back."

But if she did, it wouldn't be soon. Tomorrow would take her into
the city, where it was harder to stay hidden but easier to disappear.

II

The Discovery Channel

One

ROBERT TOOK LONG DETOURS to and from work, peering into ditches and shadowy doorways, trolling through neighborhoods that made him nervous, searching in all the wrong places for her. I didn't tell him he should try Dinkytown, and the thought never occurred to him on his own.

That's where she was, though. The people there fascinated her. This was, she knew, where the radical fringe of our culture hung out—the politically minded, the social and sexual deviants, the art students and the wannabe rock stars, all those people who'd broken their minds open and somehow freed themselves from the machine.

She sat on a ratty sofa at a coffee shop and watched the crowd. One guy was barefoot, dressed like a Buddhist monk, with a long braided beard that he flipped over his shoulder like a scarf and milky blue eyes containing a hard intensity. Another guy had a tattooed head and smoked hand-rolled cigarettes as he hunkered over his MacBook. A girl not much older than Cheryl, with hair done up in childish pigtails, handed her a flyer for a show at the Boom Boom Tick Club. "You should check it out," she said. "They're the best band in town. I know. I'm the bassist. Just looking at you, I can tell you'll like it." These people were intimidating. She wanted what they had, even if she wasn't quite sure what that was.

Propped against the whitewashed wall outside Ron's Tiny Diner, she saw a forlorn-looking boy with a pale moon-shaped face. Next to him was a sign: SPARE CHANGE—HELP ME FEED MY DOG. A scrawny puppy hunkered between his raised knees; it couldn't have been more than a few months old and it kept trying to get at the single crumpled bill in the shoebox at the boy's feet.

Something about this boy and his dog, maybe it was the dog itself, pulled Cheryl in. She watched him for a while from across the street, wishing she had the courage to speak to him, working her way closer a few steps at a time until, before she was ready, she was standing right next to him.

The greeting she gave the boy was hardly a whisper. He glanced up sleepily, then went back to doing nothing.

The puppy, though, perked its ears as she knelt next to it. A mutt with coarse mottled fur and a thin foxlike nose, its eyes had that sparkle, and when she sadly cooed, "Hey, puppy, hey-ya, pooch," it pounded its tail on the sidewalk and inched toward her. When it rolled over and splayed its legs, she scratched its emaciated tummy. She cupped her hands around its ears and shook its head back and forth. The gunk in its eyes, thick and crusty with deep canals running through it, looked like something you'd see on a barnyard animal.

"Is he sick?" Cheryl asked.

The boy mumbled something she couldn't catch.

"What?"

"She's a she. She's a fucking girl." Talking to Cheryl seemed to piss the boy off, and she nearly scurried away, mortified, but a slow second later he tipped over and laid himself down on the sidewalk, scratching the dog behind the ear. "Aren'tcha, pup?" he said. "You're my little bitch." The puppy licked his face. "Fuck yeah, you are."

"What's her name?"

"Dog." He broke out a sheepish smile, which faded immediately back into blankness.

"How old is she?"

The boy shrugged. "I found her."

His name was Jarod and he didn't talk much, but he didn't seem to mind Cheryl hanging around, either. They sat there, watching the people with someplace to go walk past. Sometimes these people dropped a few coins in the box, and though Jarod never broke his trance, Cheryl couldn't help nodding up at them to mouth a quiet thanks. She was surprised at how easily this game was played; even if most people averted their gaze and shook their heads in disgust, the dog was a helpful prop and when it wagged its tail and panted a little, it earned them not just coins but dollar bills too. Jarod hid these away in his pants pocket as soon as the donor was off down the street—he never let more than one bill linger in the box.

As the afternoon crept forward and the air turned thick and sticky, the dog's energy flagged. Eventually, it gave up on movement completely, flopped down with a sigh, its muzzle in Jarod's lap. Its tongue dangled out of its open mouth, quivering a little.

"I bet she's thirsty," Cheryl said.

Jarod shrugged. This was his response to everything.

She begged a cup of water from the Nix Bar down the block and the two of them watched as the dog dug its snout into the tiny plastic cylinder and flicked its tongue across the surface of the water.

"I should have gone and left you here with Dog," Jarod said. "People give more when they see you're a girl."

Tucking this information away for later, Cheryl twisted up the edge of her shirt and sucked on the node she'd made until it was soaked through. She braced the puppy still between her legs and daubed at its eyes, wiping the gunk away. When she could see what was going on underneath, the dog didn't look so bad off after all.

"You know, you let this stuff build up and pretty soon its eyes'll seal shut."

She and Jarod were sort of like dogs themselves, sniffing each other out, circling, hanging back, only gradually allowing small parts of themselves to show. By the time the light began to fall and bounce off second-story windows, they'd become a tiny bit less skittish with each other.

Reaching out toward the scratches on Cheryl's arm, Jarod asked, "What happened there?" His hand hovered for a second, charged, like he was afraid to touch her.

"I was bored," she said, reaching up to cover the wounds. Under her fingers, the dots of dried blood felt like words written in Braille, a secret message hidden on the surface of the *K* and the *Y* and the *O*, encouraging her toward strength.

The people walking by repeated themselves. The boy with the brown leather satchel and the sloppy part in his dense hair must have gone back and forth at least fifteen times. The anorexic girl with the fringe of pale blue beneath her black bangs and the green knee socks dangling around her ankles was crying the second time Cheryl saw her. And then there were the worker bees—carbon casts of each other, they blurred together, there were too many of them to keep track of. All these people—all these good Midwestern people. Their movements were organized around particular rhythms. It was only Jarod and her who stayed in one place.

"I thought there'd be more . . ." She didn't know quite how to put it. "You know, like a scene or something."

Jarod shrugged.

"Like other kids or whatever."

"Trent and them are all around here somewhere," he said.

What she'd wanted to ask was where the good places to sleep were. She'd been on the street for four days now and last night it had rained and she was freaked out and sick of being alone. But she didn't want to come off as a poseur. She didn't want to look like a hanger-on. He could probably tell from what she'd already said that she didn't have any idea what she was doing.

"Last night I got stuck up on this fire escape. It like broke or whatever. I climbed up there and pulled the thingy up, the ladder, and then when it started to rain, I couldn't get it down again. It was like jammed or whatever and I had to sit there getting all wet and shit. My Discman got ruined."

As she babbled, Jarod watched her. She couldn't tell if she was annoying him or not. His face had a wet, wounded look, like he was two throbs away from crying.

"Man, that sucked," she said. "You think it's gonna rain tonight?"

Jarod tugged one of the dog's paws. He looked up at the sky and scratched at a glossy canker sore on his lip. Turning to her, his thin eyebrows arching high up on his forehead, he said, "You can stay with me if you want, but you'll have to put up with my ho-bag mother."

He spat a thick gob of saliva onto the sidewalk and she realized he was blushing, hiding his face. He had a little crush, and in his awkward and furtive way, he was trying to let her know about it.

Then, suddenly, he turned cranky and officious, pulling the wadded bills out of his pocket and dumping them into the shoebox. One by one, he rubbed them flat and stacked them against the corner. They'd made more than Cheryl had thought, close to thirty-eight dollars all told, including change.

Shoving the money back into his pocket, he stood up. "Can you hang out with the dog for a minute?"

"Where you going?"

He shrugged. "I gotta go do this thing."

He was taller than she'd thought, somehow lanky and doughy at the same time, and the odd little stutter step in his walk made him bounce down the sidewalk like an extremely slow-moving windup toy. He'd come back, she was sure, and then she'd have to decide what to do. She plucked a dandelion out of a crack in the sidewalk and, using her fingernail as a wedge, split the hollow cylinder down to the flower. The puppy sighed in its sleep. When she tickled just the right spot behind its ear, she could get it to twitch and that was amusing, at least for a while.

The sun was gone and the temperature had started to drop again. It was probably a waste of time to get too close to this guy. There was that canker sore—and the whatever about his mother. But, she didn't want to spend another night hiding and worrying about what might happen to her if she slept. And she definitely didn't want to return to me. The mother she didn't know had to be better than the one she did. Or not. It could go either way.

She had this idea that somewhere out there she was going to find a new vision of the world, like a kind of Burning Man illumination. She could already tell she wouldn't find it with Jarod. But he might have friends. One of them might be cool.

He took forever. When he came back he had a bag of pot.

"So, yeah," she said, "I guess I'll check out your place." She could always take off again if it really sucked.

As they hiked away, he seemed oddly dejected. He refused to look at Cheryl when she talked to him and she decided he must be a virgin.

Two

THEY SPRAWLED for Cheryl had no idea how long on the floor in front of the couch, smoking pot and zoning out on the television. Jarod was all keyed up about the Discovery Channel, hour after hour dedicated to different regions of the world: the American West, Patagonia, the South African veldt. By the end of each program, an entire ecosystem would be explained, one exotic animal at a time. He wouldn't let Cheryl watch anything else.

"It's educational," he said. "You can see how animals are like people too." He looked at his puppy. "Right, Dog? You're a person too. You're just a really stupid kind of person." He picked something brown and unidentifiable out of the carpet and held it out for the dog to gobble down.

Cheryl clamped her mouth to the end of the bong, then pulled the plug and watched the smoke whoosh in.

I want to say this was the first time she'd tried drugs. I want to say she'd been innocent and sheltered right up until the day she stomped away, that innocence and shelter were part of what she was so bent on fleeing. I don't know if this is true, though. I might just be wishing. What I do know is that, as she and Jarod got stoned, she felt something unravel around her, like some kind of thin leaden wire she hadn't realized was constricting her movement was beginning to peel away. Her skin tingled. Her brain breathed. Muscles that she didn't know could be unclenched now relaxed and sank into a kind of restfulness. I see her in shades of purple and blue. She lies on the carpet, her head propped on an arm, and her heart radiates with wavy gold vibrations. Above her, sprinkled through the streaks of smoke, little puffs like popcorn burn themselves out. These are her fears and her sadnesses.

On the television, a giant sea turtle slowly descended into the thick Pacific, its paddles spread like it was parachuting, its heavy lumbering form casting shadows in the streaks of white light streaming through the water.

"Look at that," Jarod said. "I could be a turtle." He watched it hover for a long moment until the image broke abruptly into a commercial. "Not like that one, though. Just a little one."

Cheryl pictured him crawling along the side of a road, tucking himself up inside his shell, waiting for a car to come along and crack him.

"I'd be a moth," she said. Then she laughed. "I'd like fly into lightbulbs and pound my head against them and then get all frustrated and go chew up somebody's clothes or whatever."

The mother Jarod had warned Cheryl about didn't show up until three a.m. She limped in on a metal orthopedic cane and gazed for a second at the mess of the two of them, the beer cans and chip bags and the big purple bong. Her baggy pink sweatshirt was unzipped, exposing a shapeless yellow t-shirt with a peeling iron-on festooned across it—I'm Not Getting Older, I'm Getting Better spilling out of a tilted wine bottle. Cheryl felt like she should hide her eyes, like there was something shameful in letting herself look.

Jarod had buckled into a defensive ball. He stayed that way, silent, waiting for his mother to shuffle off and shut herself into the dark room behind him. Then he repacked the bong and sucked more smoke into his lungs.

A single heavy creak of a mattress. The sound of a television zapping on. The flick, flick, flick of a lighter. Jarod's mother slipped away for the night and not even the drugs could stop Cheryl's mind from wandering out to the northwestern suburbs and hovering there over me.

"What's wrong with her?" she whispered, warding me off.

Jarod just shrugged. He ticked his head like he was shaking off a fly.

Later, she asked, "What about your father?"

"What about him?"

Any question would be the wrong one.

"I mean, like, what happened to him?"

Jarod shrugged again.

"Or, don't you know?"

"What the fuck, hey?" His voice constricted. "You think you're my fucking shrink or something?"

For a moment she was afraid he'd hit her, or tell her to leave. But then he collapsed back in on himself and she knew she was going to be okay.

"Sorry," she whispered.

Watching walruses slip to their deaths at the bottom of a hundred-foot cliff, he didn't show any sign of having heard her. It seemed like the thing that was supposed to happen next was for her to crawl up and wrap her arms around his waist, nestle her cheek against the back of his neck, hold him and give him the little warmth she contained. He was closed off now, though, he'd disappeared, and since he wasn't willing to tease it from her, she decided she was allowed to keep her heat for herself.

They passed out on the living room floor that night, and the next night and the night after that. Jarod had a bedroom upstairs, but getting there would have meant a conversation, a recognition of what might happen inside. Cheryl wasn't sure she was up for that.

She was happier just to be stoned all the time, to lie with her back to him when she got groggy and let him hug the dog if he wanted something to hold. She liked the way time warped and twisted, how it hung upside down with the bats on TV, or stretched so thin that, if she twirled her hand just the right way, she could slip right through it, curl up and hide in a place far away from it. When she came out, she'd be a different person with a different name and a different face. If only she could stop her thoughts like she could time. No matter which direction they ran, they always butted up against my yearning face. She battled with me. She couldn't thrust me away and she couldn't make sense of what had happened between us. Days slipped by like this, she didn't know how many. With the lights so dim and the blinds always down, it was hard to tell what was going on with the sun. Anyway, she didn't want to know. Counting the days meant acknowledging she'd left something important behind. She needed to get away from thinking like that.

When they absolutely had to, they went out for necessities: more beer, more cigarettes, more Cool Ranch Doritos, more marijuana— her hundred bucks was depleting quickly. And when they remembered, when it simpered and pawed the carpet frantically enough, they walked the dog a few yards down the street for a dump. Sometimes, after Jarod kicked the shit into the gutter, the three of them would hang out on the curb, tossing stones and smoking cigarettes, blinking in the light. Then they'd head back to the house for more Discovery Channel or, if Cheryl complained, one of the two videos Jarod owned, *Blade Runner* and *Pitch Black*.

Jarod's mother hid behind the thin door to her room all day, sleeping late, chain-smoking and watching talk shows on the TV propped on the overcluttered ironing board in the corner, emerging only to use the bathroom. Some time later, she'd hobble out to her rusty station wagon and drive off to wherever it was she worked.

Even to her face, Jarod called her ho-bag. He'd shout, "Hey, ho-bag, you gonna get up sometime today?" or "Turn the TV down! I

can't even think! Ho-bag, you hear me? Turn the fucking TV down!"
She responded to these taunts in the same way as she had to the
cloud of smoke clogging the living room—by not responding at all.

There was one day in there when the ho-bag wouldn't stop howling, deep bellowing sounds, moans like shifts in the earth. Jarod
cocked his head, taking in the noise, then he told Cheryl to ignore it.
"She's just trying to get my attention," he said.

A while later, she gave up and went quiet.

"See?"

But then she started calling out, "Jarod? Jarod, honey? Jarod?"

He glared at her door, willing her to shut up.

"Listen, will you . . . Can you call the factory and tell them I'm
sick?"

Jumping up suddenly, he ran into her room. He barked at her.
"Stop it. Get up now." His voice was stern, vicious.

"I'm sick," she said.

"You're not sick. What do you have?"

"My leg hurts."

"That's not sick. Your leg always hurts."

Cheryl tried to focus on the sponges and starfish floating around
on the television, but the tranquil life of these sea creatures only
made her feel more embarrassed. The whole house seemed to be
drowning.

"It especially hurts. I need to rest it."

"Get up." Jarod's shadow sprawled out behind him into the open
doorway. As his voice rose, the shadow seemed to grow.

"Really, Jarod, I need to rest. You have to . . . Can't you call in
for me?"

"Get the fuck up!" The shadow began to twitch. It clenched and
unclenched its fists. Cheryl imagined Jarod turning into a werewolf,
the frayed edges of the shadow taking on bulk, sprouting fur.

His mother was crying now.

"You want them to fire you?"

"No, but—"

"Then don't be a fucking ho-bag."

Cheryl knew what I'd do if she spoke to me this way. I'd cry and beg her to join me in analyzing why she thought I deserved this flood of rage. Then I'd construct hypotheses in my head involving dark forces beyond human control and convince myself it was them, not her, carrying out these attacks on me. She could only imagine where it would all lead.

Stomping back to the living room, Jarod looked bigger, meaner. He dropped to the couch as though he'd been shot.

"Is everything okay?"

"She'll go." He craned his neck to peer at the doorway. "You going?"

The moan from the bedroom was noncommittal, and Jarod repeated, "She'll go."

And she did, eventually. She limped out of the house, carrying herself with spiteful self-possession.

Jarod fell into something close to catatonia, his eyes half shut, his head lolling forward, his gaze fixed abstractly, dumbly, on the puppy. He'd ignored it all day, and misunderstanding this niblet of attention, it sat up, tense and proper, flicked its tail like a strobe light, dragged itself with tentative, shuffling steps across the carpet. Jarod just kept staring, a blunt indifference in his eyes. The puppy was confused. It scooted. It stopped. It grinned and panted. Thumping its tail incessantly, it pulled another few inches forward and waited, hungry for some sort of response from him. It cocked its head toward Cheryl, back to Jarod. Another scoot, just a foot away now. And then, suddenly, Jarod lunged and growled. Flinching, the puppy seemed to know not to come closer, but it wanted to play and it wasn't quite sure if, maybe, it wasn't already playing. This might be a fun new game. Or it might not be. The puppy let out a nervous yip, and Jarod slapped it upside the head.

"Fucking bitch," he said.

Then he was over it, the bong clasped around his mouth like an oxygen tube.

More disturbing than Jarod's insolence—she found that inspiring, wished she were so daring—was his contrasting devotion to the ho-bag. He made her SpaghettiOs and tuna sandwiches, popped frozen dinners in the oven for her. Cheryl even saw him sometimes run the dishwasher.

One day, they snuck into her room while she was sleeping, naked from the waist down. Her knotted pubic hair called out to Cheryl like a haunted house. Jarod strode by as if he didn't see it and the tenderness in this act was, to Cheryl, nearly unbearable. They'd come to peel money from the meager stack she kept tucked in a broken music box on her dresser, money that wouldn't go toward drugs and beer—they'd been using Cheryl's hundred bucks for that—but toward groceries. For her.

"The ho-bag needs her kibbles and bits," he said.

It was too much for Cheryl, all this complicated emotional bondage, exactly the sort of thing she was fleeing. When they returned from the store, she sat on the lip of the couch, her head propped glumly on the balls of her hands, and took inventory of her belongings, trying to decide if she should get out of here or just get stoned again. It would take two minutes to pack up her shit.

She pulled her cell phone from the corner where it was charging and a harsh lucid thought went shooting through her brain: What if Robert and I had sent the police out to find her?

I cried when I heard her voice and she hung up on me. Then five minutes later, she called back.

"Hi." The hardness in her voice was brutal, as though all the love had been vacuumed out of her. "You're not looking for me, are you?"

I sputtered some inane thing, I don't know what. I was scared and my fear made me angry and confused.

"Don't look for me."

"Cheryl—"

"Just don't look for me."

"Maybe if you tell me where you are and whether you're eating and those sorts of things—"

"Just don't."

"Cheryl—"

"And don't call the cops. Or put me on milk cartons or little signs at Cub Foods, either."

"Cheryl, stop."

"I'm not lost, okay? I'm not missing."

"Please stop."

"You can't make me do anything."

"Enough! Cheryl! Enough! Shut up now!" I was screaming. "Listen to me now! You. Are. Not. Going to make me crazy. There're lots of things I'll allow you to do, but I'm still your mother, and when I say—"

"So?"

"What did you say?"

"So maybe you plopped me out, so what?" She knew she'd gone too far. "Mom?"

"What."

"Just promise me you won't come looking for me?"

I sighed. "I can't promise you anything, Cheryl."

"I need you to promise me. I'm sure Dad probably hasn't even figured out I'm gone, but—"

"Don't make too many assumptions about him, Cheryl. He might surprise you."

"Yeah, right. You should have seen him while you—" She seized up. The instinct to protect me was still powerful in her. "Look, I've got to go, Mom. Don't look for me, okay?"

I was in the kitchen. The flecks in the faux-marble countertop were vibrating. A sudden energy surged through me and I knew I'd do anything, anything she wanted, if she'd just stay on the phone a little longer.

"I'll make a deal with you," I said. "You keep me up-to-date on what you're doing, and I'll try to keep your father off your back."

"And what if I don't tell you what I'm doing—'cause it's really, like, none of your business, right?"

"That's the deal, Cheryl. Take it or leave it."

"Fine."

"Is that a whatever-leave-me-alone fine, or an okay-Mom-that-sounds-great fine?"

"What if I said I could take care of myself? Better than you can, anyway."

I didn't know what to say. I didn't know how to defend myself against this.

"It's not your fault, Mom. You've got to be able to take care of yourself before you can take care of another person." She said this like she'd read it in some self-help book and been saving it up for the right time to throw at me.

While I cried, she gave me the barest of facts about where she was and what she was doing: some kid named Jarod—no I didn't know him, no she wasn't lying. He had a cute little mutt named Dog and a freaky mother who could, like, barely walk, and maybe she was still in the Twin Cities, or maybe not, those details were classified. Finally, she said, "No, Mom, I'm not happy, happy doesn't exist. That's a kind of completely stupid question. This interview's over. I'm hanging up now. Say goodbye, Mom, I'm hanging up."

"It's not fair," I said. "Everything was supposed to get better. Why wouldn't you just let everything get better?"

"Nothing ever gets better, Mom."

This she said with absolute conviction.

Three

THE BEER CANS SPREAD like a ruined wall around them, multiplying by sixes and twelves. The water in the bong thickened and darkened—gunky things hung there like pears in a jello mold. Jarod sometimes tried to stare down Cheryl's shirt while she was smoking. He found unending excuses—reaching for the crackhead cheese, maybe, scratching the dog behind the ears, extended, unnecessary searches for the bottle opener—to reposition himself until he was close enough to graze her arm hair. Then he'd freeze there, charged and pulsing. If she wanted to stretch her legs or scratch her neck, she felt guilty, like she was rejecting him. He'd sulk away and the cycle would start all over again. When he handed her something later, a beer, a slice of pizza, he'd take great care not to let their fingers touch, and if they did anyway, his hand would spasm as though he'd been shocked.

She discovered him once, or she thought she did, peeking through the crack in the bathroom door, trying to catch a glimpse of her while she peed. The wood had bloated in the humidity; there was no way to get it completely closed. She saw a darkness flit past, then return and linger, and she knew it was him because what else could it be. His longing at that moment seemed like a parasite on his body, a wart that he couldn't freeze off. While she sat there, she wondered what would happen if she called his name, invited him in and gave him a better view. His gaze felt almost pleasant as it touched her skin, teasing and caressing and reassuring. As she wiped herself and pulled up her shorts, he fled, taking the sensation with him, but the possibility it had sparked stayed with her.

He was a watery version of the skater guys she'd hung around with before she left. "They're not worth knowing, Mom," she told me once. "We just do nothing. It's boring. We play *Tony Hawk's Underground* on their Nintendos and then I have to watch them try out new tricks." She called them the "alt-consumers," the "burnout bimbos." They didn't know who the vice president was or why she might think it was patriotic to refuse to stand for the national anthem. "If they were worth mentioning, Mom," she said, "you'd know." This hadn't stopped her from sleeping with one of them.

Now, here with Jarod, she was bored again. And it's not like she hated him. He'd let her stay. He'd fed her and they'd shared their drugs with each other. She felt tenderly toward him, sort of indebted. Something, even an ambivalent hookup, was bound to be better than nothing. There are lots of ways to care about someone, and pity's as valid as any other.

On their last night in the living room, the humidity crept in and covered everything like a thick and filmy layer of shellac. There was no way to escape it. Lying on the carpet, sweating out the beer she'd drunk, Cheryl kept thinking bugs were crawling over her. The idea of touching another warm-blooded thing—of letting herself be touched—was almost unbearable, but next to her, Jarod wasn't sleeping, either. She knew because his eyelids kept flickering as he watched her through the webs of his lashes, and she couldn't help wondering what it would take to get him to finally make a move.

"Don't you have like a fan or something?" she said.

He twisted onto his side, making a feeble effort to act like she'd woken him up. His ratty t-shirt, saturated with sweat, drooped toward the floor. "It's in my mom's room." This meant that, even though his mom was off at work, they weren't going to touch it.

The last time they'd smoked had been hours ago, but the oily smell of marijuana clung to the air; it was something viscous, slithering and twisting, coming to strangle her in the dark.

She sat up and propped herself against the couch. "It's so fucking hot," she said. "Can't we open the windows at least?"

Taking his shrug to be a yes, she went over and broke the windows loose from their sills, pounding them up with the base of her palm. The fresh air didn't help anything. It was too heavy to move. When she returned to her spot on the floor and closed her eyes, the creepy crawly things seemed to move faster.

"How can you wear that shirt?" she asked him.

"You're wearing a shirt."

"Yeah, you're right." She thought about this, then peeled hers off. For a second she felt like maybe this would help, but the heat wrapped right back in and sucked at her skin. "Now I'm not," she said. "So?"

"So, what?"

"Are you gonna take your shirt off?"

Jarod reluctantly sat up and yanked his shirt over his head. His skin was pale in the darkness, like a glow stick losing its charge. He seemed embarrassed, more embarrassed than she was.

"See?" she said. "Much better."

Pretending to be oblivious to the sexual dynamic of what they were doing, she laid down on her back, her head resting on a cushion she'd slid off the couch. His eyes kept veering toward her breasts and she wondered what he'd do if she took her bra off too. That would be too much.

Any thought other than how hot it was soaked through and wilted and curled at the edges. She felt like she was rotting. At home we had air-conditioning in every room, and the way she felt now, this comfort alone seemed almost worth returning for. She cursed herself for being so weak. Air-conditioning was a form of class warfare, unnatural, disastrous to the environment; it emitted freon or toxins or something, ate up the ozone, guzzled electricity. Jarod put up with the horrible muggy heat, and he wasn't even political.

She could tell from his breath that he still wasn't sleeping. How many ways did she have to say it's okay?

"Do you ever think of, like, going away?" There was no answer. "Like going somewhere with better weather? . . . Getting away from your mother?"

He tensed up behind her and she turned onto her side, facing him now, each of them loosely curled, knees almost touching, heads almost kissing—a big empty upside-down heart. She waited. Every time she moved, some part of her rubbed against him and he pulled a little tighter into himself. After what felt like an hour, she flung herself onto her stomach. Then in a quick burst of action, she draped her arm over his waist. He shivered. If this was a mistake, she couldn't take it back now.

Unwilling to make it any more explicit, she stayed like that, gradually dozing off.

In the moments of consciousness between intervals of sleep, she registered the changes in their positions. Jarod cradling her arm like a teddy bear. Later, his nose squished into the back of her neck. At some point, his mom was there and then she wasn't. Cheryl's back was to Jarod. He was holding her, his hand not quite cupping her breast, tense with the effort to avoid her nipple. She could feel his hard penis, through their layers of shorts, pressing up against her tailbone. But a greater tension stiffened his whole body. He was terrified. Even in his sleep.

When the air finally began to cool, she snuggled into him, and didn't wake up again until noon the next day.

Four

Sprawled on the couch in her cutoff cargoes and bra, Cheryl watched Jarod doze. For someone so lethargic in waking life, his sleep was a mess of neurotic tics. He jittered. He rolled. He kicked. He repeatedly slapped at his face, itched his scalp. He wrapped himself around the puppy and spooned it in the same way he'd been spooning her earlier, like it was salvation, sweetness and succor and safety itself. She could be these things. She thought, Maybe I want to be these things. She'd have to put up with his tedious silence, the unreadable grunts and hours lost to the TV, but once she got past that, she might achieve a small degree of fulfillment in wrapping his hidden dreams up in her arms. She leaned over his head, and with a spit-daubed finger, scrubbed the dried drool off his cheek.

To distract herself until he woke up, she watched VH1, *Behind the Music.* It was entrancing even with the sound off. What tragedies had befallen Adam Ant in the years since he was all the rage? She wanted to know—or she didn't not want to, which was a pretty good way of approaching the world. No expectations. She didn't have to think about the show, and it stopped her from thinking about anything else. Just the way she liked it. She could spend years like this, remote in hand, waiting for nothing, becoming nothingness.

But excitement and meaning were rushing toward her, whether she wanted them or not. Trent was on his way, about to barge in on her comfortable boredom. Without a knock, with no regard for the peace he was disrupting, he and his pack of boys slammed the door open and spilled like floodwater into the room, shouting to hear themselves shout, slap-boxing, jumping onto each other's shoulders and falling in heaps over the empty beer cans. Three white guys and one black, young like her and punky, their tattered shirts covered with slogans, knobs of steel riveted into their faces. They were kinetic and startling.

As the puppy launched into a series of sharp yips and clambered away to hide behind the kitchen door, Cheryl zapped off the TV and hid her breasts with her knees. She wasn't scared, though maybe she should have been. Instead, she felt a dark thrill, temptation, trepidation; this was what she'd longed for, the lords of destruction come crashing in to beckon her forward.

Jarod just lay there, refusing to accept this disruption of his sleep. He twisted crankily, draped an arm across his eyes.

In these first few moments, Cheryl experienced the boys less as individuals than as a large mass of undulating chaos, spiraling through the room, then into the kitchen, a voice yelling back, "Jarod, man, where the fuck's the food?" Though she sat still, watching silently from her perch on the couch, she felt like she was being swept along with them. It was only when one of them peeled away from the group—a fierce-looking guy with short cowlicky brown hair and a tattoo of binary code strung around his right arm—that she was able to orient herself and differentiate them from each other.

The guy lurked over Jarod, kicked him in the ribs—softly, but still. When he saw Cheryl glare at him, he smirked and kicked Jarod a little harder. Jarod groaned. He curled in to protect himself. "What the fuck, man," he said. "I'm sleeping."

"What the fuck, man, it's two fucking o'clock in the afternoon."

"So."

"So."

The other boys rummaged around in the kitchen. They'd quieted down. The only one shouting now was the puppy. Someone opened the refrigerator door.

Glancing at Cheryl again, the smirk expanding and sinking in, the guy with the tattoo said, "Get up, man. We've got shit to do."

"Stop kicking me."

"Get up."

She'd made up her mind that she didn't like the guy. "Hey, why don't you leave him alone?" she said.

The guy stopped kicking. He leered at her. Then, making connections, he glanced at Jarod and chuckled. "What's your name?" he asked her. The question came like an accusation.

"What's *your* name?" Cheryl sneered, hoping to bluff herself as much as him.

"Trent." The way he stared disconcerted her, made her feel like she'd done something to be ashamed of. "So?" he said.

"What."

"What's your name, Betty?"

"Why should I tell you my name?"

"Fine. Don't, then. I'll call you Betty, Betty."

"You do that, then."

"I will, then." He went back to kicking Jarod. "Listen, Jarod, fucking get the fuck up, or I'll fucking really kick you."

Jarod rolled into a sitting position. "Jesus Christ," he said. He slumped against the edge of the couch, head drooping between his legs. "Somebody turn off the fucking dog. My mother's trying to sleep."

A voice from the kitchen barked, "Fuck your mother," and Jarod lurched toward it, suddenly charged, ready to propel himself into action. "What?"

"Fuck. Yo. Mother," said the voice.

Cheryl felt like she should intervene. Why, though? None of this involved her. Besides, she was excited, enthralled. This Trent guy was a dick, but he was reckless and charismatic. Jarod had finally shown a tiny hint of backbone. Something interesting was happening.

"Hey, Mike . . . Shut the fuck up," said Trent. She wasn't sure how she felt about that. It was harder to hate him if he took Jarod's side.

"Gee, Dad, the fuck did I do?" came the voice from the kitchen.

Jarod shrank back and closed his eyes again. Trent touched him lightly on the top of the head.

"You know the fuck what you did."

The black guy stood in the doorway, scratching his shaved head, looking skeptical. A series of earrings curled up both his earlobes, like they used to on big-haired girls in the eighties. "I do?" he said, grinning.

Trent flexed his fist, faked a punch toward Mike.

"Whatever, man," Mike said. "You know who'd win." He disappeared back into the kitchen.

"Look at all this shit," Trent said. He nudged various bits of trash with his combat boot—an empty twelve-pack, a dried-up pizza rind, a childproof screw top that had once belonged to some now disappeared prescription bottle. "Jarod, man, you've got to get yourself together." The boys had kicked the cans and bottles around. They'd knocked the bong over and a brown circle of water was seeping into the pile rug, letting a musty, sweet stench loose across the room. "Clean the fucking house, man. I know you've got Betty here and you want to impress her and shit but—"

"Hey—hey!" Cheryl couldn't help herself. "What do you mean he's got me? Nobody's got me. I'm my own person."

Trent paused for a moment to scrutinize her. And then he gloated. He'd gotten to her.

"I mean, fuck!" he said to Jarod. "You look like ass too. How long has it been since you were out in the fucking daylight?" He plopped onto the lip of the couch, crashing into Cheryl, sitting on her feet, and began to roll a cigarette.

Digging at the corners of his eyes, Jarod said, "I go outside, man. I walk the dog. What do you want, anyway?"

All of Trent's weight pressed into Cheryl's knees. He was forcing her to hold him up and she could smell him—tobacco and mildew and his sour BO—but she refused to back down; no way was she going to cede her space to him. When he leaned forward to rough up Jarod's hair, she felt slighted and weirdly incomplete.

"Come on, Jarod, get up. We're all waiting for you."

Jarod just stared at the blank TV screen. The puppy was growling at someone in the kitchen. "Where are we going?" he finally asked.

"Edina. The Galleria. We stole Little Tornado's mom's car for the day."

"I don't want to go to the fucking Galleria. What do I want to go to a mall for? In Edina."

There was a thud and the puppy let out a howl. Its claws could be heard clacking across the linoleum and then there was a crash and what sounded like a mass of cookie sheets tumbling to the floor.

The three of them—Trent, Jarod and Cheryl—peered toward the door, but the kitchen was still now.

Then, "Smooth move, ex-lax, it's dead." Cheryl recognized this as the voice of that black guy, Mike.

Another voice shot back, "You're dead."

"Hey, man, I'm not the one who kicked it."

Jarod bit at the raw spot on his lip. "Hey, what the fuck, man? What did you guys just do to my dog?" He looked like he was fighting back tears, but he didn't make any moves toward the kitchen. "Those fuckers are gonna wake up the ho-bag." There was pleading in his voice and he looked toward Trent as though the guy could magically fix everything.

"Don't cry, man, Jarod. Nothing could wake her up. She's on so fucking many sleeping pills you could fucking blow up the house without waking her up."

"Yeah, well . . ." Jarod lost himself in dead air. He ran his hand like a washcloth over his face. "Where are we going again?"

"The Galleria," said Trent. "Come on. Get up."

The puppy came racing out of the kitchen and crawled into the arch under Jarod's legs.

"Yeah. So, why?"

"Fighting the good fight, man. Fucking bring down the fucking motherfucking system."

It was Cheryl's turn to smirk. "How are you gonna do that?"

Twisting around, Trent rested his arm on the shelf of her knees. "It's a competition. Whoever steals the most shit—or no, the most money's worth of shit—wins."

"Wins what?"

"Wins the satisfaction of being the best thief."

He wouldn't stop giving her that heavy look and she couldn't stop returning it.

As Jarod begrudgingly pulled himself to his feet, the other boys shuffled back into the room. They'd found some cheese balls and were trying to bank them into each other's mouths. Cheryl got a better look at them this time. There was Mike, the black guy, a blond kid with a scraggly goatee and two silver rings pierced through his lower lip, and a grungy little boy, no more than twelve years old, with thick-rimmed plastic glasses and acne all over his face.

"Fucking finally," Trent said. "Oh, and hey, Jarod, tell your girl-friend she can come too." He shot Cheryl a look to see if she'd bite again, but this time she restrained herself. She was preoccupied with figuring out what expectations Jarod had for her and whether or not she owed him anything.

Five

AT THE GALLERIA, she avoided Trent. She tagged along with Jarod, whose idea of fun was sitting on a bench and watching the people walk up and down the stairs. They blurred together, these women who all looked like they did too much yoga and spent too much money on haircuts that made them look like they had roosters sitting on their heads, these men shaped like hockey pucks, wearing pleated chinos. They all drank the same brand of bottled spring water and pushed strollers the size of SUVs. Cheryl couldn't tell what Jarod thought of them, or if they registered on him at all.

Each time Trent circled past, he snuck up and pile-drove his shoulder into Jarod, called him a lazy fuck, tried to goad him into wrestling matches. He acted like Cheryl wasn't even there. This either meant that he liked her or he didn't—it could go either way—but whatever the tactic was supposed to achieve, it succeeded in spurring on her hatred of him. And the more she hated him, the more she hated Jarod, without whose existence she would have been able to like Trent without the guilt of betrayal. This prompted her to hate Trent more. Which prompted her to hate Jarod more. Which prompted her to hate herself most of all.

To be safe, she scowled whenever he glanced at her.

"Listen, Jarod," she said when they were alone, "your friend Trent is an asshole. He's, you know? What the fuck? He doesn't have any respect for anything. The way he comes barreling in this afternoon? That didn't piss you off?" Jarod shrugged. "And then he was, like, kicking you? I would've . . . I mean, you know? What a dick! And he acts like—I mean, what am I? Like nothing? Like nobody? I'm sitting here and I'm your friend or whatever and he's come by like five times now and I don't even get a hello. You know what I mean?"

If only Jarod had agreed with her, they could have formed an alliance, sustained the awkward stasis until maybe one of them finally made a move. But Jarod just fidgeted and stared at the floor, not saying anything, acting like *she* was the one who was an asshole. She was asking him, begging him, to put a claim on her. Did he not understand what was at stake here? Or was he just incapable of fighting for what he wanted? It made Cheryl sad, but it also allowed her to feel like, whatever, she'd given him a chance and his hurt feelings wouldn't be her problem.

After the mall, they returned to Jarod's house to check out each other's loot. It was already dark outside. The ho-bag was at work and wouldn't be home until three a.m. Trent made them sit around the kitchen table and lay their catch out in front of them. He kept a running tally. The kid with the goatee—Devin, his name was—had nabbed a respectable eighty-six dollars and twenty-three cents' worth of merchandise: two cut-out-bin CDs, *Snowed In*, by Hanson, and *Hot Dance Hits of 1993*, retail value nine ninety-eight each; the current issue of *Tattoo* magazine, retail value four ninety-five; a Black & Decker power drill, fifty-nine ninety-nine; and three Milky Ways (eaten along the way but with the wrappers as proof of purchase they still counted), worth sixty-five cents apiece. Mike, claiming he was at a disadvantage because he was black, that he was watched too closely, he couldn't pull the shit the other guys could, had only a cheap pair of stainless-steel earrings, worth a mere fifteen dollars, to show for himself. Little Tornado, the kid with the skin problem, had a whole bunch of shit, a cornucopia of worthless checkout junk: five packs of Doublemint gum, two tins of Altoids, a tiny green water pistol, four key rings with Japanese doodads hanging from them, a ten-pack of blue Bic pens, a handful of brown replacement dress shoelaces and a Koosh Ball, coming to a grand total of thirty-two fifty-six. Trent turned out to be the big winner—how could he not?—though he had only snatched three things: a fourteen-dollar book by William S. Burroughs called *Cities of the Red Night*, a small but high-tech telescope worth fifty-nine forty-nine, and the real prize, a pea-green army jacket worth ninety-five dollars. Cheryl and Jarod both came up empty.

"That's cool," said Trent. "That's cool, because at least you fucking didn't just go grabbing shit you didn't even want like those mother-fuckers." He pointed in the direction of Devin and Mike and Little Tornado.

"Who says I don't want these?" said Mike, holding up his earrings.

"Yeah, alright, you're exempt."

"I took shit I wanted too," said Devin.

"Like what?"

"Like . . ." He perused his pile. "I want *Tattoo* magazine."

"That's it, though. What are you gonna do with a power drill?"

"A power drill is a useful addition to any toolbox. Every self-respecting handyman should have one."

Everyone but Trent laughed.

"Look—all I'm saying is, alright, look." Trent's tone was severe and overblown. "The whole point of stealing shit is that you want to take shit you want. If you don't want it there's no point."

"You're still fucking up the system," said Little T.

"No." Trent glared at him like he was astonished by the immensity of the kid's naiveté. "No. You're not. Not if there's no redistribution of the motherfucking wealth. If you're just gonna throw the shit out, then, you know? I mean, what the fuck is that?"

"I'm not gonna throw this shit out. Look. See?" Little Tornado began unwrapping sticks of chewing gum and shoving them into his mouth. "See?" Saliva trickled down his chin as he talked. "See? I want this gum. And anyway, you're a fucking hypocrite, man. You've already got a jacket like that."

"Yeah, this is for Betty here."

Trent threw the jacket into Cheryl's lap. His arrogance was repulsive and appealing, and she'd wanted a jacket like this for a long time. Though she attempted to come off as if she didn't care, she couldn't stop herself from trying it on.

Balancing on the back two legs of his chair, Trent thrust his chin at her.

"S'it fit?"

"Sort of." She flopped her arms to show how the sleeves drooped over her hands.

"Well, if you fucking don't want it—"

Jarod was furiously chewing his lower lip, staring intently at the parquet table. His ears were red. What was she supposed to do? Give it back? Should she touch Jarod's leg, reassure him? That would be a lie. The thing to do was to forge ahead ruthlessly and pretend not to see the pain she'd caused.

"No, I like it," she said to Trent.

"Good, 'cause I got it for you."

The slapping of moths against the kitchen window, the sound of Jarod's heel rattling against the leg of his chair, the motorcycle roaring past outside—all of these noises slowly intensified, began to swirl, a windstorm in her stomach, an unwanted trill. She was disgusted with herself. Sneering at Trent, she said, "I s'pose you think I'm gonna fuck you now?" and hearing these words spurt out of her mouth gave her a further thrill, sent her heartbeat shooting down between her legs.

When I'd started talking to Cheryl about sex, way back when she was in the fourth grade, I'd been frank with her. "It can be pleasure and it can be pain," I'd said, "but if you get too caught up on the pleasure, if you go seeking physical sensation and lose track of all the emotions underneath, you're liable to find yourself in a lot of places you'll realize you don't want to be. That's where the pain comes in. I'd hate to see you cause yourself pain." I told her, "Look for love. Go seeking companionship and communication." I gave her a copy of *Our Bodies, Ourselves* and let her make her own decisions. I'm not sure any of this did much good. There are times when the adrenaline rush of transgression can propel you forward like destiny, when the changes you want to enact in your own being appear fully formed in somebody else.

That night, while the other boys slept in the living room, Cheryl and Trent scampered upstairs and shut themselves into Jarod's bedroom. The dank aroma of long-unwashed clothes had sunk into the walls and all the soft surfaces. It smelled like Jarod, like Jarod gone stale. A sad smell, Cheryl thought. She and Trent threw the junk piled on the bed to the floor. But once they were squeezing and pulling and slipping, probing and tasting each other's skin, the smell of Trent's breath and his sweat and his hair and the slapping of the chain padlocked around his neck with each violent movement he made inside her overwhelmed any hint of Jarod in the room.

When she heard the front door open downstairs and the distinctive shuffle of Jarod's mom's lame leg, the tap, tap, tap of her cane, Cheryl tensed up. She imagined the woman looking at the boys strewn all over the living room floor, recognizing her son there asleep among them and wondering where his girlfriend had gone. The bed rattled and squeaked and Cheryl was sure the sound carried downstairs. She could almost see the woman standing there, exhausted and sad above her sleeping son, listening to the rhythmic creak upstairs and wishing she could reach down and smooth the boy's hair, stopping herself because her leg hurt so badly and she knew it would hurt more if she tried to bend.

"What's wrong?" Trent said.

"Jarod's mom just came home."

He laughed. "The ho-bag? Don't worry about her. She's cool. She doesn't give a fuck what we do."

After it was over, the two of them fell asleep, clutching each other, naked. She was surprised that Trent wanted to hold her all night long. He wasn't so tough. Earlier in the day he must have been pretending—like her—that he could restrict what his heart allowed in.

The next morning, he was cool, but subtly attentive. She'd be in the kitchen, getting a glass of water, and as he walked behind her, he'd twirl one dry finger against the back of her neck, hold it there just long enough for her to notice, before continuing out into the backyard, leaving her just before she could respond. He fumbled periodically at her ass or her elbows, grinning into her face, then tumbling away. His fingers left impressions, pricks of stimulation that tingled and faded slowly from her skin. She found herself waiting for each next jolt, tracking him with all five of her senses as he moved around the house.

There was no way Jarod could have not known. But he watched TV like they weren't there, like nothing had happened, like Cheryl was simply another stranger wandering through this house he couldn't control. Sometime in the afternoon, he stepped into his mother's room and shut the door. They spoke in hushed tones—Cheryl couldn't make out a word they said—but nothing seemed to be any more wrong than it ever was. Jarod's mom hobbled off to work with his help, and the boys all did bong hits late into the evening. They watched *Blade Runner* and a show about insects on the Discovery Channel, and when Trent scooted up and wrapped his arms around Cheryl, she laced her fingers through his and gave a hidden squeeze. Everything was fine. There were no repercussions.

Later that night, once they'd smoked out the pot and finished off all the junk food in the house, Trent disentangled his arm from around Cheryl's waist. As he stood and stretched, his shirt inched up to expose the wisps of hair around his belly button.

"Later, Jay," he said. Then, raising an eyebrow, "So, Betty, you coming, or what?"

She shoved her shit into her backpack and sprinted up the stairs to Jarod's bedroom, grinning once she was sure no one could see her. The room reeked of mildew and sex and when she saw the sheet bunched along the edge of the mattress, she vaguely remembered kicking it off her feet during the night. She'd come to find the army jacket Trent had given her, but as she grabbed the sheet with both hands and snapped it straight, what she saw was the stain in the middle of the bed, the evidence—scaly now like dried egg white—that had leaked out of her during the night.

This was real. She felt bold and brave and mean, like she'd passed some marker beyond which she could be anything she wanted.

Jacket in tow, she raced back downstairs and out to the driveway, where the boys were waiting to drop Little T and his car off, all except Jarod—he wasn't coming. He and his dog were staying put to watch whatever showed up next on the Discovery Channel.

III

One

WHEN I WAS TWENTY, I lived in Dinkytown in a second-floor apartment above a store called Just Lamps. My two friends, Sammy Theissen and Rose Baker, lived there with me. It was a bad, a horrible time. We'd all dropped out of school and we were hanging around these rocker types who knew how to make themselves look moody and sensitive while tromping all over other people's lives. We were doing drugs. Some scary things happened. I won't go into it. If Robert hadn't appeared to lead me away, I probably would have died there.

I mention this only because it's relevant.

Leaving Little T and his car in the parking lot of the condo unit where he lived, Trent and his friends took Cheryl to a similar place. The Sabotage Café is what it was called, and I'd known all along she'd end up there.

Throughout the nine years it was in business, the Sabotage Café had been an unofficial countercultural landmark, the place where misfits of all sorts met and mingled. This was where the Hare Krishnas meditated over their tea, where the weathered hippies, still pulling their thinning hair into ponytails, tried for the nth time to settle the debate over whether the walk on the moon had been faked, where the junkies landed to nod out in peace and where the strays hid from the blistering wind. Now it was boarded shut, Trent said, because the cops had clamped down like they always did on anything that challenged the social order—scared, as they should be, of insurrection—but the truth was probably more blasé: shady things going on in the dimly lit corners, a nest of rats found by the health inspectors. The boys had shown up the winter before and taken over the ruined rooms on the second floor.

Cheryl hunkered down with them, that first night, in the large space that served as the living room—the Wreck Room, they called it—drinking beer and killing time. Two-by-fours rose at intervals from behind the jagged plasterboard where the top half of one wall had been partially torn away. The other walls were all dented and gouged, papered in grime and graffiti. There was no electricity, and the boys, even Mike, looked somehow hollow and pale in the weak beams of the flashlights they'd propped in the corners. The place both thrilled and repelled her. It was hardcore.

Speaking, as boys often do, in postulates and hypotheticals, Trent and Devin could have been talking about anything—Doctor Who, comic books, Romulan spacecraft. The topic they'd chosen was revolution.

"Fucking all you need is a couple of pipe bombs and fucking—bang—you fucking smash the window and the place goes up like a fucking hellhole. Piece of cake. Just like they did back in Seattle." Trent threw his whole body into his words, and Cheryl, seated below him, could feel his emotions pressing into her through his knees.

"Pipe bombs are for pussies," said Devin. "We should make, like, a dirty bomb."

Mike threw a bottle cap at him. "You guys are a bunch of assholes," he said.

"It's called civil disobedience," Trent spat back. "Fucking fight the fucking power."

Hunched forward in the beanbag, Mike aimed his beer at Trent. "If you pull that shit at Chipotle, I'll fucking report you myself." He was intimidating. Muscular and severe. When he looked at her, Cheryl got the feeling that he was seeing through to the parts of herself she wanted to hide. She felt small and exposed, like an impostor, playing at nihilism, caught in the act of doing it wrong.

"What's the big whoop about Chipotle?" she asked.

"I work there."

"It's owned by McDonald's," said Trent.

Devin lobbed the bottle cap back at Mike, aiming for the top of his head. "And it's where he picks up his jailbait."

Catching the bottle cap and spinning it around his fingers, Mike leaned back in the beanbag like a proud king. "Man," he said, chuckling, "you should have seen the one today. She was like . . . damn. Maybe fifteen, sixteen, you know, still with the baby fat, and wearing one of those tiny little skirts—you know what I'm talking? Like two inches long? Like those fucking loincloths that start about there." He drew his finger across his crotch. "Fucking . . ." His head rolled slowly back and forth, a connoisseur savoring a fine smell. "And no underwear." He pulled a torn corner of violet notepaper from his pocket, held it high like a coin between two fingers. "You better believe I'm gonna tap that."

The way the boys all laughed appalled her. She feared she'd made a mistake, letting Trent pull her into this crude den of theirs. Now she was stuck here. Prey. Unless Mike was boasting, putting on a display for his friends' benefit, and maybe trying to impress her as well. She admonished herself: stop being such a girl.

Trent held her shoulder steady with a firmness she chose to read as validation of her alarm. "See?" he said to Mike. "Fucking, you won't get that kind of ass in the Marines." He let go, but the assurance he'd given her lingered.

"I'll get better than that, man. You know what those Arab chicks look like. Damn."

She was still spacey, the tiniest bit stoned, and her mind leapt in unwanted directions, following synaptic trails thick with paranoia, rich with police officers chasing her through shadows. Though her father often came across as inattentive, she knew, he would set the system on her. She saw him on the phone, sitting behind a large computer console, telling the cops on patrol where to turn as he followed her movements on the screen in front of him. She had to keep herself off the grid if she didn't want to be dragged back home.

"See, Betty?" Trent popped her out of this nightmare. "Didn't I tell you Mike was a cocksucker?"

The other guys were gone. She gathered Trent toward herself like a comforter, enwrapped his lower lip in her own, but instead of settling onto the floor with her, he led her into the bedroom next door. Mike was crashed out in his underwear, asleep on an army cot, his clothes folded neatly in stacks below it. On the ceiling, where some boys might have taped centerfolds, he'd pasted a poster for the Marine Corps. The line where his space ended and Devin's began was marked by the rise of Devin's mountain of crap. Random cuts of plywood and broken umbrellas; rolled-up posters, yellowed and frayed at the edges; a coffeemaker missing its pitcher. So much junk was piled there he didn't even have room for a mattress. He'd just thrown himself on top of the overstuffed trash bags and dug out a little cradle. Trent's area was bordered by masses of books, stolen by the stack from Barnes & Noble. Using them as a defensive perimeter, he'd confiscated half the room. Behind this low barrier, his space was a near void: a tattered old Minnesota Vikings sleeping bag, a mildewed futon, an ashtray—that was it.

While Devin and Mike slept a few feet away, Trent twirled his hand around Cheryl's belly button. He removed her shirt and inched up her bra. His fingers roamed her body like metal detectors. He slipped one, two, under the lip of her shorts and scraped his nails along the fringe of her pelvis, knocking, can I come in, can I come in? She didn't know what he'd do if she said no, but she kept imagining Mike and Devin watching them.

"You don't want to do this," he said.

She nodded. Then she shook her head no. Then for reasons she couldn't quite identify, she started to cry and he yanked his hand abruptly away. Her pussy stung like he'd just ripped off a band-aid. He hadn't meant to hurt her. The concern on his face said he hadn't meant to hurt her. He traced the line of her shoulder blade.

Then, tipping his head toward his friends' sleeping bodies, he said, "Is it too weird? Because they're here?"

It was and it wasn't. She didn't know what it was. She felt dumb. Conventional. But the alternative was too vast and overwhelming, filled with dangerous hidden consequences. She pounded her temple with the flat of her hand.

"Betty, if you don't want to do this, you should tell me to fuck off. You know what I'm saying? I'm not a dick. I'm not like Mike."

This made her cry harder. She pulled him toward herself. She scratched at his arm, clawed at it, hating him, clinging to him. Somehow she ended up on top of him. A pool of her tears was forming on his chest, and for reasons she had no means of understanding, she felt like she was turning into me. Her rage and self-pity had blurred together. She placed her lips to the pool, then her ear to his heart—such a hollow sound, but heavy too; it sounded like drowning.

"So," he said quietly, "you do like me." Muted by the lack of light in the room, his expression appeared almost tender.

"Yes," she said. She couldn't remember what had set her off.

Some confusion shook through him. "But, don't love me, though, okay?" His voice was barely audible. "You love someone and you just get disappointed." He slid out from under her and went up on an elbow. "You get all caught up and start needing each other and then all of a sudden you're no longer a person. And the other person's not a person, either. You're both just a collection of expectations. Responsibilities, you know what I mean? It's fucked. It becomes all, like, me, me, me." For a second, he gazed at her. "Once you start to love me, you won't like me anymore."

She wondered if he was speaking from experience. There was nothing he hadn't prodded with his mind, in search not only of the right answer, but of the hard one, the true one. He was challenging her now to join him in turning away from the world she'd been taught to trust. Here was a boy, she thought, who could help her burn the school down.

"That's cool," she said. "I'm cool with whatever."

It was hard to tell if Trent believed her, hard to tell what he was thinking at all. Wanting to make sure he understood that, whatever happened later, she wanted him now, she did the only thing she could think to do. She took him in her mouth. Then remembering the other boys in the room, she pulled away and looked up at him.

"Let's at least go into the other room," she said.

If I could have told her . . .

She wouldn't have listened, though. She was enraptured.

Two

I COULD SEE THEM, Cheryl and Trent, trying every second of each day to get into each other's pants. In her first month or so at the Sabotage Café, that's all either of them could think about. Sex, and the urgent rush toward sex, and the damp exhaustion, the clinging and panting that echoed afterward, allowed them—Cheryl, at least—to imagine, for as long as it lasted, that she had landed in a secure location where her terror and hunger couldn't get in.

Opportunity was everywhere, but to find it took searching. It crouched in the shadows under fire escapes, in the alleyways behind Crazy Eights, the pool hall on Twenty-second Avenue. It hid in the tunnels linking the University of Minnesota buildings together. It lurked in the bathrooms at Starbucks and Caribou Coffee, the bathroom at the Viking, at the Den and the Blue Room and Positively 4th Street and all the other bars and college hangouts crowded around the U of M campus. It waited under shrubs, behind ferns and reeds, in the dark crannies along the Mississippi. The two of them seized it wherever they found it—a rushed kiss, then another, a tug of a lip, a handful of ass, of hair, of tit or dick—then they pulled apart, palm to breastbone, not here, but then where, God, where can we go? There was always a stranger or five or six nearby, someone knocking at the bathroom door—What's taking you so long?

What are you *doing* in there?—witnesses everywhere leering and scolding.

Even at home, in the Sabotage Café, they had to be on guard, they couldn't luxuriate; Devin or Mike or some other random kid was always threatening to break up the fun.

"What's the big deal, Betty?" Trent asked her once. "They won't come in. They know."

"What do they know?"

"That I'll fucking pluck their fucking eyes out if they do."

But they did come in. She'd be lying on her back between Trent's outstretched legs, the two of them sprawled across the leaky bean-bag, on something—they were always on some drug or other—watching the colors shift behind their eyelids as their hands pressed buttons on each other's bodies. And there would be Devin, willfully obtuse. "Hey, check this out." Standing over them, pulling up his sleeves to show off his track marks while he held his cigarette out for them to see.

He took a drag and blew a smoke ring. "I've got to get it to there first," he said, pointing to a spot half an inch from the filter.

"Yeah, that's great." Trent kicked at him. "Now go away."

"Hold on. Watch. It's ready now." Devin demanded attention, forced them to indulge him. Clamping the cigarette between his teeth, he held up a finger—"Wait"—then began flicking it in and out of his mouth. He twirled the cigarette around in there. He put it out on his tongue without getting burned.

The fingers stopped prowling. The opportunity dwindled. Cheryl's hands remained yoked around Trent's neck, his under her shirt, where he could still tickle and probe in a limited, ineffectual way.

"Fucking Devin, man, what does it take to get you to go fuck off somewhere else, huh? We could give two shits about your fucking parlor games."

Cheryl pulled at Trent's earlobe, at his greasy hair. She wanted to shut her eyes, to stretch, to shudder. There were currents streaming from her nipple to her navel. She tugged Trent by the neck, twisted his face over hers. She bit his lip.

Devin crouched and scavenged, then threw the pennies and junk he found on the floor at them. "Whoa, man, whoa, I don't need to see that shit."

He wouldn't take a hint, or taking the hint, he perverted it. He crouched and watched them. "Ouuu, ahhh, baby, more, more." He mocked them. He lingered, a mosquito hovering in the corner. They tried to ignore him, but he kept returning to buzz in their ears until Trent finally flopped back on the beanbag.

The current stopped flowing. Trent controlled the switch. He flicked it back and forth, but he wouldn't leave it on. Cheryl was frazzled, dazed and exhausted, but still unsatisfied, her heartbeat slowly returning to normal.

And then, having won, Devin swaggered toward the door, kicking the beanbag on his way out. "See ya. Wouldn't wanna be ya."

A faint whiff of mildew floated through the air.

Trent scowled at the ceiling. When Cheryl tried to touch him, he batted her away. "We're the oppressed," he said. "Just like the fucking Palestinians." Then, prying himself out from under her, he said, "Fuck it. Let's go get some forties."

Oppression entered and exited the café, mocking them, giving them just enough time alone to remember what it was they couldn't have. Mike would leave for Chipotle and five minutes later, Devin would crawl in from spanging, and when Cheryl and Trent fled the building to search the streets for cracks they could pry open and hide inside of, oppression would roll in on the northwestern winds, catapulting south, storming down on them, waves of rain flooding and washing them away; they'd float toward the river and eddy under the bridge, swirled together with a mess of other street kids, with the rest of the runoff that had been carried out of the Dinky-town gutters.

For a few days, they found relief in a culvert that jutted out over the river along the West Bank. That was fun—if chilly—rocking to the rhythm of the rain, banging their bodies against the corrugated steel. But oppression eventually found them here, too, in the form of a girl, sickly, with scabs riddling her face. She was cowering under a jumble of army-surplus blankets, bunkered behind a massive frame pack. Trent said, "What the fuck? Where'd you fucking come from?" "Iowa," she answered. Her voice was shot, hoarse and drowsy. Then the other end of the blanket rustled and another face popped out, as gaunt and shattered as the girl's, this one hidden by patchy tufts of blood and beard. "Leave us alone. We're sick," the guy told them, and because compassion was part of the code Cheryl and Trent tried to live by, they fled, oppressed again, this time by the implications they couldn't scrape off their minds.

Oppression seeped across the city like packing foam, caulking up even their most secret nooks. They might as well stay home and try to reason with Mike and Devin, the two unreasonable quantities they knew. Couldn't Devin see that his gross-out schemes, the zits and sores and boogers he was so proud of, didn't amuse them? Couldn't he find someone else to annoy? And didn't Mike understand that they thought it was great, terrific, that he'd nabbed that goth chick's number after slipping her a free order of chips and guac, but they didn't care? If she was so desperate for his dick inside her, why didn't he chase her down right now and fuck her, leave them alone.

Just leave them alone.

"Why can't you all just leave us alone?" Cheryl yearned to shout it, to stomp her feet, to scream.

But being left alone would be too easy. It would be too nice. If she really wanted to be left alone, she might as well have stayed in Plymouth, where being left alone was all there was to do.

Anyway, even when the two of them did find solitude, oppression often snuck up and ransacked them. Trent would pass out, too drunk to fuck, leaving Cheryl frustrated and wide awake.

Sometimes, when they managed to stay sober, when they were able to outlast Mike and Devin, they'd linger in the living room, dry humping. Gradually articles of clothing would come off, Cheryl's boots, her jeans. Her shirt would be smushed up into her armpits. Trent's cargoes would be down around his knees. If they muffled themselves they could almost pull it off. But it wasn't fun. The beanbag was uncomfortable, Trent's belt buckle had a way of stabbing Cheryl's thigh. She couldn't relax; she was always aware of the guys in the next room, afraid of discovery, and she inevitably became so anxious that she patted Trent's shoulder and made him stop. "Just pretend they aren't there," Trent said. "They won't wake up." She couldn't, though. When she closed her eyes and tried to concentrate on the sensations he was drawing out of her body, she imagined Devin snickering in the doorway, heard Mike muttering and shouting in his sleep. Trent was determined, though, once he got going, and if he was quick, she could usually keep herself from freaking out by biting her lip, digging her nails into his back, until his thrusting and hoarse grunting was done. What tortured her most about nights like these were the tantalizing intimations they contained. He'd change position, and just for a moment, she'd see the place she was so desperate to reach, boxed in glass, surrounded by a web of laser-triggered alarms, and all she could do was stare at it and wish.

She touched herself sometimes, but it wasn't the same. The physical sensation was a lesser thrill than having him, his presence over her, inside and around her, taking her consciousness—her soul, she sometimes thought—and submerging it, overwhelming it, claiming it briefly as his own. This is what she yearned for: to feel him rushing over her. To be obliterated beneath him.

The problem this time was Benny, the balding twenty-three-year-old meth-head who smothered the rims of his bloodshot eyes with thick black liner and plastered black polish over his splintered fingernails—a pathetic specimen from the black place their infatuation with darkness might one day lead them. He'd shared his stash with Cheryl and the boys, mocking them for their refusal to shoot, and now he was dancing, in his peg-leg jeans, around the ruins of the Wreck Room.

Cheryl, who'd never done the stuff before, was fighting off nervous visions of frying eggs—*This is your brain; this is your brain on drugs.* After two razor-thin lines, she began to turn down the jewel case circling round and round the room. "Naw, I'm alright," she said. "I'm cool." When she looked to Trent for how to behave, he didn't seem all that bent to her—a little friskier, maybe, that was all. Her eyes felt like pinwheels. She sat on her hands. She gnawed at her lip, trying to come off as less tweaked than she was. And then she discovered she was craving the stuff. Watching impatiently as it made the rounds of the party gathered in the café. Worrying over the size of her portions.

Since the kids weren't paying, they had no choice, once the drugs were gone, but to ride out Benny's interminable ramble about his struggle to find his dealer that day. He kept losing the drama in the mass of details, and if no one told him to get to the fucking point, he'd linger for twenty minutes, half an hour, over the terrors of a broken stoplight. The various randoms who'd shown up that night—kids going by names like Torque and Scab and Ivan—had found excuses to bolt hours ago. But Benny just kept jabbering on, giving up altogether on his story and spewing out the random junk in his head. He was on to Jelly Bellies now, how there were so many flavors you couldn't keep them straight, you had to eat them one at a time and concentrate, strain your brain, to connect the taste in your mouth with the list on the back of the bag. "It's hard, man! And they're all fake and chemically, so half the time all they taste like is sugar."

Devin nodded like a drone—"Yeah, man, exactly"—but everyone else was trying to ignore him. Mike, the only one of them who had stayed clean, leafed through a year-old issue of *Bounty Hunter*. Trent and Cheryl sat on the floor a few feet from each other, playing cat and mouse games; their fingers perched and scurrying along the wood, trying to catch and not be caught.

Leaning in to kiss her ear, Trent whispered, "What do you think, Betty? Let's light his fucking hair on fire."

"You think he'd notice?"

"Fuck, yeah. Prince noticed when it happened to him, and how high must he have fucking been, you know?"

"You mean Michael Jackson?"

"No—Prince. In the eighties. When his hair lit up onstage."

Prickly, more anxious now that she was high to resist the sickly side of her emotions, she pushed it. "That was Michael Jackson. During that commercial he did for Coke."

He pulled back. "Don't fucking tell me what the fuck I mean." A smile stretched tight across his teeth, and his eyes darted cruelly over her. A warning: If you cross me, you must be my enemy.

"Sorry," she said. She tapped his wrist with a tentative finger. "I'm sorry," she said again, but he wasn't giving. The meth exaggerated her insecurities, contorted the signs she was getting from him, it made every moment fraught with the possibility of catastrophe. To prove her contrition, she wrapped herself around him, smothered him under her weight and warmth. His rancor had never been aimed at her before, and she was scared to utter the plea on her lips: *Let me in, see me, understand, I adore you.* Instead, she rubbed the tense muscles in his shoulder, apologized unrelentingly until he finally softened beneath her.

Benny's patter continued to fly over them. ". . . those ones are easy 'cause they're just what they are, like blue: blueberry. White: coconut. Crimson: raspberry—or is it cinnamon? There's an apple too that looks like that. See? Everything gets so complicated!" Like migrating geese, his words whizzed by, at a distance, on an altitude unrelated to their own. "But anyway, it's the speckled ones that can really fuck you up. There's like fifteen different versions of green with green specks and they're all—"

Her lips pressed to Trent's chest, Cheryl kissed him through one of the ragged holes in his t-shirt. "I'm sorry," she said again. "I was just being a bitch." Her smile was weak and it disappeared quickly.

He nodded, slowly, sagely, then it was over. His arm was around her, his fingers trailing up and down her spine. He pried under her cargoes, worked his hand in and palmed her ass cheek, and she kept on kissing him, violent kisses, as though she was trying to climb into his mouth, leave her skin behind and pour herself into him. The way his hand clenched, fingernails digging skin, pulling her pelvis toward his own—she'd give him anything, let him shred her to pieces, if that's what it took to retain his desire.

On the other side of the tapestry-draped box that the boys had set up as a coffee table, Devin and Benny were shouting at each other now. They'd left Benny's Jelly Belly anxiety behind. Cheryl couldn't tell what they were on to, but whatever it was, she was sure it was stupid. A struggle for dominance over nothing at all.

"Benny! Benny! Listen to yourself!" said Devin. "I know you've got less brain cells than a fucking retard, but come on!"

"Devin, man, if you only knew how I listen to myself. I hear myself all day. I can't shut it off." Benny pointed at his lower eyelid, peeled it back like an alien from *Cocoon*. "It keeps me up. Days go by. Weeks. Lifetimes. Forever."

"I'll shut it off for you." Devin pulled at the blond scraggle on his chin, picked at it, like scratching would uncover something.

"Hey, man, it's cool, okay? I'm just talking, you know? Right? Conversing." When Benny smiled, his black rotting gums made him look like a creature come back from the grave, something Cheryl's old skater friends might have stumbled across in a video game and blasted to smithereens without a thought.

"Well, converse differently," said Devin, " or I'll get my boot to converse with your ass."

Benny held his hands out in front of himself, palms down, patting air. It was hard to tell how frightened he really was. He always looked spooked; if you said hello to him in the street he'd wince.

Not that Cheryl cared either way how this turned out. She just wanted him gone, and Devin too, and Mike. Trent's fingers dug deeper into her ass, and she let out a little moan. Then she rolled off of him. "Let's go somewhere," she whispered. "I can't stand it."

She could feel his thoughts in the pulse of his fingers against her shoulder blade, his ideas ramming up against each other as he ran through the secluded places he knew—Pillsbury Park with its curfew and its trolling cops, that cinder-block outpost at the top of the Stadium Village parking ramp. He was calculating the probability of diminished desire in relation to distance and time. Maybe Cheryl wasn't making herself clear: all they had to do was leave the room. She'd fuck him in the stairwell, in the middle of the street, anywhere, just let's get rid of these guys. She slid her hand up the leg of his shorts and his eyes bulged, his groin rose.

"Come on," he said. "I want to check something out."

They fled to the kitchen. Rectangles of caked grease and soot framed the spaces where appliances had once been. Mouse droppings spread across the floor like spilled Tic Tacs. Trent yanked open the window. On the other side, maybe two feet away, was a stucco wall. He traced the path for her: a short leap to the drainpipe, then a quick, careful scramble up to the roof; they could use the rusty bolts as footholds. Dangerous but worth it. She followed him up.

The roof was vast and empty, an expanse of tar paper glittering in moonlight. It was heaven, salvation. They were finally alone.

That night, for the first time, she let the desire rush through her unmitigated. It was oceanic, a salt-heavy weight roiling under her skin, lapping at her pelvis, dampening everything, condensing on the surface in filmy layers. She imagined taking him whole into her system—like that weird spiny fish she and Jarod had seen on the Discovery Channel—and holding him there, soaking him in her juices, until the two of them became a single organism, sharing veins and arteries and internal organs, never to be parted again.

A few days later, they dragged a torn inflatable kiddie pool up to cushion their bodies against the grit and tar. They worked out a code involving obscure hand gestures and references to Debbie Harry. Trent would flash a sign, Cheryl would say, "Debbie's hungry," and then they'd race off, poking and pulling each other, scaling the wall to the roof and the release that existed for them there.

Fuck was the word she preferred to use. *Fuck* kept everything on a level, helped her deny, at least to Trent, whatever else might be going on. But with every new entry he made in her body, he penetrated deeper. *Fuck* helped her focus on the physical act, on the bodies bumping into bodies, helped her overlook the other stuff her body held, all that spiritual muck she felt him probing. Whatever part love played in her feelings had to be hidden, from herself as well as him. Love wasn't cool. Love just fucked things up. And this thing between them would last longer without it.

Three

THE PAGE SHE SENT ME had been torn out of a 'zine of some sort. It was crinkled and stained and ripped in the corner where the paper had been yanked from the staple. On one side someone had drawn a crude cartoon of Uncle Sam, giddy and naked, masturbating while bouncing on top of a geyser of oil. On the other, a frame of anarchy symbols surrounded a list of what seemed to be meant as incendiary assertions:

TRENT'S BILL OF RIGHTS

We have a right to a Starbucks on every corner.

We have a right to a shitty job in a tiny cubicle in a windowless room in a giant corporation and a right to be fired from this job if we surf the internet or make personal calls or if the boss finds out we've got a weak handshake.

We have a right to watch crappy TV right up until the day we die.

We have a right to believe the hype.

We have a right to say whatever the fuck we want and have the shit we say ignored.

We have a right to get totally shit-faced and do fucked up things in the name of boredom, then pretend the next morning we can't remember the fucked up things we did.

We have a right to secretly feel bad about having done all those fucked up things. (I'm sorry I ripped up your stupid poster, Mike, but I'm not sorry I pissed on it. What the fuck's wrong with you, man? The Marines?!!)

We have a right to starve for everything we don't have and never will.

We have a right to destroy ourselves when we realize that, really, we have no rights at all.

She'd drawn a heart pierced with an arrow around the name Trent. I would have thought it was silly if it hadn't been just so sad.

Four

THE GUY WHO OWNED the Sabotage Café knew they were there. Cheryl'd never met him. He was never around. But his influence was strewn across the place like stale crumbs.

"He's a legend," Trent told her. "You've heard of Nobody's Fool? The drummer, Cap? Rick Milton? That's him."

Of course she knew who he was. I'd told her about him many times, described things she shouldn't have ever had to hear. I can't justify myself. It was a mistake. But except for Sarah, and Robert sometimes, Cheryl was the only one I knew who would listen.

Trent's awe of Cap disturbed her. This first time he mentioned him, they were at the St. Anthony Park branch of the Minneapolis Public Library, taking advantage of the free Internet to check out the web sites of anarchist groups around the country. Trent clicked out of the Black Bloc report he'd been poring over and Googled up a page about the band.

The official story, as told by some guy named Douglas Braun and posted on his blog, Braun Candy, went like this:

> Nobody's Fool could have become the voice of their gener-
> ation. They were *supposed* to be the voice of their genera-
> tion. Of all the bands to rise out of the '80s bubble, they
> were the one that best melded the chaos of second-wave

American punk with the catchy melodic sense of the Stones, the Beatles and the Clash. Over a prodigious four-year period from 1984–88 they recorded five albums—two and a half hours' worth of music—for the tiny local TallTales label. The first two, *Who Wants to Know* and *Not Again,* were laid down on a modular four-track in the unfinished basement of Rick "Cap" Milton's parents' house. There was a moment there in 1986, after the release of their masterpiece *Would That It Were,* when the A&R men couldn't get enough of them. Every label in the country was vying to sign them. But as Epic, the label that eventually succeeded, soon discovered, except for Swope Johnson, the band's front man and songwriter, Nobody's Fool was more passionate about bagging the gnarliest girls and sampling the hardest drugs than doing the hard work of building a lasting career. Their life's ambition was not to be rock stars but to be able to drink free at their favorite local bar, the CC Club, for the rest of their lives. This "slacker" attitude (a term that years later would come to characterize the sort of people Nobody's Fool most resembled—and predated), with its unfocused energy and Midwestern fatalism, was the very thing that the critics adored about them, but eventually it did the band in. They recorded one album for Epic—a spirited effort entitled *Say It Ain't So, Joe*—went on one nationwide tour, saw one song rise into the top ten on the college charts, and then Swope realized that if they were to sustain the grueling workload that the majors required of them, the band was going to have to sober up and get serious. When Cap, Jake Jones and Denny Preston had other ideas, Swope ditched them and took off for New York, where he hired a bunch of session musicians to help him record Nobody's Fool's last studio release—a collection of quirky up-tempo ballads called *Action Figure* that, though a massive commercial failure at the time, prefigured the po-mo stylings of Pavement and Beck and the Flaming Lips and the whole slew of geek bands that rose to prominence over the next decade. Cap, Jake and Denny can still be seen most nights swilling whiskey at the CC Club, or catching a new act at the Boom Boom Tick, the same grimy joint where the band performed their first gig. Swope, in the meantime, now works in advertising, writing jingles about prescription drugs and sugared cereals. Both camps are still convinced they made the right choice . . .

Douglas Braun went on to assess in endless detail each of the songs on *The Edge of Nowhere*, the compilation of outtakes and B-sides that was released in 1994 to fulfill the third and last record the band owed Epic.

"But, see, that's all bullshit," Trent said. "Candy-ass crap that's supposed to fucking make you forget how fucking dangerous Nobody's Fool really was. It's ad copy. Middle-class fucking suburban bullshit. They weren't a product. They were a fucking idea." He preferred the counterhistory, the hipper, darker, messier story of a bunch of radicals blown through with chaos.

While they wandered through the streets of St. Anthony Main, he told Cheryl how Cap and the band had been kicked off the Midwestern leg of a Dead Kennedys tour because they were too rowdy even for Jello Biafra, how they used to do pickup shows with Hüsker Dü, sharing top billing, until the deal with Epic threw Bob Mould into a paranoid frenzy and he began to sabotage their equipment, snipping wires in their amps and stealing the extra strings from their guitar cases. He said, "I can't believe you've never heard of them."

And protective of me, she lied: "The name's sort of familiar. Maybe my mother was into them once, I don't know."

She didn't mention the things she knew Cap had done, how, one hilarious night after his girlfriend Rose Baker passed out, he and his buddies lit her hair on fire, or the way he had of buckling with laughter while Jake and Denny smoothtalked young girls into shooting up with them. And even though it might have impressed Trent, she didn't let slip that Cap had dated me too—what a joke it had been to him, his two girlfriends sharing a single apartment. Instead, she listened. She hung on Trent's every word and let his version of Rick "Cap" Milton replace mine.

Trent ran through the legendary anecdotes: the time Bad Brains stumbled through town and HR crashed on the floor of Cap's apartment, disappearing the next day (Cap found out later) with all the band's amps and the half gram of cocaine Cap had hidden inside his bass drum. The time GG Allin showed up at a party and pulled a knife on one of the girls there—Cap took a bottle of rye to Allin's head, split it open, knocked him unconscious and then the party continued on, people tromping over Allin's bloody body every time they wanted a beer from the fridge. How Cap had even met Iggy Pop once; they'd shared a needle and stared silently at the cracks in the wall together.

Cheryl could infer from the timbre of Trent's voice the power these names exerted over him. She liked that he'd steeped himself in a reality with which I hadn't been able to reconcile. Here was the world that had shattered me, and hand in hand with him, she'd liberate herself from all the fears she'd inherited.

When they arrived at the Sabotage Café, it was late afternoon and the Wreck Room was full of shadows. They found Devin sprawled on the floor, listening to something that sounded like whale calls. One forearm was thrown over his eyes and the other arm extended out above his head, palm up and pulsing, like he was worrying an invisible rosary. Instead of a hello, Trent stomped on Devin's fingers, and when he lunged up to defend himself, slapped him quick upside his head. Exhausted, still prying himself loose from the night before, Devin sagged back to the floor and twisted at one of the loops in his bottom lip.

"What is this shit?" Trent said, marching toward the boom box. "It's like something's fucking dying in here." He jabbed at the buttons and killed the noise, then, prying the lid open with a flattened paper clip, flipped the CD out of its chamber and sent it sailing toward Devin's head. "Betty here wants to check out Cap's stuff."

The snarl Devin flashed at her had no fangs. Of the three boys, he was the youngest—fifteen, sixteen, maybe, the same age as her—and his nastiness made him seem even younger. He loved gross things for the grossness of them: boogers and dead birds and fat-lady porn. A few days earlier, after Trent had taken off to print up his manifesto and Mike had already left for Chipotle, he'd straddled Trent's wall of books and sullenly watched her read the "Freaks" issue of *ReSearch*. "What are you after?" he eventually asked. Glancing up, annoyed, she told him, "Nothing." "Come on, I know you're after something. You all are." "Who all?" "All you feminist bitches." She stared at the pictures in the magazine, grainy black-and-whites of grinning pinheads and cyclops babies. "Name a woman who's not a bitch," he said. "Um, me." "No, you're a bitch." "How would you know?" "Because I know. Because you're a female. Quid pro quo." She laughed in his face. "You don't even know what that means," she said. "What?" "Quid pro quo." "Sure I do." "No you don't." He thought for a moment, and then, befuddled, said, "Okay, so tell me, what does it mean?" "I can't remember, but it doesn't mean what you're trying to make it mean." "See, there's the proof. You're being a bitch. Type A: Feminist." "Jesus Fucking Christ," she'd said. Heading downstairs and into the street, she'd walked off toward the Green Tea Smoke Shop for a package of Drum, more annoyed at the way he was grinning behind her, gloating, thinking he'd won something, than at the possibility that he might actually believe the crap he'd been spewing.

"She's never heard Cap's stuff?" he said now, sitting up to make sure she saw his sneer. "What is she, like a mental retard?"

"No, I'm not a mental retard. What are you, like eight years old?"

He squinted and spit her words back at her. "What are you, like eight years old?"

"Hey, Devin," Trent said over his shoulder as he dug through the loose CDs and broken jewel cases strewn around the boom box. "Fucking shut the fuck up."

Devin scratched his forehead with a stiff middle finger. "Make me."

Shuffling the discs around like puzzle pieces, Trent continued his search. "If I could fucking find it, you'd see," he told Cheryl. "They were the best fucking Midwestern punk band ever."

Jealous and annoyed by the intensity of Trent's focus on Cheryl, Devin leapt in to refute him. "They weren't punk," he said. "They were a garage band."

"Devin, didn't I tell you to shut the fuck up?"

"I'm just saying, they weren't punk."

"Okay, what's punk, Devin? Why don't you tell us?" Trent stopped his searching and waited for an answer.

A blank look, a few tugs at the ring in his lip later, Devin said, "Hardcore's punk. Fucking Agnostic Front. Henry Rollins and shit."

"Whatever," Trent said. "It's a continuum." He went back to rummaging. "Alright. Here. Check it out, Betty. This is *Not Again*."

A wobbly bass line set the tone for the first song—down tempo, almost countrified—until the drums crashed in and sped things up and a guitar, heavy on feedback, started stabbing around the melody. Swope's weedy drawl broke in, "Shit, man, hold up. I—fuck, hold up, hold up," and the instruments collapsed into a jumble of screeches and snare rolls. Then they started again, the same as before, this time meandering into a surprisingly melodic and moody song about the desolate winter streets of Minneapolis.

Until now, Cheryl had stayed away from the music of Nobody's Fool. She knew one of their songs was called "Julia's Drowning," and she was scared to hear what it might contain, what previous incarnations of me might be illuminated. She didn't want to think about it. Me with black rings around my eyes, my chin and teeth covered in the charcoal I'd been fed after the band had dumped me at the hospital. But that song was on a different album. This one was okay. This one made her feel closer to Trent.

"They used to just trash places." His words tumbled into her. She longed to be filled up completely by his voice. "Like clubs and shit, Betty. They'd get totally blitzed and throw raw hamburgers at the audience. Or, like, they'd take a break halfway through their set and come back fucking wearing each other's clothes and playing each other's instruments. Like the clothes and instruments would stay together, but fucking the band members would have all moved. I mean, fucking brilliant, right? Fucking kick-ass. Once they played a place, they'd never be invited back."

Devin let loose a whooping noise from deep in his throat. He was trying to scoff, but it sounded like he was having a seizure. Trent shot him a look. He rolled a joint and held it to Cheryl's lips.

Eyes closed, listening, she felt like she was rising out of the muck that connected her to me, hovering over it, floating away. She'd expected the music to be seething and hateful; instead it was aching, a dim flare sent up from a desolate lost place.

"Can I have some of that, or what?" said Devin, moving over to the beanbag.

Trent ignored him. As he twisted back to flick the ash from the joint, he was careful not to jar Cheryl's head in his lap.

"This music is great," she said. "It's so sad."

"It's not sad," said Devin. "It's pissed off."

"Well, I think it's sad."

That wheezing half laugh lurched out of Devin's throat again. "Hey, Trent, you gonna give me the fucking joint, or what?"

"It's amazing how they did it," Trent said. "They were totally smashed the whole entire fucking time. Like stumbling, lurching, lay-on-the-floor-and-spin drunk. And they—"

"That's such bullshit. You're so full of shit, Trent. They were on acid. They weren't drunk."

"Devin."

"What?"

"Shut the fuck up."

"Give me the joint."

"I said shut the fuck up."

"And I said make me!"

Cheryl's head hit the floor with a thud, and the joint fell onto her stomach as Trent dove across the room, legs stretched behind him, arms cocked in front of him. He wrapped the waistband of Devin's underwear around his hands and stood over him, excited, his fists up near his chin. "Shut the fuck up, dickwad, cocksucker, bitch." Suspended like a baby in a swing from two feet of thin stretched-out fabric, Devin squirmed and yelped between Trent's legs. "How's that? You like that, you want some more of that?" He was laughing, pulling with all his might, lifting Devin right up into the air. Then the beanbag shifted. Trent toppled onto his back. The cardboard box they'd been using as a table collapsed beneath him, but he kept pulling, inching across the floor, his fingers turning white inside the waistband as he dragged Devin behind him. He adjusted his grip, tugged until Devin howled, until the fabric tore and he had the waistband up around Devin's ears, scraps of gray-white fabric fluttering below it.

Exhausted, the two boys flopped gasping on their backs, arms and legs twisted all over each other. They were laughing, both of them, giddy, content.

Trent propped himself up on an elbow. "Where's that joint?" he asked, and Cheryl handed it over.

"Fuck, man," Devin said, "that fucking hurt." He was rubbing his ass crack, tugging at his jeans. "That was my only pair of underwear, you ass-wipe."

"I got him good, didn't I?"

"I'm serious, dick, you gonna get your girlfriend to buy me another pair, or what?"

"You know what, Devin," Cheryl said, leaning in to bring herself closer to their fun, "I'm gonna *sew* you a pair, how's that?"

This shut him up, but it seemed to secretly please him as well. Grabbing at the joint in Trent's hand, he said, "Give me that," and once he had it, he took a deep drag and lay back down to stare at the ceiling and chuckle to himself. Eventually, he slinked out to go spanging and it was just her and Trent again, curled in the beanbag, snuggling under the coat he had given her.

"This was their symbol, see?"

He found a Sharpie and after sniffing its fumes, he sketched a large circle on the back of the coat. He drew three vertical lines inside the circle, then one horizontal and one diagonal. When he was done he had the letter N superimposed over the letter O, both of them caught in the sights of a rifle scope:

"Cool, huh?"

"Yeah."

They listened to the music.

In one of the photos on the CD insert, Cap sat alone on a wooden fold-ing chair in the middle of a vast concrete room. Ten, fifteen, twenty empty beer bottles lay strewn at his feet. Above his head, there was a sign, a cartoon sombrero. MEXICO, it said. 6B. Cap was dressed in tight black jeans and combat boots, a bandanna wrapped around his left knee. The military blazer he wore over his ripped t-shirt was cluttered with buttons. The photo was a cliché of its time, really, but something about it resonated for Cheryl. She could imagine Trent daydreaming himself into Cap's place in the photo: junkie-thin, crumpled in on him-self, his arms shrouding his head, his one leg hiked up on the chair as though to protect himself from incoming shrapnel. This was a man defeated, utterly so, yet somehow also defiant, as though he knew the fight was hopeless, that the mall and the concrete and everything else would destroy him whether he submitted or not, so why not make some noise as he was going down? This was the stupor before the bat-tle, the drunken sob of despair before he blazed back again, returning to the stage to lead the doomed insurrection. She could see, when she looked at the photo through Trent's eyes, the little boy trying to become the man. It didn't matter if the myth was a lie. It made her smile.

How many hours had she spent in her room, blasting Rage Against the Machine and wishing she were somewhere dangerous and real instead of stuck way out here in Plymouth? How many times had she gone into the city to see an exhibit at the Walker with me and been more interested in the folks on the street—those coiled creatures, beaten but somehow not beaten down—than in the totems to the human spirit hanging on the clean white gallery walls? Or driven in with her friends, escaped for a day, to wander through

Uptown trying to look cool and smoking cigarettes and dreaming of how great it would be to escape like this forever?

She hadn't been able to imagine at that time how a person went about transforming herself from the thing she was into the thing she wanted to become. But here, this boy Trent stood now like a hooded shaman, his eyes glowing amber, his arm around her shoulder, his lighter held out to show her the way. He spoke in a language that she'd heard in whispers but never fully understood before, words that rattled like keys on the end of a string, slid into sockets and unbolted doors she would have been afraid to open alone. "This country's fucked-up. We have to tear it down and start fucking over." Words that pulsed and grew and enveloped her mind like those of the saviors she'd embraced before him: the Dalai Lama, Hillary Clinton, Rumi. "We have no idea what's really going on. The media's job is to keep us confused." He saw through hypocrisy. He shook with outrage. "See, that's what it means—the fucking Second Amendment. When your country's sold you out, it's your job, it's your fucking responsibility, to rise up and resist. To burn the motherfucker to the ground." Alienation was a galvanizing force in him, and in the few weeks since she'd arrived at Sabotage, he'd changed the rules by which her world operated.

On a Wednesday night, or a Sunday afternoon, they'd head to the Boom Boom Tick Club and hang in the gutter with the other grimy kids, sniffing around for a party to crash, waiting for someone to pop out for a smoke. "Hey, Tim, hey, Flake, hey, Little Tornado, come here a sec. You got a stamp? You already pay? Come here, Benny, I need to talk to you a minute." Trent knew everyone and Cheryl did too now. She was fearless as long as he was around. There was a whole society, fueled by glue fumes and nitrous and whatever else they could get their hands on, hiding in the ruins of bombed-out buildings or just bumming along the river all night, lurking and scheming and pulling away from the world she'd so recently fled. The bands were mostly local, kids like them, from the suburbs or sometimes from the U of M, thrashing their way through their first, second gig. It didn't matter. The music was just noise. They congregated here, at the all-ages shows, to listen to war cries and manifestos, to embrace the chaos storming through their cells.

The trick was getting in. Trent pressed the back of his hand to Benny's, clasping tight until the smudged Masonic eye on Benny's bloated skin peeled away onto Trent's, a temporary tattoo. They all took a turn at it—Devin, Mike, Cheryl—stealing stamps from whoever was around. Then, flashing their fists under the black light, they rammed through the door and ricocheted into the vast empty space. Stomping boots, butting heads, slamming shoulders and chests, they climbed bodies and speakers so they could dive. They pulverized every cell in their bodies—each other's, their own, it didn't matter whose—pummeling each other, sometimes, out of joy, other times beating themselves bloody with rage. Somebody's glasses would fly across the room and there'd be a stampede to shatter them. A bruise, a welt, a broken tooth. They learned to recognize themselves through pain.

Then, stumbling, limping back to the Sabotage Café, they felt transcendent, beyond the reach of the cops and social workers, unable to be tempted by the born-agains passing out bag lunches from the backs of vans and offering hot soup and candy and pop to anyone desperate enough to climb aboard and take the ride back to Shepherd's House. They'd learned how to reject worldly things on their own and their squalor gave them all the comfort they required. They'd been embraced by the refuse of the world and now they had nothing, were becoming nothing, and dreaming of ways to turn everything else into nothing with them.

And I thought, okay, my job is to stay out of the way. Maybe Cheryl will have better luck than I did. Maybe she's found a better way to be. I didn't believe it, though. Experience had taught me there was a lot to fear.

Five

SHE CALLED TO TELL ME I was a bad mother. She remembered one day when she was ten years old and I'd yanked her arm almost out of its socket as she was about to cross the road. Yes, she'd seen the car speeding toward her, but so what? I didn't have to pull so hard.

"But every mom does that," I explained to her. "It's one of the things they teach you in Parent School."

"That doesn't make it right," she said.

She remembered how I'd made her practice her violin for one full hour out of each day, even though she sighed and complained every time. "Couldn't you tell I hated it, Mom? Did it never occur to you that I was tone-deaf?"

"You never told me."

"I did tell you, and anyway, you're my mother. You're supposed to be able to notice these things."

"I notice things, Cheryl. I notice all sorts of things."

"Yeah, but half the time they don't exist . . . you know, Mom? Your world, the way you see the world, it's fucked-up. It doesn't work."

"All I ever did was try to provide you with the things I thought would make you happy. And protect you."

"I don't want to be happy," she told me then. "I don't want to be protected. Not by you."

.   .   .

Is this when she exploded? Is this when that bright restless girl I used to know turned her will to fight against herself? I'm not sure. I lost her for a while after that.

The haunted voices I'd fled when we moved to Plymouth returned to blot out what I could see of her. They'd changed over the years; they'd thinned and lost their richness, lost their complexity; they'd screamed themselves hoarse in their search for me. I could no longer make out what they were saying, but through their wailing nonsense, I understood they were angry at me.

I suspected that Cheryl had pointed them in my direction. To shut me out. To sever our bond. She knew it was one of my jobs to listen. Maybe more acutely than was good for her, she knew I'd been cursed with too much empathy, that I was liable to be overwhelmed by the sorrow washing over me. But she also underestimated how hard I'd fight, how primal my need for her would be.

For weeks I heard nothing. She didn't call. She sent no coded messages. She found a way, somehow, to push me from her mind. That's the part that scared me. She'd been my shield and my reason, my touchstone, and without her I didn't know what to believe.

When I was in her room, I could almost make her out. I stayed there virtually around the clock now, lying on her bed, lying under her desk sometimes, sitting on the floor with my legs straight in front of me, holding my body incredibly still. If I found the right spot and turned my head the right way, I could block out the voices and, for brief intervals, catch bits and pieces of where Cheryl was hiding.

On the West Bank. The buildings nondescript and gray, bleached and chalky. It was all pale roads and sidewalks and parking meters—two in the morning and everything was dead underneath the trees. And Cheryl, walking down Washington Avenue, had bulk and mass. The dust in the air gravitated toward her, clung; it mixed with her sweat and caked her skin with mud.

Her boyfriend was speaking. There was violence in his voice. "All these fucking money-grubbing lawyers, reading the bylaws and finding the fucking loopholes. You know what they had to do? Fucking they had to change the fucking name. As long as it was Kentucky Fried Chicken, they still had to give free meals to the homeless. It was in their charter or whatever the fuck it's called. But if it was KFC, fucking they could do whatever the fuck they wanted. It was like a whole new company. So, see? Capital wins again. Not even the Colonel can ward it the fuck off." His bony arms swung loose as he walked. Turning the corner, he jumped and slapped a street sign. "It's true. I'll show you the web site sometime."

They were heaving themselves into a massive dumpster out behind a fast-food restaurant. Standing on slick black bags. Buckets of chicken were lodged in the corner. Cheryl picked one up and found it was still warm.

"Federal law," Trent said. "Everything gets thrown out at the end of the day. Perfectly fucking good food. But no, they can't give it to people who need it. Fucking that would be fucking anti-American."

They plopped to the ground, and as they headed back across the river toward Dinkytown, they dug in, gnawing on drumsticks, ripping the skin off of thighs. They sucked the meat from the carcasses, and when they were done, the bones flew behind them and rattled on the pavement for stray dogs to fight over.

Then she'd disappear again in the din of voices.

She was testing me. Gauging how complete my submission would be. I couldn't call her, not if I hoped to keep her. Robert, I was sure, was tracking my calls, trying to discover where she was through them and drag her home before she was ready.

All I could do was wait, locked in her bedroom, and strain for further glimpses of her. In the back of her closet, I found the baby-blue cashmere sweater that I'd given her on her fourteenth birthday. "Jeez, Mom, just what I've always wanted," she'd said. "An old-lady sweater." She only wore it once, and then just to please me, careful to choose a time when we were far away from anyone who might get the wrong idea. Still, once was enough. It had belonged to Sarah and it connected the two of them together. My thought was to put it on, but it didn't fit. The best I could do was lie on her bed and snuggle up tight with it, listening, watching. Sometimes Gremlin hopped up and balanced on my hip; he helped me search.

There she was, holed up on the second floor of the Sabotage Café, sitting cross-legged in the Wreck Room. The cardboard box they called a table buckling under the weight of empty bottles. Old copies of *City Pages* strewn everywhere. It might have been noon, or three in the afternoon. The two windows hid her from whatever was outside; one was boarded up, the other slathered in dull black paint, pin-points of light streaming in and mapping constellations across the walls: the surfboard, the ice cream cone, the vacuum cleaner. A different universe.

She liked the darkness. She liked being nowhere.

She wielded a razor blade, cutting slits in the cuffs of her army jacket so she could stick her thumbs through when she wore it. It was tattooed with patches now, a mohawked skeleton smoking a ciga-rette, a smiley face with a bullet through the brain, the logos of bands that had died before she was born, the Subhumans, the Germs, the Slits and the Cramps; their names alone expressed her aspirations.

Or she'd be drinking from a bottle of cheap whiskey, bracing her-self for the stick of steel through her eyebrow or her nose, the double hoop snakebite through her lower lip.

She was transforming herself, letting Trent transform her. "It's about ownership," he explained. "You can let *them* fucking own you, you can shop at the places *they* want you to shop and believe the fucking things *they* want you to believe, help them fucking build their fucking empire, all that bullshit, be a fucking drone like fucking everyone else, or you can, you know, fucking fight the power. It's like that Clash song, you know?" He crooned, "I came here for a special offer / a guaranteed personality."

Her lip was twisted around his fingers, pulled taut like dental floss, and he was stabbing at her with the stud. The rest of her body went chilly and damp and then there was a pop and a sudden burn, a surge of adrenaline as he pressed again, harder this time, forcing the stud out the other side.

There were things she was supposed to do after that—douse the wound in alcohol, twist the stud twice a day, stop herself from toying with it while it healed—but she forgot. Infection crept in. She didn't mind. She sort of liked it, actually. The mild warmth, the itch were somehow comforting; they reminded her of how far she'd come.

I was scared for her. She was becoming feral.

Rooting around in her closet, I searched for evidence of the girl she'd been before. The shelves were filled with distressed jeans, tattered, threadbare t-shirts, Catholic schoolgirl skirts and ripped tights in black and blue and sometimes blood red. Watching me, Gremlin twitched his ears. He leapt from his perch on her desk and dug through the old shoes and bedding on the floor, revealing a black trash bag in the closet's corner. The bag distressed him. He wouldn't stop clawing. When I pulled it open, I uncovered aspects of her earlier selves: an old North Face jacket, the cords she'd worn during her anti-leather phase, all those t-shirts with their quaint ideals—Keep Your Laws Off My Body, Race for the Cure, Free Mumia. I piled them next to the sweater on the bed. Something told me that if I could arrange these items in the correct configuration, I'd be able to coax her back to me. I buried myself in them, breathed in the scents embedded in their fabric—incense and perfume and patchouli oil and that other smell, that complex essence of her.

And there she was, kneeling in the Wreck Room, her arm braced flush against Devin's as they waited for Trent to drop a lit cigarette into the seam. It was a game. Who was the toughest? Who would flinch first? The three of them watched as the cigarette burned down to the filter, leaving a blister of singed skin on each arm.

She did whippets.

She sniffed glue.

She popped Valium, Percocet, whatever she and Trent could steal from the dorm rooms of the undergraduates gullible enough to let them in.

She crushed Ritalin tablets under a CD case until she'd rendered them into a fine dust, then she and the boys—even Mike this time— took turns doing lines until sunrise.

And that's just the stuff I can bear to mention.

There was nothing she wouldn't do. There was no order, no rules, except those Trent or Mike or, rarely, Cheryl or Devin made up—*for the next three days, no one's allowed to speak, we'll only point and grunt, and every time anyone says a word out loud, everybody gets to hit him*—and these rules were made to be broken, to be shattered as proof that rules inevitably constrict the human spirit.

At Tattoo U., the dingy storefront parlor on Fourteenth Avenue, she studied the designs tacked across the wall. They were all inadequate, striving for beauty or for a refined, stylized sort of ugliness. A mermaid, a rose, a black widow's web, a pot of gold, a sacred heart, an elaborate gothic alphabet. She wanted something harder on the eyes, something that would make people look away in shame.

"What if I wanted, like, a splotch?" she asked the guy behind the counter.

"A what?"

"Like a, you know, just solid black ink."

She'd been thinking for weeks about what she should get, comparing her every idea against the binary code Trent had wrapped around his bicep; he'd translated it for her, a poem by Arthur Rimbaud called "The Drunken Boat" that she hadn't been able to follow completely, but from what she picked up seemed to relay, in nightmarish detail, the shattering of souls at the end of the world. Her ideas ran more toward the bar code on the neck, the chain around the wrist, the Pillsbury Doughboy, the toxic waste symbol, or words, maybe, EVERYONE KNOWS THIS IS NOWHERE or QUESTION EVERYTHING or just WHY? in heavy dark letters snaking down her leg. They all felt like clichés. A copyright symbol on the shoulder had seemed pretty fresh for a while, but then she saw the same thing on a shaggy college kid in a retro-seventies sun visor, dribbling a hackey sack on his foot as he stood on the steps of the U of M Mall.

"Solid black ink?" the guy asked.

"Yeah."

"Like a starburst or something? Like that?" He pointed at a cartoon of an Aztec sun god.

"No, just a splotch."

"I don't know. Did you bring a drawing?"

She grabbed the pen off the counter between them and fished a scrap of paper out of her back pocket, a flyer for yet another all-ages show. "Here," she said, scribbling indiscriminately. "Like this. But totally black inside."

"That's gonna look like shit."

"So?"

He glanced at his coworker, who was daubing his towel at the lower back of a strawberry-blond girl with glittery lip gloss. "So we're artists here."

"If it's what I want . . ."

The guy held his palms up as though he were helpless.

"If I'm willing to pay, I should be able to get whatever I want. I mean, what about the customer's always right?"

"I don't know what to tell you," he said.

For a while, she glared at him and tried to come up with a new line of argument that would force him to give in. If Trent were there, he'd have known what to say, but all she could think to do was scowl and gnaw at the ring in her lip. The guy wasn't breaking. He went back to the comic book he'd been reading.

"How 'bout a moth?" she said. "Can you do that?"

"Sure. Where do you want it?"

After half a second's thought, she held out her forearm, the one she hadn't scarred with invective against me. "Right there."

But when the guy finished drawing on her arm, the moth he'd etched looked more like a butterfly. She told him, "That's not a moth. Moths have furry antennae. Do you think I'm another one of your fucking sorority girls or something?"

He chuckled. "Sure. Okay." He drew some fur on the butterfly's antennae.

"So, if you'll change your precious art just 'cause I tell you to, doesn't that make you a hack, really?"

His needle paused an inch above her skin. "What?"

"I mean, if you were an artist, wouldn't you just do whatever the hell you want and not let me decide how it should look?" She'd found the correct logic, but it didn't have the same fire coming from her as it would have from Trent. He'd have broken down the capitalist system and shown the guy exactly what kind of cog he was by now, but her tone of voice was off, anxious and timid. "You know what?" she said. "Forget it. But listen, can you at least fill in the wings?"

"With what color?"

"Uh—" Her sarcastic expression floated right past him. "Black."

As soon as she left the place, she ripped the gauze off and assessed the damage. The moth filled up a roughly two-inch square of skin. She hated it already. The borders were so crisp, the wings so symmetrical, even the inflamed skin around the tattoo had an appalling elegance. The antibiotic lubricant the guy had rubbed into it just made it look worse, glossy and new. She did exactly what he'd told her not to: rubbed her thumb vigorously across his work, vandalized it, smudged it, pressed the ink across the lines he'd so carefully stayed within until she started to bleed.

I should have told him to tattoo my face, she thought, I should have asked for something bigger. She imagined her whole body haphazardly covered in ink, misshapen blue and black smears, maybe some yellow too—she'd be one big bruise, one big internal hemorrhage. A blot on this world. One day she'd catch herself in a car window and see she was a person she didn't recognize. Her body itself would be a kind of protest against everything that she hated.

Or maybe just a protest against me.

They were on the sidewalk, Cheryl, Devin and Trent, scaring up change for a bottle of Thunderbird, old-man wine, wine for Native Americans. They liked to drink it sometimes for the novelty, the romance of it. They were in a playful mood. Their sign this time said BEER FUND.

Some young guy walking past, a U of M student, Tevas and shorts and a faded red t-shirt that proclaimed his ironic fidelity to RC Cola, cut a wide arc around their outpost. Contempt rose off him like gasoline fumes. He made it around them without saying a word, but waiting for the light to turn at the corner of Fourth Street, he looked up at the sky and slapped himself a couple times on the leg. He shook his head. He turned, hesitated and stalked back to them.

"You people are a bunch of leeches, you know that?"

"And you're a fucking zombie," said Trent.

"I mean it. You're everything that's wrong with this country."

There was a chuckle. "Oh, are we? And what are you?"

"I'm—" The guy stopped.

"A fascist?"

"I'm—no, see? That's why you kids piss me off so much. I bet you don't even know what a fascist is."

Another chuckle. "Sure we do. You."

"You know what the problem with people like you is? You make it more difficult for other people who actually care about what's wrong with this country to do anything about it. You're a bunch of selfish kids, pissed off at Mommy and Daddy."

"And you're a fucking fascist who thinks those do-gooder organizations are gonna do something to solve anything. You want to get into this? We can get into this. I read the Internet. I read the fucking paper. You want to know the percentages? You want to talk about what these fucking *legitimate organizations* really do? Fucking Meals on Wheels. You ever heard of a tax break? You ever heard of complacency? Middle-class guilt? Governmental—"

"You know what? Forget it. I don't know why I . . ." The guy ran a hand through his sandy hair. He shook his head. His contempt was gone. In its place was pity, and this was maybe the gravest of his mistakes.

As he turned his back and wandered away, a chunk of broken cinder block sailed after him. "You're the fucking problem, asshole fascist." It hit him in the shoulder, inches from his head, and it wasn't Devin, it wasn't Trent, who threw it.

It was—no.

I can't look.

I don't want to see this.

You think, when you've crawled through dark places and survived, that the things you've learned might be transferable. They're not, though. They're not. They're just useless memories clinging like grit to the crevices of your brain, grinding and chafing and tearing you up. They don't help you. They don't help anyone. All they do is fill you with dread.

Six

I FIGURED IT OUT, EVENTUALLY. Cheryl wasn't guiding the voices toward me, Robert was. Like an electric conductor, a Tesla machine, he drew the souls toward himself from all over the city, focused them and then bounced them back in my direction. Their murmuring rose in both volume and pitch whenever he was around.

The clothes piled around me in Cheryl's room could only filter the voices so much. The buffer they created was full of holes. What I needed was a solid airtight wall, more layers, closer to my skin. I needed to wrap myself completely in Cheryl, to climb into her clothes and disappear inside her, but I understood that this wasn't possible, not with her so far away.

And then in that way solutions have of appearing as soon as you finally give up on finding them, I knew what to do. I slid open the double bolts on Cheryl's door and peered through the crack.

No Robert, nowhere.

I tiptoed out.

He was home, though, I knew—the voices had grown stronger over the past hour and blocked out even the faint glow of Cheryl's hair—but where he was exactly, and what he was doing to manipulate my mind, I had no idea.

In the hall the voices flicked past me like whips. *Help me. Save me. Where's your light? Help me see. Shine your light. It's so dark.* Each one cleaving, scraping, pressing its mark on me. Slowly, with wary steps, I made my way through them, keeping my mouth shut so they couldn't jump in.

The door to the master bedroom was open, the bedside lamp on. Steeling my face, narrowing my vision, I lunged past it.

The voices were pounding me now like hailstones, threatening, hissing like raccoons. He'd sent them to distract me. To keep me occupied while he and whoever it was he'd enlisted—the police? Dr. Rahajafeeli? Yeah, him, it would have to be him—worked out their plan to trap Cheryl and me.

"Julia?"

A glance—he was sitting on the foot of the bed, his thin talon feet hidden inside sheer black socks—and I forged on. The linen closet was just a few feet further. It contained something I needed.

"Julia?"

The voices swirled so fast here that they stung my eyes. Tears streamed from the corners. I was blind. But when I squeezed the knob on the closet door, they faded slightly. Brass. It's a conductor. It took what little defense I had against him and magnified it.

"Can we talk for a second?" He was next to me, leaning on the doorway, his one leg bent like a crane's across the other. The rest of his body was—I don't know. I refused to look at him. "What are you doing?"

The tiniest gesture of refusal, that's all I would give him. I couldn't speak, couldn't open my mouth, not with the voices trying to get in.

"What are you being so secretive about?"

I shook my head, a warning.

"Julia, please. You have to let me help you. What happened to us talking things out together?"

Then he squinted at me. His silence was as threatening as his speech. I had the sense that he was gathering his forces—that's why the voices had grown so muffled. He'd pulled them into himself. That's what he was doing. And once he'd turned them into something hard and ruthless and quick, he was going to hurl them at me through the doorknob. Brass was a conductor, but not for me—he was the one who controlled the energy. I suddenly remembered the studded belt Cheryl had started wearing low on her hips that year; were those studs made of brass? Yes, I thought, yes, they were. And who'd bought that belt? It hadn't been me. Was she wearing it now? Was that why I couldn't find her? I wondered what kind of stories Robert had told her during the three months I'd been away. What absurd ideas had he installed in her head? Maybe the belt was one of the tools he used to beam messages to her and drive her away from me.

Terror gave me strength and I yanked again, releasing the knob quickly as the door swung open. The sewing kit was in the back corner of the third shelf, behind the guest towels, past the washcloths. Cradling it tight to my chest, I turned on Robert. He was giving me that look that always meant trouble, like somehow I was trying to wound *him*. I shook my head, kept my mouth clamped shut.

"Julia." The way he kept saying my name, like he was afraid to upset me, it was disconcerting, like he was invoking something hidden inside me, trying to take it away.

"STOOOOOOOOP!" Once my mouth opened, I couldn't shut it again.

And suddenly he had his arms around me, his hands clasped behind my back, flexing, squeezing as tight as he could. "Calmdowncalmdowncalmdown," he said.

When I bit his shoulder, I could feel his muscle fighting back under the tight knit of his oxford.

"Julia. Calm down. Now." His voice was clipped. Dictatorial.

"Let me go!" I screamed. "Stop torturing me!"

The more I fought against him, the tighter his grip became. I made myself limp and sank out of his grasp, onto my knees, then further, onto my back. I flailed there.

He said it again: "Julia." Crouching in front of me, he struggled to make himself look like he cared, held his palms out in front of his body, as though I were a dog he could lull into trusting him. "Okay? I'm not gonna hurt you."

I spat at him.

"You're not taking your pills, are you? Julia? Are you? You, really, you need to take your pills." He said this with the same soothing tone of voice I remembered him using all those years ago when he'd agreed to help me manage without them. I was beginning now to understand what that word, *manage*, meant to him.

"You're trying to kill me," I said.

He kept on going, not even a flinch. "If you take your meds—Julia, look at me."

Grabbing me by the chin, he held my head straight.

"If you take your meds, things will be a lot easier." The skin on his face was thin and translucent. I could see his skull through it.

Once, a long time ago, he'd known just how to be around me. He'd loved me. He'd been on my side. But that Robert was gone. Now, he was a man who hid behind obscure threats. *Things will be easier.* What things? And for whom?

"What things?" I asked.

"Things, Julia. Everything. Your life."

I searched his face for what he was hiding, but all I could find were crow's-feet—and inside his eye sockets, mirrors, shiny, silver, my face reflected back at me. How'd I get so haggard? When'd I get so tired? What had he done to make me so exhausted? The voices. That's what it was. But now, weirdly, as though he'd been reading my thoughts, they'd vanished. "Where'd they go?" I said. "What did you do with them?"

"With what?"

"You know what."

Pinching his eyes, he said, "No, Julia, I don't. I really don't. Not if you don't tell me."

"The people!" I shouted. "Don't pretend you don't understand what I'm saying! I'm not crazy! I know what you're up to! What did you do with the goddamn people?!"

Then he broke. He broke and he cried and instead of reflecting me back to me, now, he was showing me another different him. The soft, malleable Robert he'd once been. The one who cared so much and was so affected by the troubles I couldn't shake that he responded to them as though they were his, as though he were living my life along with me. He was putting the Robert I used to trust on display. The one who had offered me alternatives at that time in my life when I'd reached the limits of my possibilities and been lost and drowning in Dinkytown, the one who, with Sarah already six years gone, had been the only person I could confide in. He was showing me—taunting me, trying to bribe me with—the Robert I'd taught myself how to love.

Well, I could be tricky too. I narrowed my eyes. "Fine," I said. "I'll take your stupid fucking pills. But"—nose quivering, finger jabbing in his face—"Dr. Rahajafeeli has to stay out of it. And Cheryl—" I had to stop myself so I wouldn't cry. Crying would give him control over me.

"I'm doing everything I can to find Cheryl," he said, as if I would somehow be comforted by this.

"Keep away from her," I snapped.

His eyes picked slowly over my face, searching for soft spots he could exploit and attach his barbs to, but I was hard, I was glacial and barren, and when he knew there was nothing to hold on to, he dipped his head slowly and whispered, "It's going to be okay."

My pills. They were worse than a straitjacket, restraints on my mind, making me foggy, dizzy, meaningless, unable to discern the meaning in anything. Even the new ones, the atypical ones. They rid me of myself, destroyed my reality and forced me into an alternate one, a reality of surfaces without substance and life without living that wasn't really an alternative at all. They thinned my blood. They made me fat. If I took them long enough, I'd get diabetes. But by then, diabetes would be a gift, a step closer to death and escape from them. Robert knew this. He'd sympathized, years ago. He'd been the only one. And now he'd changed his mind. This most recent episode had changed his mind. Dr. Rahajafeeli had finally convinced him. Well, I still had me, and it was my body and I'd faked taking these pills before.

I hissed at him, "Stay away from my daughter, and I'll take your stupid pills."

He'd find out, eventually, that I'd lied to him. Then he'd release the voices again, send them stampeding back, and call Dr. Rahajafeeli in for reinforcements, to provide another front and block any possibility of escape. If I worked fast, though, I might be able to build my defenses before this happened. I had to. For Cheryl's sake as much as my own.

Rolling over, pushing myself up, I turned my back on him. As I scurried away, I checked the sewing kit—scissors, yes, needles, thread, yes, thimble—everything was there.

In Cheryl's room, I threw the bolts, turned off the light and lay down on her bed. I listened. I closed my eyes and looked past the room. Nothing.

I dug through the clothes piled up on her bed. Burrowed. With scissors and teeth, I ate at the seams, split them open and separated each item into its parts. First the cashmere sweater that had been Sarah's, then the brown cords, the nylons, the North Face jacket. I cut the political slogans off the t-shirts and piled them together for later use. Then I began sewing, constructing something new from what I had destroyed, knitting the pieces into one large cloak that contained everything she'd left behind. I had to keep sewing, as quickly as I could, create a tapestry big enough for us both. When I was done, I wrapped it around my shoulders. I stood very still in the center of her room, arms spread, ready to embrace her.

I called out her name and waited.

Gremlin was at the door, digging, mewling to be let in. I opened it a crack, bolted it behind him. He tipped his head. He was listening too. We waited together.

And waited.

And waited.

Until we found her, the only one still awake, stumbling through the dark Wreck Room, her hand trailing along the unfinished wall from one wooden strut to the next. She was able to see—gray on gray on black on gray—that wasn't the problem, the problem was moving, the problem was thinking, the problem was convincing her feet to land in the places she tried to put them, and doing all these things without tipping over or vomiting. She reeled her way toward the cubby off the kitchen where, behind a black flag nailed to the doorway, the toilet—that cracked basin, rust stains licking from its drain—was hidden. One step, another, one more. She had to rest. The room careened around her. She had to shut her eyes. She longed to wrap herself around something hard and immobile, cling to a buoy and keep herself afloat. She wavered in the dark. Her stomach twirled. There was a gypsy inside her, thrashing and swinging and clamoring to get out. She lurched and grabbed at the blackness, her whole weight pulling on the lump of fabric until she heard a tear— the flag ripping from the nail—and she fell.

A noise like cicadas pressed at her from all directions, and some-where on the other side of it, she faintly heard her boyfriend calling out to her. "Fucking . . . what's going on out there . . . Betty?" She couldn't respond. Just getting her brain to turn his sounds into meaning was hard. She broke into a sweat. Pulling herself along the floor, she found the toilet and propped her head on the lip. The spins wouldn't stop. She'd used up her energy. All she was capable of doing now was opening her mouth and letting the water, the bile and everything else, the various colors of her self-loathing, flow out.

As I stood in the bedroom she'd deserted in Plymouth, Trent pulled himself from the sleeping bag to navigate around his walls of books and tiptoe across the dark space of the Sabotage Café, searching, whispering her name, until he found her. He knelt beside her, rubbed her back through the dry heaves, gave her a knee on which to rest her head and a piece of cloth to wipe her chin. He brought her a half-empty bottle of Coke and held it to her lips so she could wash the taste of vomit from her mouth. Then an arm around her ribs to shoulder her weight, he walked her through the Wreck Room and past the sleeping forms of Mike and Devin, into the corner of the bedroom they shared. He laid her down, careful not to let her fall, and watched her sleep.

I was too late, but at least I'd found her again.

Seven

I SAW HER AT PARTIES that erupted out of nowhere.

One night it would just be the four of them, silent in the Wreck Room, each with his own bottle of Midnight Dragon, all of them separately regressing into the stricken soft tissue of their pasts—those memories, so similar and shameful, that they could neither obliterate nor share: that one time Mike's Army Ranger dad had snuggled up next to him on the couch, feeding him cognac while they watched *The X Files,* and his hand inching up Mike's inner thigh, boasting how he'd been inside Area 51; the time Devin had finally hit his father back and instead of laughing or pummeling him harder, his father had said, "Finally, you pussy. What took you so long?"; Trent's long week of holding his mother down, braced like a brick over her shaking body, while wiping the sweat away with a warm washcloth and whispering, "Everything's okay, it's going to be okay," telling himself as much as her, erecting one last edifice of hope for her to later shatter; and Cheryl, Cheryl, secretly missing me—and the next night, the kids would be at their door, demanding that Sabotage open for business, bursting in and overrunning the place, every rat in the Twin Cities suddenly squatting inside its dilapidated walls.

Kids sat in circles, passing one-hitters disguised as cigarettes. They hovered over the portable boom box, rifled through the CDs scattered around it, laughing and scoffing, and sometimes, when they found an especially awful disk—anything by Green Day, Devin's stolen copy of Hanson's *Snowed In*—they'd whip it across the room like a saw blade. They stomped to the rushing beat of the Rollins Band, bowing and bouncing the floorboards. They punched more and more holes into the wall.

The scabbier kids, who'd been on the scene longer, searched their veins shamelessly, and when they found one that was still uncollapsed, they shot up right there in the Wreck Room, the kitchen, right there on the futon where Cheryl and Trent slept.

When Mike came home from his job at Chipotle, kids would cascade over him as he opened the door. He'd press through them to drop his shit in his locker and find junkies nodding off on his army cot. "Motherfuckers have no sense. See? This! This is the problem with this fucking town." He'd try to pull them off and push them out, to shut down the party completely, but there were too many kids. New ones kept streaming in all the time. "We're chaos, dude," they said. "You can't control us."

These parties metastasized. They went on for days. A solid mass of kids, puking, fighting, making out, fucking. Aching. Jostled loose, whisked to opposing sides of the room, Cheryl and Trent lost each other in these parties.

Devin, one afternoon, couldn't control himself. He flailed, naked from the waist down, wagging his limp penis in people's faces. He couldn't get it hard no matter how much he rubbed. Everyone laughed at him. He didn't shock them. They'd lived through worse explosions of despair themselves.

Sometimes kids cried in the corners, hiding their faces. No one knew why, but no one asked, either.

Eventually, two, three, four, five nights later, the drugs would be cashed and the alcohol gone. Anyone still around would be passed out on the floor, bodies strewn at random, a frozen half-finished massive game of Twister.

I remember one night like that in particular.

The scent of hops mingled, in the dank Wreck Room, with the smell of sweat and smoke and street. Some girl no one knew was wailing in the bathroom. Except for her, Cheryl and Trent were the only ones still awake. They crawled through the dark, feeling their way over wobbly bodies until they reached each other's voices.

"Betty?"

"Yeah?"

"Betty?"

"I'm right here."

"Where?"

"Here. That's me."

He groped up her arm and she cupped his hand, warm, against her cheek.

They huddled there, listening to the crash of breaths around them, and Cheryl wondered why comfort and sadness felt so alike, why she lost herself whenever she couldn't find him.

Trent nibbled her ear. "Maybe we should go see how Debbie Harry's doing."

"Sure," she said. "Okay."

As long as she was near him, she didn't care what else went on. Stepping carefully, they picked a path over the carpet of kids and climbed out the window, crawled up to the roof, and laid themselves down in the kiddie pool up there.

A muggy heat had lingered into the night. The edges of her body blurred into his, like her skin was made of tissue, disintegrating. Tonight, Trent moved slowly, a quiet dream inside her, picking up speed for just a moment near the end, staring into her eyes possessively.

When he rolled off her, he gazed at the billboard across the street—a pointing McGruff, TAKE A BITE OUT OF CRIME—and said, "Wow."

"What's the matter?"

"I'm just thinking. That's forty, Betty. I've been inside you forty times."

She winced. She startled. "What? Is this a race?"

"I'm just saying . . . It's like I know things about you now, you know what I mean? Like I—like"—he paused, then said almost daintily—"your pussy is mine."

She shot up on an elbow. "What do you mean?"

"I mean, like"—he stalled, quickly backing down—"I didn't mean it like that. It's, like, it's one of the things I understand in the world."

The idea thrilled her. Then she thought about all the parts of herself this understanding excluded. She stopped herself. He was trying to be sweet, and she didn't want to ruin it.

Above her, the streetlights bounced off the clouds, turning the night sky a veiny orange, as though there was something organic up there. A breeze coasted down over the rooftops and hooked across her sweaty body. "How many girls have you been with?" she asked.

"I don't know. A few."

"A few, like ten? Or like—how many?"

He squinted. "A few, a couple."

"You can't remember?"

"A couple."

"Like two?"

"What do you think a couple means, Betty?" He glanced at the billboard, at McGruff's finger jabbing back at him. "Why does it fucking matter?"

"I'm curious. I don't know." Now that she'd started, she was desperate for every last detail. She wanted to contemplate and obsess and compare, to torture herself with his memories of them. Trent, tense, defensive, was trapped under her leg. His body felt weak and scrawny there, but she knew this was an illusion. A further question kept scrolling through her mind, an angry dot bouncing over every word: *Do you love me? Do you love me? Just say that you love me, you don't have to mean it.* It was hard to resist the urge to chant along. She felt queasy and shameful. Like a stupid girl.

The breeze was gone. Sweat was filling up in the kiddie pool, their intermingled sweat, sucking at her skin, gluing her to the plastic.

"Were their pussies yours?" she said.

He slid his arm around her shoulder and pulled her gently toward him.

"Were they?"

"Come here," he said.

"No."

"Fucking just come here."

She could only oppose him for short, concerted bursts. Her cheek on his chest, she listened like she had that first day at Sabotage to the plodding sound of his heartbeat.

His fingers rooted lazily through her hair. His lips rested against the top of her head, almost but not exactly kissing her. He whispered something, but she couldn't understand him and she didn't ask him to repeat himself. It was safer to believe he'd said the thing she yearned to hear.

I wanted to tell her, don't put your trust in men, especially not if they're little boys. But I couldn't. Not yet. I had to wait. I was too upset to say anything right then. She was making all the same mistakes I had.

IV

So What?

One

JAROD SAT halfway up the wooden staircase leading to the Sabotage Café's second floor. By now it was late July. Nearly two months had passed since Cheryl had ditched him for Trent, and in this time, she hadn't seen him. She'd hardly thought of him. She'd filled herself up with her new situation, with Trent and everything that came along with him, resisting the überculture, fighting its lies, building this gritty new world for herself out of all the crap it discarded. Jarod existed in Cheryl's memory not as a boy she'd almost loved but as a casualty of the corpora-capitalist system that had lobotomized America. He wasn't committed to the cause; the pull of his mother had been too strong. When the revolution came, he'd be left behind.

He looked somehow even more pathetic than she remembered him. He was shriveled, cowering, even in the muck of summer, under his hooded sweatshirt, his wide, watery eyes fixed on a nowhere spot in the broken step below him as though his last scrap of self had fallen through the gap.

Her first thought when she saw him was to cut and run, to hide out among the reeds and hubcaps in the empty lot next door and wait for him to go away, but he glanced up—briefly, indifferently—before she could.

The dog named Dog was crumpled like a limp towel under his feet. Its snout was long and pinched, thinner than Cheryl remembered, and uglier. The fur on its back had grown long and coarse and its coloring had deepened into rusty brown streaks, but it was still a sort of spindly little thing, its paws two sizes too big for it. It gave a little bark when it saw her and slipped out from between Jarod's legs, tumbling down the six, seven steps to slobber over her knees.

"Hello. Yes, hello. Yes, hello, little doggie." She crouched, letting its tongue flip over her face. "You remember me, don'tcha? Yeah, don'tcha? He's gotten bigger."

"She's a she," Jarod mumbled. "She's a fucking girl."

"Oh, shit, right." She flushed, but he didn't seem to notice or care. He was busy digging his fingernail under a thick splatter of green industrial paint adhered to the step next to him. "How's your mom?" she asked.

No response, not even a pause in the picking—he'd found an edge and was now working at prying it free.

"Something interesting there?" she asked.

"No."

She'd forgotten how petulant he could be, like an eight-year-old, glum and pouty after having been forced to put the Lucky Charms back. A sudden anger—just a flash—bolted through her. He did this on purpose. He wanted something, or he knew something, and he wanted her to guess what it was. A tedious exercise, yet she felt compelled to play along. She was worried he might be here to fuck things up with Trent.

The dog stood almost three feet tall when she raised it by its front paws. It waltzed with her, taking clumsy steps forward and back, side to side, until it was able to shake her off. She tickled it behind the ears and ran her hand in circles around its nose, teasing it, waiting for Jarod to give himself away.

He just kept picking. Then, once he'd detached the splotch from the stair, he studied it like it was an ancient coin, rolled it in his fingers, scrutinizing its ripples and dollops of texture. "Hey, Dog," he said. "Come here."

Cocking its head, the dog peered at him, wagged its tail. He beckoned it with an open palm. Then he crumpled the paint into a pellet and held it out like a Scooby-Snack.

"Don't do that," Cheryl said.

"Why not?"

The dog chewed, smacking its mouth like it was sucking on peanut butter.

Cheryl climbed up and dug her finger in the dog's gums, under its tongue, around its teeth, trying to rescue the paint. She was too late. "It'll get sick. There's probably lead in that paint," she said.

Jarod slumped back on his elbows and gazed sullenly at his puppy.

"It's poisonous."

The way he stared at the puppy frightened her. His eyes were hard and dull. He reminded her of a sponge, not because of what he absorbed but because of the way he just sat there in a state of suspended animation—or a mushroom cap.

"You don't care?"

"I care," he said, pushing the words out, finally willing himself to look at her. The blood vessels were rising to the surface of his eyes.

Didn't he know he'd lost his chance with her? He should leave her alone. Just because she'd cared once didn't mean she gave a shit anymore. She willed him not to cry. The urge to comfort him was already returning. She implored herself, Fight it off, don't give in. "I know you care," she said.

Leaning against the shaky wooden railing, she stared, pitiless, as he tried to corral his tears. The dog lingered on the step below them. It watched Jarod too. Then it lost interest—he was just sitting there, not even talking. It dropped to its belly, laid its head on its folded paws and, sighing, turned away.

"Where is everybody?" said Cheryl.

"That guy Mike's upstairs."

"He won't let you in? He's a dick," she said. "Come on. I can handle him."

She started up the stairs, preparing herself for an attack on Mike, but Jarod just sat there. "You seen Trent?" he asked.

"I don't know. He's around. You don't want to go inside?"

There was that shrug again.

"Well, I'm gonna go in."

When she tried to step around him, he placed his hand on her leg, held her there with his hangdog eyes, silently pleading, begging for that thing she'd closed off to him. What really pissed her off was that she couldn't stop herself from being affected. She plopped down on the step.

"You gonna tell me what the fuck's wrong with you?"

He patted the dog and it nuzzled its head up into his lap. "I'm just sad," he said.

She softened. "I figured I'd see you around here sometimes," she said.

"I've been working."

Jarod working. Jarod counting money. Folding clothes. Busing tables. Jarod spearing litter in a park. It was too absurd. A smirk cracked across her face.

"What?" He frowned at her. "I'm not a fucking retard. I can do things. I'm working in the stockroom at Rainbow Foods. Listen, where's Trent? I gotta talk to him. It's an emergency."

Something in her seized up. She tried to remember her time at Jarod's house, all the little ways they'd circled each other, sniffing and gauging the distance. Though there wasn't anything tangible to point to, it would be a lie to say nothing had happened. She'd tromped over him just like everyone else, but he didn't yearn for everyone else, he hadn't hoped to possess everyone else. At some point along the line, she'd made him an implicit promise, and then when Trent showed up she'd denied the whole thing.

"So, what, you can't tell me about it?"

"Uh-uh," he said. "I'm just sad, okay?"

How could she have thought there'd be no repercussions? What did he have on her? Nothing. She'd done nothing. But he might lie. Who knows what he might say? And Trent would believe him. Jarod was his friend and she was just a girl—wasn't that the way it always worked with boys?

The conversation in her head bubbled over and suddenly she was shouting at him. "That's why we haven't seen you, isn't it? It's not his fucking fault you couldn't make a move. It's not my fault, either. Why do you have to come fuck everything up?"

He looked at her like she was acting crazy.

Calming herself, she said, "I mean, because—"

"I know what you mean," he said. Withdrawing again, he peered at the dog, batted at its ears. Something had turned suddenly cold in him, and the thought that he might have more important problems than whether she was into him or not bounced through her mind like a wasp trapped in a kitchen window. She remembered how terribly she'd wanted to hold him during those torturous, she thought now, tender nights when they'd lain side by side pretending to sleep. "I'm sorry you're sad."

She allowed her head to sink onto his shoulder. His body relaxed slightly, melting toward hers, and they sat there for a while, bearing the weight of the immutable past.

And in that moment, I believe, her sympathy for me expanded a tiny bit. She took one small step toward returning to me. She recalled the outrage that had coursed through her all those times she'd invited friends for sleepovers at the house only to watch them lose interest in her discussions of school crushes and join me in the kitchen, pouring all their troubles onto the table as we sipped Red Zinger tea and shoveled microwave popcorn into our mouths. They told me about the secret feelings they feared would turn them into failed human beings. The sexual impulses they couldn't control. The self-disgust that crept through them like mold. The raw places in themselves that everything outside said shouldn't exist. I treated them like I was a friend, not a parent. They knew that instead of frowning, instead of reciting the creaky platitudes that most adults used to dismiss their problems, I'd just feel. And maybe cry with them. That's why they trusted me. Jill Swenson. Danielle Reid. Jessie Clowen. Those are just the ones I can think of right now. It was as though Cheryl had delivered these girls to me. I soaked up the emotions they couldn't handle, told them they were good, normal and good, that they had a value beyond what they could see. We'd stay up late playing Boggle or Yahtzee, and all the while, Cheryl would be sitting there staring into her tea, her face sinking into a hard little airless padlocked place. Eventually, she'd hump off to watch TV and make a point to blare the volume. Then, the next day, they'd leave and I'd never see them again. Cheryl would drop them out of her life. "They're mine!" she'd scream at me after they were gone. "They're mine, not yours! Why do you always have to monopolize? Why do you have to steal everything from me? Can't you at least let me have my own friends?" It was a test I was always going to fail. I think, here with Jarod, though, she began to comprehend that I'd had no choice but to embrace her friends. Despair is a sickness that I understand and I had no choice but to feel what they were going through.

Slipping her arm through his, she clasped Jarod's hand. Their fingers knotted together, and for a brief moment she felt submerged in a current, large and continuous and imperturbable. It was as though, drilling toward his pain, she'd tapped her own, and now they were bleeding together.

The dog suddenly jumped up. Footsteps were approaching. It lowered its head, ready to lunge toward the doorway at the bottom of the stairs.

As the clomping drew closer, she yanked her arm free from Jarod and waited.

The dog started growling, a gurgle deep in the back of its throat. Then the person walked past the door: some short Asian woman with aerodynamic sunglasses and blond streaks in her hair. Some nobody.

Cheryl punched the wall. She'd taken what had been mere insecurity and turned it into evidence against herself. Given Jarod something real to tell Trent. The head on his shoulder. The holding of his hand. All that complicated intimacy. "Fuck!"

The dog barked at her and flipped its tail. Slapping her fingers around its snout, she shook its head back and forth until it reared up. It bucked and whined, but she held on tight.

"Hey!" Jarod said. "Hey, let her go!" He slammed Cheryl into the wall and cradled the dog's head lightly between his hands, examining it.

The sidewalk outside the doorway glowed, a blinding rectangle of white at the end of the shadowy tunnel. She tapped at the wall with the side of her skull, unwilling to look at Jarod, unwilling to apologize, though some kernel of her being felt she should. The swath of bright light kept pulling at her, changing shape, pulsing. She was transfixed, unsure which she hated more, herself or everyone else in the world. Then a shadow cut through the light, and a moment later Trent appeared in the doorway.

Jumping to his feet, Jarod ran down the stairs. The dog lumped behind him, leaving Cheryl alone to gauge exactly what she was about to lose.

One of his hand-rolled cigarettes wedged in that odd way of his, deep between his middle and ring fingers, Trent glanced at her with a hint of a smile as though he were looking at her for the very first time and he approved of what he saw. She'd seen him like this maybe two, three times before and each time had hit her like a revelation. She told herself to remember this expression in case she never got to see it again. After tonight, she was sure, all her alternatives would be used up; her life would turn out like mine and there was nothing she could do to stop it.

Jarod had Trent by the elbow, tugging him backwards, and as Trent let himself be led out the door, he held up two fingers and aimed a casual what's up at Cheryl. He turned the corner and disappeared before she could respond, but his and Jarod's long evening shadows lingered in the frame of sunlight, weaving and melding and separating again. They spoke in low tones. Jarod's shadow hands wavered in front of Trent, telling figurative stories, describing and pleading, building the case against her. Trent's shadow was still, head bowed in concentration. It seemed to be coiling, preparing to pounce.

Stop being crazy, she told herself. The only conspiracy that exists against you is the one in your head. But it didn't help. She was my daughter, and doomsday thoughts came quicker than optimism, fantasy came easier than logic, and the urge to fill the gaps in her knowledge with morbid delusions overwhelmed her.

When the boys returned, the evidence was clear: Trent's body had shrunk into a tight knot. His face was hard. His lips thin. A cold rage narrowed his focus and he leapt right past Cheryl, ignored her, raced up the stairs two at a time and slammed into the squat. Jarod chased after him. The dog let out two shrill yips and galloped behind.

Alone now, she slumped against the wall and tapped her head against the flimsy banister, waiting for Trent to come flying back out with her shit in his arms, her backpack, her t-shirts, her one pair of jeans. She wondered, Would he remember the army jacket? Ha. Of course he would. He'd recognize how much it meant to her and leave it behind on purpose, fling it across the room, into one of Devin's piles of trash.

Someone was watching her from the top of the stairs. It was him, she knew. She could feel his rage burning up the back of her skull. Don't look. Don't look. Don't let him see your eagerness, your weakness, your need. He moved slowly down the stairs and sat next to her. She had to be strong, to be the first to attack.

Turning, she glared. "What?"

"What, nothing," he said. He'd left her clothes upstairs. "I need you to go somewhere."

"Where?"

"I don't know. Somewhere. Wherever the fuck you want."

Beneath his furrowed brow, his face was tense, every muscle squeezing to withhold his emotions. She wanted to touch him one last time, but she couldn't—if she did, she knew, one of them would explode.

"So, pick a place," he said. He pulled a green lighter out of his back pocket and nervously tapped it end over end against his knee.

She tried to make herself as cold as he was, to turn herself off, but she couldn't.

"Fucking pick someplace, Betty. I'm gonna need to fucking find you later."

The tears came suddenly. She couldn't control them. And knowing he wasn't going to comfort her just made them that much worse.

"Fucking—"

She screamed at him. "Where do you want me to go?!"

He showed no pity. "Why do you have to be such a fucking—" An abrupt rage spasmed through him. "Goddamn it!" He whipped the lighter as hard as he could toward the doorway. It ricocheted off the sloped ceiling and clattered onto one of the steps below them in a way that left his gesture incomplete, flimsy, impotent. He leapt down the stairs and grabbed the lighter, threw it again, this time out the door.

"The cross," he said, turning on her. "Alright? Go hang out at the fucking cross."

Two

As she raced along Fourth Street, angry shapes streaked past, places she hadn't ever thought twice about, coming at her like insults—the Mobil MiniMart where they'd stolen so many ham and cheese sandwiches, the lampposts and mailboxes mummified in leaflets, the faded, torn awning of the Nix Bar, the Chinese joints and the Green Tea Smoke Shop, all these places where she and Trent had spanged, all these bitter, insipid associations. The goodness was seeping quickly out of each of them. She tainted everything she came in contact with.

Maybe she should vanish, just cease to exist. What would Trent do then? He'd keep doing whatever. Nothing would change. He'd forget all about her in, like, five minutes. It wasn't even worth it to go to the cross.

But then, where else was there? St. Anthony Main? There was jack-all to do in St. Anthony Main. Or she could head toward Hennepin, wander downtown, but then she might run into Robert, who'd drag her home, who'd lock her up and never let her out again. She could climb down that drainpipe—those junkies couldn't still be hidden there, could they? Well, if they were, maybe she could score from them. Infect herself with whatever they had. She could go anywhere, but somehow each place would still be the same nowhere—nowhere worthwhile. Her too many choices made for no choice at all.

On the West Bank, she wandered through the granite and concrete plaza around which the University of Minnesota's arts buildings were clustered, and wondered, like she did every time she saw it, why everybody called it the cross. Okay, the different grades of stone were laid out in a kind of a quad, which, if you looked at them slantwise, she guessed, could be considered cross-like, but really there was no reason for such melodrama.

A handful of skater kids loitered in the plaza. It was a favorite hangout, a wide tiered bowl with a variety of obstacles for them to bounce off. Cheryl kept her distance. She climbed one of the pillars dotting the perimeter and watched them fuck around, skittering down railings and surfing along the arched ledges of the bowl. They competed against each other, picking up speed and popping their boards, flipping them back and forth on their toes as they leapt over tipped trash cans, then landing with arms outstretched and amazed grins on their faces. Or, more often, they tripped and tumbled, sprawling face-first on the vast pink granite plain.

A year ago, she would have been one of the mousy girls lined up like cheerleaders along the steps, pretending to be impressed by the skaters' prowess—or rather, willing themselves to be as impressed as the boys they adored were of themselves. Now she loathed these kids, the girls and skaters both, not just because they were blind consumers, their resistance a style, a fashion choice, another way to check out, but also, more urgently, because they didn't know how good they had it. They were poseurs, into the lifestyle not the life, sequestered waist-deep in their middle-class comforts, and here at the cross to, more than anything, show off their purchasing power, their kick-ass old-school Vans, their killer Birdhouse rides. Their lives were stable. They didn't know fear. To think she ever believed she might have something in common with them. Not with a mother like me, she didn't.

Small clusters of runaways and gutter punks were scattered

around the plaza as well. They clung to the edges, far away from the skaters, and banded together like refugees around campfires. Though the day had been sunny, they looked somehow soaked through, as though they'd been caught in a flood.

When the sun started to set and the lamps blinked on, the gutter punks seemed to multiply. Alone, or in cohorts of two and three and four, they gravitated toward the light like bats. Hunger streaked across their faces, as well as a desire she recognized as her own, the dream of combustion, of the world in flames, all the parking lots cracked, the concrete pylons shattered, the power lines severed and the schools in cinders. Hemorrhages of mayhem blossoming out of the charred ruins. Civilization razed to the ground and ready to be rebuilt differently this time. They conspired, these starved children, at the edge of darkness, each of them eager to enter the action.

From her perch, Cheryl watched their small communities grow and shrink. She could see them but they couldn't see her. Even when they looked her way, they gazed right through her. She recognized them—most of them, anyway—but their names were a blur. They'd been to parties at Sabotage. She'd had them in her home, or the place she'd called home—she was going to have to forget this word again. To be surrounded by so many people, separate from all of them, a unit of one, too unimportant to even be scorned—it felt somehow right. It was what she deserved.

She'd hoped that maybe these could be her people. But she'd been wrong. The only person who'd ever understood her, the only person who ever could, was me. She had no place—not even a place among people who, like her, had no place. Where, she wondered, did exiles go when even the land they'd been banished to kicked them out?

In the right hip pocket of her cargo shorts, she felt something pulling, like the insistent hand of a child. Her cell phone. For almost two months now, she'd been ignoring it, denying the connections buried there like fossils. She couldn't anymore. The names and numbers lodged in its memory cried for attention. They were all she had left of her identity.

When she pushed the button that powered the phone up, she didn't expect anything to happen. She couldn't remember the last time she'd charged it. But—ding, ding, dong—there was that chime, and then the crude magnifying glass roaming the screen for a connection. It uncovered five bars, a sliver of battery. She searched the contact list for a name besides mine—someone she could replace me with, a girlfriend, a former intimate, anyone, so long as they couldn't see through her. But every name came with a complication, some ruinous story she couldn't undo. She was just stalling, anyway. The tug in her navel allowed only one choice.

She gave in.

It was almost nine p.m., and I, at that moment, was lying on her bed, listening to her paranoia and loneliness. I'd spaced out. I'd lost track of her, just for a second. This one time when it mattered, I wasn't prepared.

By the time I reached the phone, the machine had picked up. What I heard was "Mommy?" One aching word. She hadn't called me this in years.

I grabbed the receiver. "Cheryl," I said. "Honey, Cheryl, I'm here."

And then there was a slippage. Her voice was yanked away. The machine screeched with feedback and dead air rushed in.

Her battery had run out. I knew this explained it, but I couldn't stop wondering if, had I picked up right away, her phone would have lasted just a minute longer, time enough for me to tell her I loved her. *Come home,* I would have said. *I don't hold anything you've done against you.*

I want to make this clear. Those pills, they're like a lobotomy on a drip, bit by bit scraping my brain from its shell. But if she'd stayed, I would have kept taking them. I'd have happily sacrificed my mind for her.

That's not what had happened, though. She'd left. And now that the connection was dead, time seemed to shift. It skipped and it hovered. It threatened to swan-dive, come to a full stop before staggering on like it always does.

A whole new set of strangers overran the cross. Some skater kid across the expanse pulled a Casper and before she knew it, she'd watched him grind and ollie for ten, twenty minutes. She remembered the exuberance of her skater pals in Plymouth. There was one she'd been sorta-kinda going out with, Matt was his name, and they'd sit around in his driveway, just the two of them after school. He'd try and try again to get his board to 360. "Wait, wait though. Watch this one!" Holding his hands out like wings. "See, it's—just wait, let me . . ." Requesting patience as though he thought she had somewhere else to go, had anything better to do all afternoon than sit on the hood of his mom's car and watch him fuck around. "It'll work this time." No embarrassment at all. Like a flirtatious child who understands that the inept flailing is more endearing than the success. She'd teased him—"Yeah, okay, whatever"—tickled by how hard he worked to get nowhere, enjoying the pointlessness of it all. The course her life would take had glimmered before her: the slog through high school, the slingshot into college where what she'd learn in class would maybe be interesting, but irrelevant to the real education happening in the dorm, the social education, the learning how to float above it all while trying on lifestyles like Halloween costumes, searching for that especially vibrant one. She'd assumed she was part of the great enlightened for whom special things have been set aside, that she could create herself out of wishes and rearrange the entire world on a whim. She'd thought she'd been promised a great many things. Now she'd closed off access to all of them.

Blinking into the streetlight mounted above her head, she tried to pin down exactly what it was that had defined her life before I'd gotten sick. Contentment. But that wasn't quite it. There was too much boredom and dissatisfaction for that. Confidence. Confidence and a presumptuous belief in her own right to the future. And naiveté. Because how could she have believed she was really like the other kids living in Plymouth with us? Sickness collected in our house like gas. It was imprinted in her DNA. Madness. She wasn't allowed—she couldn't allow herself—to make the assumptions everyone else did. Even her capacity for joy was suspect.

The busyness below her caught her eye again. A girl was squatting on the polished granite, drawing invisible pictures in front of her; a bar code was tattooed across the base of her neck—Cheryl allowed herself a hiccup of pride over having decided against that one. A group of thick, happy towheaded boys spun a Nerf football over each other's heads; they looked so normal in their backward baseball caps. Then she was off again, distracted, spacing over all the ways she wasn't like them.

On and on like this, she waited, losing more hope, letting more and more self-pity leak in.

And then she saw Trent. That steel chain around his neck. That brass lock bouncing against his collarbone. He'd tied a black bandanna around his left forearm as though he was off to join the insurrection. The despair vanished. But another anxious feeling rushed in to replace it. How could she need him so absolutely? Was she even able to exist without him?

Three

ACKNOWLEDGING HER with a thrust of his chin, Trent held back and rolled a cigarette as she shimmied down from her perch. She could sense how much he loathed her dependence on him, how much he resented having to be here, and it pissed her off, sort of, that he had come. His mood was black and defensive. Even in abandoning her, he had to show off his superiority, had to make himself unassailable. Why couldn't he just flake out like a normal person, throw her crudely away so she could hate him in peace? But, no, that would be too kind.

"So?" she said. She followed his cues and refused to get too close.

He took a drag off his cigarette, studied it. Then, without a word, he started walking, and she trailed him out of the plaza like a hungry dog.

They moved in and out of darkness. Cutting across the wide cropped lawns, up the ramps and walkways of the West Bank Extension. This was the new part of the university, vast and impersonal, and except for the business school with its optimistic powder-blue windows, it was all hulking boxes made of concrete and brick plopped down on expanses of empty space.

They didn't speak once.

When Trent held his cupped cigarette out for her to take, she shook her head no. There was barely a drag left. He took one last suck and flicked the roach into the air.

She had to remember, he'd already abandoned her; what he was here to do was display the proof.

"Where we going?"

"I don't know, Betty. We're fucking just walking."

Up the final ramp into the barn-red bridge that linked the West Bank to the main campus. Then reaching the other side, Trent turned onto the bike path that wound down into the park along the river. Decorative streetlamps—their black paint chipped in places, the rust underneath peeking through the cracks—shot out fillips of light surrounded by long spans of darkness. Cheryl's gaze hopped from one lamp to the next—anything to keep herself distracted from Trent. A storm of insects battered the glass around each bulb.

He was savoring her distress, reveling one last time in his power over her. When thoughts of her flickered through his mind later, this would be what he remembered, not the curve of her breasts or her pubic hair's texture, not the pitch of her laugh or the punch of her wit, but the way she stood sometimes with her shoulders slumped, an expression of abject need breaking on her face, and the glee he took in ignoring it.

Little by little, he edged closer to her, gradually working his hand into hers, prying her fingers apart and grasping. She reminded herself, I'm humoring him, not the other way around. He can't reach me anymore, no matter what he does. But his hand was sweaty, and as he fumbled further, kneading his thumb into her knuckles, squeezing and roaming around for a response, she shook him off.

It was like he was trying to reenact some music video, the grainy kind meant to prove how sensitive the hard-drinking, hard-drugging bootjack punk really was underneath all the random destruction. She wasn't buying. No way would she play his dew-eyed girl. She'd seen this one before; the song was way too long—the melody was strained and overproduced.

Fuck that.

When he stopped in the middle of the path, she was supposed to stop too, and stand there, quivering, waiting for the blow.

Fuck him. She kept walking.

"Betty, hold up a sec."

Anger thickened her skin. Nothing could pierce her.

"Betty—"

"What?"

She turned.

"Come here a sec."

"No."

"Just come here a sec."

"You come here," she said.

He did. He came so close she smelled the ashes on his breath, the iron and acid, that slight whiff of mildew on his clothes. He slipped his arms around her waist, pulling her toward him, and thrust his pelvis into hers. When she tried to squirm away, his grip clamped tighter.

"Just let me hold you." It was all so stagy. So melodramatic.

Finally, she had to resort to violence, to dig her nails into his wrists and twist his arms around behind his back.

"You can't do that anymore. You've lost the right," she said.

"What's that supposed to mean?"

"You know what it means."

The park had been left intentionally wild. Weeds sprouted into tall grass. Half-strangled trees rose out of dense webs of shrubbery and thistle. To the left was darkness and brambles. To the right, the river—it sounded like rain. This was where Trent went, down the steep ridge, bending to grab something from the ground on his way. She could see him down there, in shadows, pressed against the iron fence, breaking pieces off whatever it was he'd picked up—a dead twig, it must have been—and lobbing them into the water.

The thing to do was to walk away and let this be the end. Or rush up behind him and slam him into the fence. Instead, she gravitated slowly toward him and pressed up against the dull iron spear tips to wait for him to send her away.

He whipped the chunks of rotting wood as far as he could. Once they hit the river they were barely visible, shadows on black water, floating toward the retaining wall and collecting in the glistening web of foam there. When the stick couldn't be broken down further, he threw the last finger as far as he could and picked up another one. He bounced it in his hand.

"We killed the dog," he said.

Then he whipped the new stick whole into the river.

Gripping the fence to hold herself steady, she refused to look at him. The water was an empty space below her, nothing but sound and an unstable pitch of black. Beyond it, streaks of muddy gray, cliffs, and then a line of pale electric yellow where the lights of West River Road were strung like some optimistic thing beyond her imagination. In places, trees jutted into the light, black furry creatures, hulking on the ledge.

"We had to," Trent said. "It kept jumping on the bed. The ho-bag said he had to get rid of it."

She'd misunderstood everything. Jarod. The sorrows locked behind his droopy face. She saw herself reaching over to muss his hair. The dog. All of this over a stupid dog.

The tall grass cut at her shins as she raced through it. Burs pulled at her shorts and bunched in her shoelaces.

Behind her, Trent was yelling. "We didn't have a choice! Cheryl! Wait! Fucking hear me out!"

Cheryl. Not Betty, but Cheryl. The same old Cheryl she'd always been.

The sharp sting of bile pierced the back of her throat. Saliva welled up and pooled under her tongue. She reeled, swallowed back vomit, continued running. When she heard him chasing her, she sped her pace. Her knees buckled. She toppled into the pathway, the light.

He wrapped her up and pinned her. She couldn't kick herself away. He was knotted around her, the rope pulling tighter and tighter as he whispered into her ear, breaking her. "Let me explain, okay? Then you can go ahead and fucking hate me."

A rhythmic padding moved toward them along the path, then a couple of women emerged into view. Their identical ponytails bounced back and forth, and though they kept their eyes fixed on the distance in front of them, they were discussing something, slinging half sentences back and forth between huffs of breath.

Trent rolled off Cheryl, and as if by agreement, the two of them scooted to the edge of the trail and sat cross-legged, their knees almost touching. They waited, scowling, for the women to pass.

"It's sort of unnecessary, though, huh?"

"Did you tell him that?"

"I can't talk to him about these sorts of things."

"That's probably the real problem."

Noticing Cheryl and Trent, the woman closest to them arched her eyebrow and tipped her head. Her friend's mouth stretched into a perfect O and they both fell silent and sped their pace.

Once they were gone, Trent spit between his legs and picked up where he'd left off. "It was ugly," he said. "I knew it would freak you out." He was staring at her, searching. He'd expected something that wasn't there.

She exploded. "Don't you understand anything? I don't care about the fucking dog!" The fury in her own voice scared her.

"What the fuck, then?" The look in his eyes. It was like she was the one hurting him.

The best she could think to do was fall back on the grass. It was stiff and prickly, a bed of nails. She pulled giant clumps out with her fists. "I thought you were kicking me out," she mumbled.

She didn't have to look to know he'd gone cold.

"Not everything is about you, alright? I know you wish it was, but it's not."

This statement would haunt her, torture her, later. She'd hold it to the light and study its color, layer it over the fragments of her life, trying to figure out how true it was. These were exactly the sorts of words she used to hurl at me when she wanted to wound me. Hearing them from Trent shocked her, terrified her. The physical world is a porous place and reality a hypothetical thing. I'd neglected to teach her how to believe in it, and in order not to slip, she'd had to be vigilant. She'd had to construct a wall of rules and surround herself with them in order to ensure she didn't become like me. Now the barrier she'd built between us was breached and that old fear came flooding back in. She couldn't trust her perceptions—not a single one.

But sitting there next to the river with Trent, she wasn't thinking of how like me she was. She was thinking about him. He'd been supposed to help her create a new world. To be her escape. She was thinking he wasn't an escape at all, now. There was no escape.

He touched her arm softly. "I'm not gonna kick you out, Betty. Why would I do that? You're all I have."

Four

"THEY HAD TO DO IT, MOM," she would have said, if we'd ever been able to discuss these events. "The world's a tough place. It doesn't matter what they say their intentions are, do-gooders like the Humane Society are really just there to make the middle class feel like they've done something worthwhile with their lives. You know what I mean, Mom? Like to sweep all the horror and death into the corner, to turn everything into white rooms and gleaming steel tables. These people can't handle real blood and guts. The truth bums them out. You know what I'm saying? How are they gonna keep their fantasy alive if they have to see how they're like everyone else? Right? I mean, right? It's bullshit. It's just like organic farming."

These words would not have been hers, not originally, anyway. They'd belong to Trent, and like a college freshman enamored with her teacher, she would have rolled them around on her tongue until they felt natural in her mouth. My job, then, would have been to respond with tolerance, to patiently nudge her back toward herself.

"Remember when we got Gremlin?" I'd say.

"Uh-huh. Yeah, okay, Mom. But so what? So we went to the Humane Society. That doesn't change it. For every cat they give away, they kill ten more."

I'd wait. I'd speak slowly and re-create that day. "There were some spectacularly fine cats there. Beautiful, full-breed cats. A Persian. A

Russian Blue. All kinds of kittens—the place was crammed with them, gazing out at you from those metal cages, their eyes wide and pleading. And what did you do?" A rhetorical question to which she'd know the answer.

This story was a favorite, enshrined in family legend. She'd heard me tell it dozens of times. And despite everything I'd put her through, despite all the ways she'd tried to kill this part of herself, she was still sentimental, still cherished the image of herself the story contained. I'm positive she would have played along.

"What did I do?" she'd ask.

"You walked up and down every aisle of the shelter. You peered into each cage one at a time. And when you found the oldest, most snaggle-toothed cat there, you pointed and said, 'That one.' I thought, My God, this cat's covered in grease. It can barely lift its head. It's on its last legs. I imagined eyedroppers and midnight trips to the animal hospital. This cat won't last a week and then what'll happen? I'll have a bawling ten-year-old on my hands. I don't think I'm ready to teach her this lesson. 'Here,' I said, 'Cheryl, let's revisit the kittens.' I tried to guide you away but you wouldn't budge. 'We have to take this one, we have to, Mom,' you said. And when I asked you why, remember what you said?"

She'd wait. She'd let me finish the story for her.

"Those other cats are easy" is what she'd said. "Those cats will find homes. But nobody but us is gonna love this gremlin."

Rancid

One

CHERYL AND TRENT spent more and more time on the roof. They scaled up the drainpipe almost every night now. They slept there. In the early hours after dark, the tar remained warm, pliable and sticky. Later, as the head abated, they'd wake briefly and nestle together under the rank comforter, missing most of its stuffing, smelling faintly of cat piss, which they'd found in the dumpster behind an apartment complex on University. As the weeks went by, other detritus accumulated: whiskey bottles; empty forty-ouncers; wrappers from candy bars and mini-mart burritos; small blue ziplock bags, so minuscule they barely fit the tip of a finger inside, ripped at the seams, licked clean of their contents; a handful of prized books from Trent's wall downstairs, Henry Rollins's journals, Charles Bukowski's poems, a few rumpled issues of *Cometbus* and a glossy coffee table book that retailed at nearly a hundred bucks but had been discounted to five fingers by Trent, the definitive photo history of an anti-culture subculture, a revolution that had disappeared into the great hegemon and died right around the time the two of them were born—I can say with authority it wasn't as much fun as it looked.

They got used to the open air and, more, to the privacy, the distance from Mike's clomping three a.m. boots and the incessant nonsense that dribbled from Devin's mouth. They began to take for granted the ease with which they could strip off each other's clothes and fuck the night away, though most nights now they were too drunk to fuck.

Since Trent had admitted his need for her, she'd undergone a profound change. Her dreams of chaos and revolution had softened, transformed into radical versions of something else, something a lot like domesticity. Not the suburban home life in which she'd been raised, not the nesting she'd been trained by years of sitcoms and baby dolls to believe in, what she imagined was more a raucous house party, but a home built in squalor, cobbled out of other people's trash. A place that absorbed every vagrant and lost child who showed up at its shattered windows, let them in after curfew, never asked where they'd been. Something like the communes of the sixties and seventies, but minus the body paint and inane optimism. A rougher and meaner capital-free zone, with her at the center of it all. They'd build a family out of the rubble. They'd still smash shit up, though, they'd still be badass.

During the day, Cheryl and Trent scrambled back inside to avoid the unbearable burn of the sun. They hid in the permanent shade of the living room. The heat hit the low hundreds in the afternoons, the air thickened like gravy, the humidity rose. Rain came in brief spritzes, offering no relief. The kids cooked like dumplings in a steamer, lumps of dough, glistening on the hardwood floor. Movement exhausted them. Better to do nothing. Once in a while, a rumor about a prospective street action floated through—burning down a Gap, defacing a Target, vandalizing a McDonald's Playland—and they roused themselves, briefly energized by the hope of combusting in righteousness and anger. Then nothing would happen, the rumor would sink under the suffocating heat and the kids would give in to their lethargy again, lying around, marking time by the trickle of sweat down their bodies.

I want to say it was the delirium of summer that made the signs so hard for Cheryl to read. Five or six days after the boys killed the dog—who could say how many, they were all the same, they all blurred together—a faint sweetness began to accumulate in the kitchen. The smell was subtle, it wafted in and out, but each time Cheryl caught it, she paused for a moment to wonder what it could possibly be. An idle thought. She'd remind herself to bring it up with Trent, then forget until the scent hit her again.

The one time she did remember to ask him about it, Trent was fading in and out of sleep, lying on his back, his head propped on the kiddie pool, limbs splayed out so as to catch the most breeze. His eyes remained shut. He grunted and mumbled something Cheryl couldn't decipher.

"I swear there's some weird smell," she said again. "No?"

His mouth formed slow, half-articulated words.

Leaning in close, she whispered in his ear. "In the kitchen, like right around the sink. I can't believe you haven't noticed it."

Nothing.

She placed her open palm flat on his chest and an immediate moistness accumulated under it. "Trent?"

Shaking her off, he rolled onto his side to face away from her. "Sleeping," he said.

"But, just real quick. You haven't smelled it?" It wasn't so much that she cared about the smell as that she didn't like him ignoring her. "Trent?"

"What the fuck?" he said, turning, staring, wounded. "I'm fucking sleeping."

"You don't smell it?"

"What?"

"I don't know. Downstairs. In the kitchen. There's a weird smell down there."

She didn't notice his shudder before answering, "It's probably just Devin."

"It's not Devin. It's—"

"Or garbage. Something. Let me sleep."

"It's like a rotting smell. Really nasty."

"Where is this?"

"I told you already. Under the sink."

"I don't know, Betty. Maybe it's a dead rat. Who cares?" He turned again, adjusted the kiddie pool under his head and that was that.

She didn't push it. She didn't wonder if maybe they should conduct a search, remove the carcass from their living space. Nothing like that. Trent was right. Who cared? Except for passing through on her way to and from the roof, she didn't hang out in the kitchen anyway. And having decided it wasn't important, she hardly noticed the smell gaining texture, slowly infiltrating the whole squat. Like the other inconveniences of their situation, it was bearable. Live long enough with it and it disappeared.

Two

SHE MOVED into a state of consciousness beyond caring, out of my reach, beyond saving.

Even Devin stopped annoying her. He spent most of his time sunk into the beanbag, leafing through the various porn magazines he'd stolen from gas stations and blue bookshops or found in gutters and trash cans, in stacks tied with twine behind public housing complexes and in the basements of co-ops. The more perverse the photo, the more he fetishized it, but his interest never seemed to be sexual—as far as Cheryl could tell, he had no sex drive at all. What he responded to in these images was the way they invoked the extreme limits of the human spirit. He took comfort in knowing that someone, somewhere, was being degraded, that contempt was such a universal emotion. And when he was especially bored and cranky, he liked to thrust the uglier photo spreads in front of Cheryl's face. Golden showers, gagging scenes, bukkake and skat, whatever he thought would upset her the most.

With one hand thrust down his pants, resting there in a way she'd once found creepy but now thought was touching, he waved a magazine over his head. "This is some freaky shit. Look—check this out."

She snatched and gawked. She'd grown to enjoy this game.

Today, what she saw was a woman with her hair up in greasy pigtails—naked, of course—balanced spread-eagle on the handlebars of a Harley Davidson while peeling her vagina open for the camera. She was extremely pregnant, but somehow still rail thin. Her breasts, which should have grown plump and heavy, were shrunken like popped balloons.

To better savor Cheryl's reaction, Devin tumbled from the beanbag and slithered up next to her, peering over her shoulder at the photo. "Check out those bruises!"

There were yellowish-purple marks up and down the woman's arms and a large welt on her inner thigh. She was only vaguely real to Cheryl; the circumstances that had led her to the moment caught on camera weren't worth getting up in a snit over. What most interested Cheryl was her contorted pose. A woman made of rubber. Gumby does Dallas. Hilarious.

Devin had this proud look on his face. "Why are you crying? She's just some skank whore," he said, and when he saw Cheryl wasn't crying but laughing, he punched her hard on the shoulder.

Grabbing him by the hair, she shook his head back and forth in mock anger. "Leave me alone," she said. They were both grinning.

That smell floated in and out of the room. It was getting so she kind of liked it. She'd dared herself toward apathy, and now, here she was. It was a kind of milestone. A victory.

Even Devin—Devin, who from the start had pestered and picked at her, who loathed women maybe even more than he loathed himself—was no longer capable of disturbing her. Where once she saw him as stupid and dangerous, she saw him now as charming, sweet, harmless. He was on the inside, along with her and Trent.

Mike was inside too, but less so now. When he was home, he glowered and muttered. He zinged Japanese throwing stars at the walls.

Disgusted by their aggrieved wastrel ways, he'd stopped bringing food back for them weeks ago, and without his handouts, Cheryl and Trent and Devin mostly starved. So what? It was too hot to eat anyway. They took turns spanging out on the street with their cardboard signs and their screwed-on expressions of utter dejection. When they got desperate, they nibbled dry pasta, which expanded in their stomachs and created a convincing facsimile of fullness. Mike didn't care. He enjoyed watching them starve. He stood, arms folded and flexed, over their crumpled forms and laughed. "Man, I'm so glad I'm me and not you fuck-alls."

Soon he'd be a Marine, and as the day drew closer, he distanced himself more and more from the rest of them. This smacked of betrayal, and Cheryl was even more wary of him now than she used to be.

Unable to wait the five days he had left, he'd begun practicing his low defensive crouch, his arms out in front of him at severe angles, knuckles cocked. He hoped, before boot camp, to smelt his body and mind together into an iron rod. Flinging his legs sideways in inept deathblows, made all the clumsier by the jackboots laced up his calves, he'd shout "ki-kou" or "pi-tang," "di-pa-mou-tow," raging mock-Asian nonsense. When his boots hit the floor, he'd find himself in cool new positions and he'd freeze, teeth clenched, lips spread wide, waiting for everyone to be impressed. Aikido, he called it. Cheryl called it crap.

Especially when, like now, she was trying to nap and he was performing his tricks over her head. "You better watch out," she said. "I've got a perfect angle on your balls."

"She stirs, she wakes, she's alive!" His foot lunged in slow motion toward her head, crept forward, his boot stopping an inch from her face. The deep treads of the sole hovered over her forehead. A pebble was caught in the heel.

"Knock it off." She slapped him away, and he plopped into the broken director's chair.

"I got some shit I want to drop on you," he said.

"*Some shit you want to drop on me?* When'd you get all ghetto?"

"Seriously," he said.

Getting cushy with Mike would only lead to trouble. He'd triangulate and manipulate, use what she told him to further his fascistic argument against Trent. She didn't want to carry any of his secrets and she didn't want him to have power over hers. But it had been a day and a half since she'd eaten and Mike had a job and the other guys had run out to sponge pot off the college kids—who knew when they'd be back. "You got any food?" she asked.

"I'll buy you something. Come on, let's get out of here."

"You got money?"

"You think I hang out at Chipotle for my health? You think I just do it for the girls?"

He better splurge for something good, she told him, or she wasn't gonna go anywhere.

"Whatever you want."

The most expensive restaurant in Dinkytown was a place called the Red Barn. It served the same nasty food as Ron's Tiny Diner or the Village Inn but charged a premium for the privilege of enjoying its rustic decor. This was where she told him to take her.

"Sure." He tapped her shoulder. "Let's go."

For ten ninety-five, she ordered a bacon cheeseburger with onion rings. The rangy girl taking her order had a teeny gold cross dangling from her neck and the willed sunniness of a farm girl, but she was haughty enough to smirk when Cheryl asked for the burger well done. "What?" Cheryl demanded. "What's so weird about that?" But the girl just shrugged, dropped a gaping grin on Cheryl and, ever so slightly, arched an eyebrow.

The coffee she'd ordered took forever to come, and when she added milk, it turned gray instead of brown. "You're not gonna eat?" she asked Mike, taking a sip. He'd watched silently, a tolerant patron, while she fumbled through her confrontation with the waitress.

"I'm not hungry."

Cheryl rolled her eyes.

"Fine, you want me to order something?" With a flick of the finger, he called the waitress back and asked for green tea with lemon. He mimed a whistle as she strode away. "Happy?" he asked Cheryl. There was something even smugger than usual about him today.

"This coffee's shit."

"They're between rushes. It's been there since ten a.m." So he knew his way around the restaurant business. The service industry. Was that supposed to impress her? It didn't.

Waiting for her food, she drew faces in the spilled coffee on the table and stared out the window at the near-empty street, wishing Trent would stumble past and rush in to hang out and mock them. "Fucking yuppies," he'd say. "Buy me a coffee." As the time ticked past and the silence persisted, she filled in this fantasy with greater detail. Him pushing down the street, his head hanging like deadweight on his shoulder, his eyes shifting about for something to pounce on. He'd be brooding over something. Some random thing. And then he'd see her. There'd be a moment of recognition and he'd brighten, his muscles relaxing, his eyebrows melting from those angry arches into wide-open curves. It would be like she was wielding a sloppy paintbrush and slathering over the ugliness of his day with a light glimmering sunshine.

Her body ached toward the burger when it arrived. The first few bites detonated in her mouth like torpedoes. The bitch waitress had brought the burger medium instead of well done, but still, it was wonderful. Hot food. How long had it been? Grease dripped down her chin, down her arms. She didn't care.

Mike remained virtually frozen in place. He watched Cheryl silently as she slid the batter off her onion rings and dipped it bite by bite into the assembly line of salt and ketchup she'd set up on her plate. He studied the pile of things she didn't want, the limp onions, tomatoes, pickle, lettuce, coleslaw. "Throwing out the healthy stuff," he said. "Nice."

"You want it? Here."

"I'll eat at work," he said. He folded his hands under his chin.

That's what was most galling about all of this. Mike was sitting there like the father in a bad TV show, full of his own virtue and capability. She wished he'd hurry up and get to the moral so she could say, "Gee, Dad, thanks. I guess you're right. Not doing your homework does sort of cause problems." His condescension was boundless. She thought about sticking her finger down her throat and throwing his charity back up onto her plate. "Here. I don't want it. You can have it back." That's what Trent would do. But she didn't have this kind of drama in her yet.

Instead, she plopped the last bite of burger into her mouth, and though she was stuffed—her stomach had shrunk, this was the first proper meal she'd had in months—she chewed and chewed, sucked every drop of liquid from the fiber, gnawed on it like gum until it was hard and dry, until her jaw hurt. Then she spit the cud back onto her plate, a gray pile of ground meat that reminded her of Gremlin's chronic hairballs.

"You want anything else?" he asked impassively. "Dessert? Ice cream? Something?"

"No."

"You sure?" he asked again. "Once I'm gone it'll be all ramen all the time."

Glowering, she shook her head again, no, and waited for him to pick up the check.

"Aren't you gonna hit on her?" she asked as the waitress walked away with his twenty.

"Nah. She's too skinny."

"You've been drooling over her since we got here."

"She doesn't have the look."

"What look?"

"She likes herself too much to get fucked-up with me." He cracked a halfway smile. He was looking Cheryl directly in the eyes. A death gaze. A gaze that confiscated the things it took in. She saw him for a second, in the back of a Humvee, covered in dust, surveying the rubble of the Baghdad streets—he'd have this same grim expression on his face.

"Do I have the look?"

"You're pretty much a good girl," he said. Then he leaned across the table. "Aren't you?" When she gave him nothing, he slouched back and smugly nodded.

A good girl, she thought. Well, fuck you too. What I am is too good for you.

He suggested they head over to Sonic Sounds, the used-record store a couple blocks away that specialized in obscure imports and hard-to-find old indies. "I'm sure they've got all of Nobody's Fool's shit. You can get yourself a souvenir."

She could feel the beginnings of a food coma coming on. All she wanted to do was go home. That and get away from Mike.

As they wandered back to the Sabotage Café, his pace slowed and slowed until finally he stopped. The faded gray siding of Sabotage was visible now at the end of the block. Whatever he was after, now was the time.

"I'm right, no?" he said. "You are a good girl."

"Sometimes, sometimes not. I guess it depends on how much I like you."

"Yeah. See? That's what I mean. A good girl."

The fucking burger was giving her a stomachache.

"I mean," he said, "what are you doing here?"

"What, here on earth? 'Cause my mother plopped me out. Or do you mean here, like here going to lunch with you? I'm not gonna fuck you if that's what you mean."

"Don't be obtuse."

"Yeah, I know that word too." What a prick. "Why are *you* here?"

She could see the blood rising to his face, turning it a deeper, more complex hue of brown. His voice was controlled, forceful. "You think I *want* to be here? I'm not like you. I don't get to pick and choose. Anyway, I'm getting the hell out."

"Well, I like it here. Trent likes it. Devin—"

"Fucking Devin. That kid's a psychopath. He'll be dead by next year."

"It's better than fucking joining the system."

"Don't talk to me about the fucking system. Where are you from? Plymouth? Edina? You *are* the system."

"Trent doesn't—"

The force of Mike's laughter was ferocious, terrifying. "Do you even talk to your boyfriend? Do you even— Why do you think he calls you Betty? You think that's a compliment? You ever heard of Betty Page? Betty's what we call girls we want to fuck and forget." He stepped back. "Screw it. You people aren't my problem anymore."

For a moment, she wondered, What if he's right? Then she remembered the terror she'd seen on Trent's face when he'd thought he was going to lose her. "You're all I have," he'd said. She had other things, she had me and Robert, but he was all she wanted. Mike was wrong. Even if what he said was true, he was wrong.

Three

THE THING TRENT AND HIS FRIENDS did to the dog lurked somewhere in the recesses of her mind. I want to think it asserted itself in the most incongruous of moments. As they sat in Arby's sucking down free refills of pop, Trent would slide a cartoon he'd just drawn—the two of them, huge heads on tiny bodies, riding a rocket ship off toward the moon, maybe—across the table, and there it would be, the dog's mottled face, its slick floppy tongue, peeking through the blotted ink. Or the three of them—her, Trent and Devin—would be dropping water balloons from the window of the squat, keeping score of their hits with an elaborate point system that ranged from zero, a total miss, to fifty, a slam dunk into a baby stroller, and as her balloon splattered onto the sidewalk, she'd think of blood and hear the dog whine. *They killed the pathetic defenseless little thing, they murdered it.* The thought would shoot up like a chunk of rotting wood unmoored from a long submersion in water. It would float around on the surface for a moment, then drift out of view.

Sometimes when she was up late, jittering after everyone else had passed out, taking the edge off with the dregs she found in abandoned bottles, the dog would peer at her out of the blackness and she'd be unable to blink its face away. What they'd done would play out in front of her.

"Hey, Dog. Come here, Dog."

She could hear them—Trent, Devin—horsing around with it, throwing imaginary balls across the room, trying to get it to run into the wall.

"You want to do something fun, Dog?" Devin had asked it while trying to grab ahold of its hind legs. Then, walking it around the room on its forepaws, "I hope you're into S&M, Dog."

When he lifted the dog up and swung it like a golf club, it whimpered a little, let out a yowl. She could hear Devin's cackle—the devil laugh he took on when he was feeling extra-evil—as he let go and sent the dog sailing, sprawled out and paddling empty air.

However Trent pitched it after the fact, Cheryl was sure he'd found Devin's antics hysterical. He always did. That's why he kept the kid around, to fuck shit up and make him laugh.

But what about Jarod? How would Jarod take this? His impulse must have been to protect his pet, even as he struggled to prepare himself for what they were all about to do. He would have scrambled after it, wrapped himself around it. Held it tight and whispered in its ear. Cheryl imagined he said, "Be brave," but that was maybe overdramatic. More likely, he said, over and over, "Hey puppy, hey Dog, hey little bitch, hey, why'd you have to go and fuck everything up?"

And Mike? Mike would just be shaking his head. "Look, if we're gonna do this, and really, I still don't get why we are, let's quit with the bullshit, huh? And, hey, no way are we gonna do it here."

Trent, always torn between Devin and Mike, would have felt ashamed, his authority threatened. Clapping his hands, he'd shout, "Devin. Stop fucking fucking around. Let's go now."

Then she'd see them downstairs in the cavernous, musty room where the Sabotage Café had once served up its sludge, that room with streaked layers of dust on the windows, with no ventilation, a concrete floor, filled with wooden tables and folded-up chairs and a dusty copper bar, all four of them—five with the dog—hearts surging, wondering what to do next.

Taking in the chalky, chill scent of the moment, Jarod might let the dog loose to roam one last time. Trepidatious at first, but curious and alert, the dog twitches her nose. She concentrates. Nostrils to the floor, she takes a step forward. A pause. Then another step. Half a step, pause, and her right ear perks up. Her head ticks a notch, like the second hand on a clock. She changes course, moving quickly but carefully toward the chairs layered six rows deep against the wall across from the bar.

The boys hardly notice. They're rummaging, themselves, in search of instruments to aid them in their cause. The curved steel lever from the espresso machine. A screwdriver. They can't find any rope and they're too lazy—or excited—to make the trek back upstairs, so Trent bundles up a hunter orange extension cord. This is what they'll use to bind the dog.

Jarod stands to the side, sinking into himself, a finger to his lips like a high-strung and apprehensive grandmother. He's the only boy not in the spirit of things—it's a game to them, they're commandos on a mission—and if his lips weren't quivering, he might be confused for the captain of this unit. As it is, hidden in the furrows of his hooded sweatshirt, he's more like a specter, a conscience haunting the proceedings.

The dog's found her spot. She splays her legs like a girl in a bar bathroom, squeamish about getting close to the toilet seat.

As soon as they hear the hiss of her urine, the boys stop what they're doing. Trent darts to the squatting animal, lifts it like a barrel. "Hey, Dog—what the fuck, Dog?" He holds it out in front of him on stiff arms, and as he spins it, the dog sprays a surprisingly long, looping arc of piss across the room.

Trent shakes the dog, but the stream doesn't stop. "Shit!" He's laughing now. "Fucking A, look at that shit."

A trail of moisture cuts across the dust, over the chairs, up the wall, onto the tables stacked surface to surface next to the bar. Then a horizontal slash across Devin's t-shirt, a dribble on Mike's ankle.

Mike just shakes his head, but Devin, behind the bar searching the drawers for a knife, raises a soup ladle. "Oh, you asshole," he says. Then he lunges.

Trent uses the dog as his shield when he dodges.

Taunting, feinting, testing their skill, they circle each other like kickboxers. They pay no attention to the hectoring from Mike, his reminders that he's got to work after this and if they want his help— and you *know* you need it—they better stop fucking around already.

"En garde!" The ladle stabs out toward Trent, catches the dog in the ribs, but the blade doesn't pierce. Devin pulls back for another attack, and as he collects himself, Trent kicks. With a quick grab, Devin has his foot. He twists and pulls, trying to throw Trent off balance.

The dog makes sounds that dogs shouldn't make. Crying sounds. Human sounds.

Jarod's found a chair. He's not watching this, he can't. He's hidden his head between his knees. Maybe the crying is coming from him. Probably not, though. He's just waiting for it to be over.

Twisting Trent's leg behind him, Devin slashes at his ribs with the spatula, yanking the leg higher, higher, still higher, until Trent starts to hop and then Devin kicks his other leg out from under him.

The boys fall and the dog flails away. She scrambles across the room in search of escape, runs in loops around the boys, barking, barking, barking.

Pinning Trent beneath him, Devin whips the ladle down indiscriminately. When he gets the right angle, it makes a nice wet sound slapping against Trent's flesh. All Trent can do is buck and protect himself. A few welts, a few cuts, it's all in a day's fun.

They're warming up, getting their blood rushing.

A second, larger collection of tables is stacked in pairs along the back wall, square slabs of treated and finished pressed-wood product, balanced on thick iron cylinders. They're lined up four by four, a double-stacked grid. The dog races into the shadowy vault beneath them and backs herself to the corner, pressing down as flat to the floor as she can. She needs to have all four feet on the ground. She needs to be poised and ready to run.

Crawling in after her, Jarod crouches, his palms out in a plea for trust.

Mike, meanwhile, has joined the wrestling match. He acts as referee, officious and scolding, enjoying in a more subdued, headier way, the few kicks and punches he manages to get in.

Jarod pets his dog. He implores it, stop shaking. What his friends are about to do doesn't feel real to him. Death isn't as familiar to him as disappearance—the slow random drift in and out of his life of people and things he doesn't trust enough to cherish. That's the way it's always been with his father. That's how it feels now, here, with the dog. He's saying goodbye, lying on the concrete next to his pet and scratching its forehead. Instead of preparing to accommodate the loss, he's steeling himself to deflect it, priming himself for the moment when Mike reaches in and drags the animal out of the cage of tables. He's detaching himself, telling himself, Feel nothing.

As Mike grapples with the dog, pulling it roughly by the front paws, the nails on its hind legs scrape along the concrete. He reaches one hand blindly behind his back. "Where's that extension cord?" Then wrapping the dog's legs tight, he lays it out in the middle of the room.

The boys are silent now, amateur surgeons surrounding a specimen. Devin's choosing his weapon. Trent stands ready to help. Their brains are flooding with rushing endorphins.

"Should we string it up?"

"What if we, like, dissected it?"

Jarod is still hiding under the tables. He's turned around. He's facing the wall, staring at the graffiti there: "Resist," it says. He's clamped his arms around his head but the sounds slide in anyway. He's thinking about the Discovery Channel, about the way the gazelles and antelope tumble over themselves, so graceful, when the lion catches up and clips them.

"Just hurry up, huh? I've got to get to work."

"Fucking here goes nothing, right?" Was that glee in Trent's voice?

Each time the scene played in Cheryl's mind, she asked herself this question, and each time, she chose to answer it no. She knew what came next too. She couldn't turn it off. She couldn't switch channels with a blink of her eyes. It kept going, there, beneath the lids, a continuous loop, varying slightly, sometimes graphic, now lyrical, now from the dog's sad black-and-white point of view. All she could do was wait for a distraction—Devin's shout for help carrying a street find, the plaintive life story of some new kid on the scene, best of all, though, hardest to come across, a drug powerful enough to knock her out.

Whatever trick allowed her to escape, these thoughts weren't gone for long. They always came back in some new variation. One thing remained consistent: the excitement in Trent's voice and her refusal to recognize it.

There are ways, I've discovered, that the things you imagine cling longer and dig deeper and cause more damage than those you've actually experienced. The lines begin to blur. You begin to have difficulty distinguishing between what's fantasy and what's real.

For a while there, I saw them every night, Trent and Devin, stabbing and stabbing and stabbing. Sometimes they noticed me and then they'd wink before going back to their gruesome game. Sometimes it wasn't the dog but my daughter tied up and bloodied beneath them. Sometimes, in my lunacy, I think it was me.

Four

THEY WERE ON THE ROOF AGAIN, Cheryl and Trent, pawing and teasing each other on, when the humidity broke and a warm rain flooded down like sudden bathwater. The drainage pipe was slick, a thrill to rappel, but back in the squat they felt hemmed in by the old oppression, by Devin's found trash and Mike's bad vibes. One look and they knew they couldn't take it tonight. They raced downstairs, and out onto the street, broke the taboo and made for the space where Cap's stuff was stored: the café itself. Cheryl had never set foot inside, never asked, never wanted to, somehow fearing it contained traces of me, dust that glowed green and was better left undisturbed.

The doors were boarded shut, so they tried a window. In the three weeks since he and his friends were last here, it had bloated and no matter how Trent pushed and pried, it wouldn't budge. While Cheryl danced behind him, her arm around his waist, fingers on his belly, then down his pants, tracing his pelvic bone, probing his damp pubic hair, he tried again. "Fuck this." He shook her off him, found an empty bottle in the alley, and warding her back, smashed it through the window. "Kick ass," he said, and then he kissed her, rough and sloppy, his saliva gushing into her mouth. Knocking the shards from the pane, he urged her to enter.

The thing that hit her first was the pull of heat, like the inside of a car left naked in the sun. Then she tasted the dry chalky grit of the air and the smell sank in, a scent with mass and weight and propulsion; it was a physical force, sweet and putrid, clinging to her like a spiderweb.

"Fucking A!" She tried to back out into the rain, but Trent was behind her, blocking her way. "This is that smell, the one I told you about."

She knew what it was—she'd known weeks ago when she'd caught the first whiff, when it had been just a trace, a fold of air in the kitchen, but still, even now, she refused to believe it.

Hands on her hips, Trent walked her backward through the room. He tried to talk the smell away—it's nothing, some dead rat, some shit like that, it'll go away, you'll see, in just a second, come here—and she heard lust in his voice, a breathy, conspiratorial excitement. He pecked at her face like a belligerent bird, palmed her ass, pulled her close. He didn't seem to be gagging like she was.

They waddled around the cavernous space, Cheryl holding her breath, gulping air through her mouth. Everything was too close—Trent, the rain, everything.

The back of her ankle caught on something. It was stiff and slick, squishy in places. Something wrapped in a plastic bag. Her foot became tangled and it gave underneath her. She could feel two frail rods jutting out from the bulk of the thing in the bag. "Trent," she said, "hold up, hold up, I'm gonna fall," but he wouldn't stop pressing, stop pulling and grabbing, he wouldn't stop manhandling her is what it was.

Her other ankle hit. She twisted. She fell. Her shoulder took the impact, but it still hurt. Trent tumbled over her, his body crushing her, sharp elbows jabbing, knees pounding her thigh, her groin.

He was kissing her. His lips were on her neck, one hand up her shirt, kneading her breast like clay. He thought she was into it, she could tell, and why wouldn't he—they'd had rougher sex than this a dozen times before. But never in a place so saturated with death.

That's what it was, the smell. It was the dog, the carcass of the dog. They'd left it there to rot. She couldn't pretend not to know anymore.

"I can't breathe," she said. "I think I'm gonna throw up."

Trent wasn't listening. Or he didn't care. He was fumbling with belts, yanking at her soaked shorts, pressing the nub of himself into her.

"It's dry," she said. "I'm sorry."

"Fuck, you want to stop?"

"No, finish." She couldn't disappoint him, not even now. "Just finish."

She lay there, every muscle in her body tense, breathing through her mouth, trying not to breathe at all. She swallowed back the stomach acid in her throat, she swallowed back the sound of her tears, and she took it.

She believed she had no choice.

And when he finally came and asked if she was pissed, she lied and she told him no.

VI

Fear

One

FEBRUARY EIGHTEENTH. A Wednesday. Over three months before Cheryl ran away.

It was going to be a dangerous year. She was coming up on her birthday, turning sixteen, the same age my sister had been when she died. Certain essential parts of Sarah had made their way through me into Cheryl, but I still worried that the wrong ancestor was watching over her. The ancient relative of Robert's whose name we'd taken had lived in a vastly different time; she knew nothing about the trouble Cheryl would face.

I'd been operating in a low-grade panic, trying and failing day after day to stop the fear from spreading. Knowing I shouldn't, but having no choice, really, I finally broke down and mentioned my fears to Robert, who pretty much responded just like I'd thought he would.

"Yup," he said. "She's reaching the magic age. Watch out! The whole house is going to turn into a pumpkin. We're all gonna go up in a puff of smoke."

He was trying to mollify me with sarcasm. It had worked before, popping my logic into cackles of laughter. This time, though, I wasn't in the mood. We'd been at it for almost an hour, and that look I loathe, the one that says I'm his toy, says no matter how loud or long I talk, he still won't hear a word I've said, was strung like an electric fence across his face.

"Go ahead. Gloat. But when Cheryl ends up . . ." The word was *dead*, but I couldn't bring myself to say it. "We'll see how much you'll be gloating then."

"Just relax, Julia. Remember where you are."

It was after eight. We were sitting across from each other at the kitchen table. I wanted to smack him. Instead I stood up and turned my back. My reflection in the sliding glass door confronted me. Splinters of frost cut across the reflection's face, and for a second I forgot they were on the exterior of the glass and thought they were actually part of my body. I reached up. My hand came between the frost on the glass and the face outside. My perceptions corrected themselves. But the slip terrified me. I had to remind myself: *Stop.*

"You relax," I said, spinning around to look at Robert.

He must have seen the change. His smirk fell away. "Just take a step back, Julia. Slow down."

"No. She's going to be sixteen," I said. "Don't you have any idea what that means?"

"Yes, I know what it means." I was giving him a headache. His finger was pressing at his eye.

"So . . ."

"Do we really have to go through all this again? What happened to sticking to things we can prove?"

"I CAN PROVE THIS!"

"Okay," he said. His hands flipped out in front of him like streamers. "Do."

The details all fit together in my head, the way Cheryl and Sarah and I were connected, but when I tried to explain them in a coherent argument, they peeled apart from each other and fragmented. "Not everything can be proven just like that," I said. "Some things you just know."

"Try."

Something moved, a quick vibration at the edge of the room.

There. A bulb of flesh. A fleck of black nail polish. I was dizzy. It was getting harder for me to breathe. I opened my mouth. I tried to be coherent, but the only word I could get out was "Sarah."

As I rushed from the room, Robert grabbed my wrist, and to get him off of me I had to bite him. Then, in the hallway, I smacked into Cheryl.

"What's wrong?" she asked. She was terrified. She'd never seen me like this before.

I pushed right past her, reeled down the hall toward the bathroom and slammed the door. After turning the lever in the tub to the right and pulling the shower valve, I settled onto the toilet seat to wait for the steam to fill up the room.

I understood exactly what was happening, but there was nothing I could do to stop it. It wasn't all just a trick of my mind. It wasn't completely psychosomatic. Some of it was real. My blood wasn't flowing. There was a pinch, like a cramp, at the base of my neck, an unstable prickle fluttering up and down my arm. When I tried to breathe, the air could get in, but something was stopping it from getting out.

This had happened before, but usually I was able to suppress it, to push through it by slowing myself down and regulating my body's malfunctions. Those previous scares had been rehearsal drills, preparing me for a severe attack. Now here it was. Cheryl was turning sixteen. Nobody was going to protect us.

The fist rapping at the door was too confident, too intolerant to be Cheryl's.

"Open up, Julia."

But Cheryl was there too. I could hear her behind him, trying to reach me. "What happened, Mom? What's wrong?"

He snapped at her. "Go to your room."

"But—"

There was rustling, more pounding. "Julia?"

"But, Dad—"

"Now. She's just upset, okay?"

Robert's voice dropped away and all I could hear was the water from the shower pummeling the tub. The steam twirled in slow pinwheels across the room, dusting the mirrors, tumbling into the two scalloped sink basins and folding in on itself, spilling up and out like a witch's brew. The air was growing heavy and my reflection in the shower door blurred.

"I swear, if you don't open up, Julia, I'm gonna break the door down."

He didn't realize the door was unlocked. He hadn't checked. Even in his rage, he had decorum, that small-town courtesy, bred into him by his mother; thinking about barging in on my privacy in the bathroom made him squeamish.

"You're making this harder than it has to be," he said, and the knob turned. The door opened a crack and paused there. Then he shoved it wide. He cut through the steam. Swiftly, stridently, he ducked into the tub and shut off the water.

When he turned on me, one arm of his pale-blue button-down shirt was soaked to the shoulder. The terror on his face enraged me.

"Happy now?" he said.

A sharp pain shot through my heart and when I tried to speak, all that came out was a hoarse whisper.

Robert sank onto the lip of the tub. He thought I was faking it, I could tell. He had no compassion.

I fished out the book of crossword puzzles Robert kept in the wicker basket next to the toilet, and unclipping the ballpoint pen he'd tucked inside as a placeholder, I performed a quick diagnosis on myself. I flipped the book open and scrawled my situation onto a page of newsprint. I'M HAVING A HEART ATTACK, I wrote.

"No you're not."

CALL 911.

"You're not having a heart attack."

CALL 911.

"What are your symptoms?"

ARM TINGLES. SHOOTING PAIN.

"How about we take some deep breaths." He reached for my hand, but I jabbed the pen at him, warding him off.

CAN'T BREATHE. HEART . . .

My hands were shaking so badly I could barely form the words on the page. I kept stabbing holes in the paper. It was hopeless and Robert didn't care anyway.

My throat felt like it was going to rip apart, but I had to push through the pain and force out a sound. I didn't want to die. "Cheryl?!"

She didn't come running.

I stared at her father until he left the room in exasperation.

Then I flipped to the back cover of the crossword book—it was less fragile, slick, heavy card stock—and wrote down the things she needed to know.

CHERYL,

CALL 911. I'M HAVING A HEART ATTACK. I HAVE TO GO TO THE HOSPITAL. DON'T WORRY. EVERYTHING WILL BE OKAY. WE'LL GET THROUGH THIS. BUT HURRY PLEASE. THE SITUA-TION IS URGENT.

VERY IMPORTANT: DO NOT DISCUSS ANY OF THIS WITH YOUR FATHER. WE CAN'T TRUST HIM. HE DOESN'T UNDER-STAND.

I LOVE YOU.

MOM

The note in my lap, I waited for her to come to me.

It took her a while, but eventually, she did.

"What's up?" she mumbled, her voice a dull monotone.

I handed her the note. As she scanned the words I'd written there, her hands shook so badly that she had to use both of them to hold the crossword book still. But she kept her composure. She refused to cry. I was proud of her.

"I just have to say, Mom." She scrutinized me, and I caught a trace of her father's intolerance curling around the edges of her mouth. "You're not acting like you're having a heart attack."

The pain spiked up my arm.

BUT I AM.

"Wouldn't you be, like, rolling around on the ground? I mean, wouldn't your face be turning blue or something?"

I AM HAVING A HEART ATTACK!! I wrote.

"Mom?"

DIFFERENT PEOPLE HAVE HEART ATTACKS IN DIFFERENT WAYS.

That was as far as I was willing to go. Even in my distressed state, I was still her mother. Even incapacitated. And there was no way I was going to debate her on the things taking place within my own body.

"This is crazy!" she said.

I was done talking. There was nothing left to discuss. If she didn't call the ambulance soon, something terrible was going to happen.

She must have intuited the severity of my position. Her face puckered with the effort to hold back her fear. She was at an age when her reality had yet to harden—the rules of her world were still permeable—but she understood that this, now, this was real. I wasn't playing games with her perception. I was as frightened as she was, and she was the only one who could do anything about it. If this angered her, she had a right to that anger. I understood. She wasn't mad at me, she was mad at the situation, at the impossibility of fixing the situation, at her own childish urge to run away and hide, pull the covers over her head while she waited for everything to end. The circumstances demanded she take on responsibilities that, as my daughter, my child, she never should have had to shoulder. I wasn't supposed to be the helpless one. We both understood this. But understanding did us no good. The facts wouldn't change. Reality refused to be altered. I was slumped on the toilet, halfway to collapse, with no one to save me but her.

I squeezed her hand, a quick, furtive pulse. *Thank you*, it said. *You're my whole life.* And when my hand dropped from hers, she pulled out her cell phone, punched in the numbers and left the room.

Later, while trying to block out the murmur of Robert and Cheryl's conversation, which was floating through the house like distant gunfire, I got it in my head that, if I were outside in the brisk air, my blood would flow a tiny bit more fluidly, my heart would beat just a tad more regularly, and I'd be able to persist and survive until the ambulance came to my rescue.

My breath was short again. The house was thick with signals I couldn't decipher.

I pulled myself to my feet, and lurching, staggering, made my way slowly out of the bathroom. Every few steps, I lost my breath completely and had to stop until it came back to me. Braced against the wall, heaving, I waited for the pain to end. Then I pushed on.

Down the hallway.

Past the bedrooms.

The whispers halted abruptly.

I made it to the kitchen, and Cheryl and Robert were staring at me.

For a moment I watched them. They looked exhausted, nervous, like they'd been struggling to trap a skittish cat. Without taking his eyes off me, Robert reached over and patted Cheryl's arm. It was like they were in some corny support group.

"Don't forget," he told her, "two plus two."

I could surmise what had come before: him filling her up with resentment toward me, saying, Don't trust her, don't listen to a word she says, when she speaks, look her in the eye and show no emotion, saying, Listen to the song playing in your head, anything just so long as it's not her; she'll try to catch you in her sticky logic and you'll want to believe her delusions could be real; they can't, though, remember this, they can't, and somewhere inside that brain she knows it too; she's more scared than you are; all she wants is sympathy, sympathy and control, but don't give it to her, make her work for your love; she's stronger than she's pretending to be and if you're tough, if you refuse to play along with her, you'll see, she'll pull herself right back together again. Oh, when he was in the mood, he knew how to argue. He could persuade anybody of anything. Never mind that the person he was describing looked a lot more like him than like me.

I refused to let him spook me. There was too much to do. Cheryl had been crying, and I'm sure, he'd found a way to blame that on me as well. But her survival was too important for me to waste energy on managing their misconceptions. I picked up one of the ladder-back chairs stationed around the table, lifted it with two hands and turned toward the living room.

"Mom?" Panic, not love, is what her voice contained. "Where are you going? What are you doing now?"

Focus on the door. Just make it to the door. That's what I told myself. Don't let them distract you. One step and two steps and three steps and four steps. Don't let them confuse you.

"Mom, answer me, at least!"

A chair toppled behind me.

"Your daughter's asking you a question, Julia. Aren't you going to answer her? Or can't you hear her?"

Almost there. Almost there. Remember to breathe. I was on the carpet. Past the antique table piled with junk mail. The heavy bench carved out of a tree trunk.

"Mom, are you going outside? You can't go outside!"

Her voice was shrill, pinched, as though someone had twisted a thick length of rope around her neck, like they were strangling her, dragging her by the throat up the side of a mountain, an impossibly steep mountain, dragging her quickly. And the person holding the end of the rope was me. It was tightening, squeezing the life from her. She saw it now, I could tell, the danger swooping toward us; she saw how little control we had over it. What needed to happen first was for me to make it through the crisis inside me. Then we'd be reunited with Sarah. The pain would relent. The rope would fray and snap. Cheryl would be released and I'd be redeemed.

"It's like zero degrees out there! Mom, don't go outside!"

Set down the chair. Turn the handle. The weather stripping crackled as I pulled the door open. My arm still tingled. My feet were going numb. A gust of frigid air seeped through the unopened storm door.

"Mom!" She grabbed me by the elbow and tried to yank me back. "Stop! Mom, stop! Stop! Please!"

If I'd been able to speak, I would have told her, Don't cry. There's no reason for you to cry. This is a good thing, a necessary thing. I'm doing this for you.

Instead, I shoved her.

She toppled back on her heels, tripped and fell to the floor and Robert came swooping in to slam the door shut. He blocked my way.

"Enough," he said.

Patience. I lowered myself onto the chair. They'd get tired eventually. All I had to do was wait. I thought of Gremlin—the insistent part of her little brain that, when an idea was lodged inside it, narrowed her attention to this single thing, how to attain it, where the dangers and obstacles barring her way were and what it would take to get past them. If Gremlin wanted to escape the house, she would sit, poised, on the arm of the couch. Hackles up, she'd watch for the split second she needed. She'd swipe and draw blood if you tried to stop her. To get past Robert, I'd have to be catlike, to focus my desire and bide my time and seize the opportunity when it arose, brutally, viciously if that's what it took.

Cheryl sobbed. She wouldn't stop sobbing.

"You see what you've done to her?" Robert said. "Don't you think we've had enough excitement for one night?"

Using hand signals, I tried to remind him that I couldn't speak. I slit my throat. I grimaced and held my hands up in an oversized shrug. I twirled two fingers in front of my mouth like I was teasing a ribbon out of it.

"Julia, come on. This stopped being funny about—" He bit his lip, shook his head. "It was never funny."

We glared at each other. A childish staredown. When he broke to glance at Cheryl, I lunged for the door. He caught me. He sat me back down.

I waited.

"Mom—"

As he turned to shush her, I lunged for the door again. He spun. He stopped me.

I waited and lunged.

Waited and lunged.

Again.

Again.

After a while all I had to do was twitch.

"Are we going to do this all night?" he asked.

I made a face to say, That's up to you.

"No. It's up to *you*," he said.

Something remarkable happened then. Cheryl spoke up again. "Can't you stop?" she said. Not to me but to him. "You're hurting her." I wasn't expecting this. I wouldn't have dared.

Robert's hands tumbled over each other, fingers pulling fingers, twisting at rings that weren't there to be twisted. And then one hand curled slowly into a fist and pounded the other. Palm grinding knuckles, he tried to walk away, turned and turned again and turned.

"Fuck it." Hearing him swear was exhilarating, painful. He couldn't even look at me anymore. "She's not going out there like this, though. Where's her coat?"

"Mom, where'd you put your coat?"

Board games came tumbling out of the closet as he rummaged through it. Ski jackets, windbreakers fluttered to the floor. Hangers twirled on the clothes rod, clattered and flew. He wasn't going to find it there, and I knew this. It was hanging from one of the dowels next to the garage door in the mess room. I'd put it there that afternoon after returning Cheryl's overdue movies.

He was in a frenzy now, throwing snow boots over his shoulder, flicking galoshes at my head. He jerked the plastic storage bin off the shelf and let it drop. The lid popped open, ten years of winter accessories tumbled out and he threw them at me, a rapid barrage of limp wool and fleece and leather and nylon and cashmere.

I let the clothes bounce off my body, gave him no reaction, no satisfaction. When something useful came my way—a pair of petrified ski gloves, cracked and peeling at the joints, a violet headband adorned with a smiling cartoon moon—I collected it in my lap.

With nothing left to strew at me, he stomped off. I listened as he clomped from room to room. A door slammed. Gremlin shrieked and scrambled. Thuds and pings and swooshes of hard-to-interpret sound followed Robert around the house, and all this while I sat still, full of wonder, gazing at Cheryl, her chin digging at her knees, her eyes pointed at me, wary, squinting. She'd tried to convince herself I wasn't human, that my behavior was beyond the realm of what it was possible for a person to do, that my mind—or what she understood of it—was alien, a thing to be dismissed and exiled. She couldn't manage it, though. She loved me, and for now, she'd stopped trying to protect herself from me.

I flashed her a shy little smile and something snapped in her. A frightening loathing radiated off her, coloring over the kindness. I was confused, disappointed. I'd thought she understood, but I'd been wrong; it would take months, years for her to understand.

Robert finally returned with my parka. He tossed it onto my lap and leaned in close. "From here on out," he said, "I'm not responsible. Whatever happens, I'm not responsible. You understand what I'm telling you, Julia?"

I refused to respond either way.

Thinking, I guess, that I'd beg him to change his mind, he backed gingerly toward the kitchen, ducked around the corner and hid just out of sight, waiting to see what I was going to do.

Heft myself up. Pry my arms into the sleeves of the parka.

Cheryl rose with me, but instead of trying to stop me this time, she just stood there watching. I held her by the shoulders, and I'm not sure how, but when I opened my mouth to speak, the words were there. "You need to know this: I'm doing this, all of this, for you" was what I said.

Then I turned. I picked up my chair. I left.

Outside, the air was dry and brittle. Snow had drifted into the house's shadow and hardened into a crust across the earth, removing all the sharp edges from the landscape. The neighborhood had been bled of color.

In order not to slip on the ice shellacked across the concrete walk, and conscious of my weight, my tendency to lurch from support to support, I marched, deliberately lifting each foot and placing it back down, testing the sturdiness of each step before I committed to it. I could hear, in the quiet, something beyond sound, a rhythmic whirring with no perceivable pulse, the sound of endurance, of hardly getting by. When I reached the lip of the driveway, I tried various locations for the chair, moving it incrementally around until all four legs had a sturdy hold. Then I sat and waited for the ambulance to arrive.

It was easier to think clearly out here. The cold froze up and sealed off stray tangents of thought. Sarah. Me. Cheryl. Those were the essentials. Anything else was a false complication, a distraction inserted into my brain in order to discombobulate me. Cheryl. Me. Sarah.

My neighbors' living rooms were lit orange and blue. The TV sets were drawing families together and distracting them from the darkness. Everyone was inside, everyone but me, all insulated and cozy and gradually, cell by cell, losing their memory of the winter numbness that had tapped their bones. But I liked the cold. Right then, I cherished it. It was purging, burnishing something within me.

I sang.

When you're weary, feeling small

And as "Bridge over Troubled Water" 's fragile melody washed through me, my symptoms receded. My heart was beating more evenly already, more slowly, easier. I could breathe again. The tingling in my arm had disappeared and my voice cut sharp and clear through the frozen air.

The cold was presenting me with an alternative. Cheryl and me both. I knew—I'd always known, now I admitted—that I was the only one to protect Cheryl, and the person she needed protection from was me.

A thought occurred to me. One last thing I needed to do.

I stood up and moved my chair, squirmed out of the parka and flapped it. Then I laid it out flat across the driveway. This would be my bridge. It would carry me across and Cheryl would be released.

Placing my chair on top of the parka, I sat down again. I didn't mind the cold. I was beyond cold now.

I had to get better. I had to fix my mind. Until then, for both our sakes, I'd stay outside, sit here, a sentry, guarding the door. I'd wait.

I'd refuse to let the vandals squirming in my brain back inside the house.

The ambulance would be here soon, and when it arrived, the handsome young men—overworked, bleary-eyed, going on two or three days without sleep—would leap out and find me waiting for them. They'd take my blood pressure. They'd ask me where it hurt. They'd rotate my arm above my head and glance quizzically at each other behind my back. They'd tell me that there wasn't anything wrong with me. Physically I was fine. A little overweight—they'd lecture me on that. But I would be adamant. I'd demand they take me away with them.

And when they asked, Robert would tell them the truth. He'd sign the forms, and then I'd be gone.

Sail on silver girl, I sang.

They were almost here. I could hear the siren twirling out on Hemlock Lane. Heads were popping up in my neighbors' windows, backlit, in silhouette. They were riveted.

Cheryl was watching too. How could she not be?

I sang about how I would ease her mind. And at the time, I thought that was what I was doing.

Two

THAT WAS THE DAY on which she should have left. Her reasons, her logic, would have made sense then. She'd watched me disintegrate, over a three-hour span, from the capable, loving woman who'd driven her to school when she missed the bus and helped her sign up for tap lessons, jazz lessons and Suzuki lessons; who'd washed her clothes, folded them and put them in the drawers, never once asking her how they came to be so saturated in smoke; who'd included a treat each day with the granola bars and yogurt of her packed lunch; who'd sat with her, eyeing the metronome, while her violin squeaked, and patiently talked her through her frustration, hiding the headache the instrument gave me and lying when she cried that she had no talent; who'd done all these sacrificial motherly things while still teaching her not to let boys run her life or trust the media and its codes of beauty, reminding her constantly of what she could become if she remained intrepid and uncowed—an astronaut, a poet, a rock guitarist, physicist, feminist, doctor, lawyer like her dad—who told her, as every woman should tell her daughter, that she could be president if that's what she wanted, but if she chose (it was her choice to make), there was nothing wrong with being a homemaker, the hardest job on earth, let no one tell you different. She'd watched me revert from sometimes-wise, sometimes-lovely, sometimes-weird Mom into the smaller thing I'd always been, the frightened animal I'd kept hidden from her. I'd winced and cowered. I'd shivered. I'd quaked. I'd shown myself to be, at least for a time, incapable of doing her any good.

And I can't fathom, I don't understand at all, why she didn't leave then when everything was broken, why she waited instead for everything to be fine.

Three

BEFORE HE BROUGHT ME HOME, Robert had told her to try to "act normal" around me, and maybe that's what she'd thought she was doing by hiding in her room each day from the second school got out until I called her to dinner. It wasn't really so different from normal—the same furtiveness, the same teenage sullenness—but in my nervous state, I felt very much like her reasons for avoiding me were more localized, less dismissible than run-of-the-mill teenage angst. "Let her come to you." That's what Robert had said, and that's what I did.

On the first night—well, not exactly the first night, the very first night was spent out as a family, Cheryl, me and Robert crammed into a booth at Outback Steakhouse, Cheryl sulking and gazing at the parking lot through the whole thing, Robert fidgeting, and me aching in helpless shame; when, finally, she did deign to open her mouth, it was only to spew out her hatred for Outback and all the evil she claimed was packaged inside it. But on the first night the two of us were alone, Robert having returned to his habit of staying at the office until late into the evening, she looked at the care I'd taken in the place settings and said, "Dad lets me watch *The Simpsons* during dinner." I couldn't argue—I wasn't sure what authority I had anymore—so I sat alone at the table in the kitchen and tried to block out the cackle of the TV. On the second night I got up the courage to join her in the living room, but once I'd settled in, she stood up with her plate. "I've seen this one already" was her excuse before stalking back to the kitchen table. Robert had said, "Don't push her." Remembering this advice, and wishing he were home to help me follow it, I let her go. I let her do whatever she wanted and made special meals: mac and cheese flecked with crumbled bits of bacon; burgers and oven-roasted tater tots; tacos, each fixing held in its own bowl—meals she'd begged for in the past, meals I hoped would please her. And slowly, over the next four days, it seemed like things got better. We became used to each other.

The thermometer hit eighty on that final day, and when Cheryl returned from school, she changed into her swimsuit, the cute lime green bikini with the pink trim that we'd bought for her the summer before, not knowing that in a matter of months she'd reject all cuteness in favor of tatters.

I'd been making cookies—peanut butter, her favorite—planning to leave them without comment on the kitchen table, one more act of kindness, one more example of my capablity. And just in case my care slid past unnoticed, I'd saved her the beaters too; I was going to leave them on a saucer in the fridge, her name in a heart on the note taped to the Saran Wrap.

"You look nice in that," I said, and she rolled her eyes, but she stopped herself from making a snide remark. The current issue of *Rolling Stone* coiled in her hand, she headed out onto the wood-slat deck that Robert had built around the pool. This restraint on her part was, I thought, a good omen. Her resentment had begun to dissolve into a less exhausting apathy. "Just holler if there's anything you need," I called after her.

While I finished my baking, I watched her from the window. For a while, she leafed through her magazine. Then she began reading a longish article I later figured out had been about the band Rage Against the Machine. She'd talked about them before, their political

engagement, which she was impressed and inspired by. After reading a few pages, she gazed off toward the creek at the end of our
property and thought for a long time, her brow furrowed like she
was working out some uncomfortable new knowledge that had
caused a breach in her understanding. She frowned. She blinked and
shook the thought away.

Her magazine spread under her head like a pillow, she laid herself out on her stomach and trailed one hand along the dimpled
blue tarp that we hadn't yet rolled off the surface of the pool. Her
leg twitched, and while she reached around to scratch it, she peered
out of one eye, searching, suspicious, maybe wary of me. I waved
through the kitchen window, grinning huge, and she closed her eyes
and dozed off.

She seemed so peaceful out there on the deck, and the day was so
perfect and sunny and warm, that I figured she couldn't hold it
against me if I wanted to join her in sunbathing. What was she going
to say? "No, you're not allowed"? If she did, I could roll out her
favorite self-defense: "It's a free country, I can do what I want," and
who knows, this might lead to an interesting debate, maybe about
morality and human interdependence, or a roaming inquisition on
how free we really are in this country.

"She's mostly just scared" is what Robert had said, and on this day
she'd seemed slightly less so.

I took a risk. I changed into my swimsuit and whipped up a pitcher
of Crystal Light—another of Cheryl's comfort foods. Then, once
the cookies were out of the oven and arranged on the platter, I carried the beaters out onto the deck. One in each hand, I stood over
her. She was content and I knew she was dreaming by the way her
eyes twitched under her eyelids. It would have been a shame to inter-
rupt her.

An intermittent breeze was blowing through, one of those breezes
that come in like clouds, blocking the sunshine just long enough for

the body to register the chill before pushing off again. Though she didn't open her eyes, it must have woken her. "What do you want?" she said.

"You're awake!"

"I've been awake." Then, peeking, "Why do you have to stare at me like that?"

"Cookies!" I said. "To celebrate! Here, I saved you the beaters. It's peanut butter. Your favorite."

"Peanut butter cookies aren't my favorite."

"Sure they are. They've always been your favorite."

"I like Nutter Butters. There's a difference."

She shut her eyes again. The conversation was, apparently, over.

"Mom," she said a few moments later, "I know you're watching me."

"I'll put them in the fridge. You can have them later."

"Fine." She sat up and stretched her arms behind her back, clasping her hands together to crack her shoulders. "I'll have one. But only if you leave me alone, okay?"

As she scooped the sugary dough from between the tines, she made a big production of her resentment. She stared diffidently at each bulb of goo on her finger, careful not to break her frown or glance in my direction or do anything that I might possibly be able to construe as gratitude. But once she got started, she couldn't stop herself. She teased every last fleck of dough from the beater, and when it was gleaming, she moved on to sucking the sugary residue from her knuckles, chewing it out from under her nails.

"What are you smiling about?" she said.

"Am I smiling?" I was beaming, I knew it.

"Yes, you're smiling."

"Well, I can't imagine why."

A gob of dough clung to the corner of her lower lip.

"Do you want the other one? I made Crystal Light too."

She shrugged and nibbled at her pinky.

"The lime kind."

"I haven't drunk that stuff since I was, like, fourteen." Her tongue was thick with dough.

"That was just last year."

"So."

"So, it wasn't—"

"Last year was a whole year ago! That's a long time!"

And something about the conjunction between these emphatic childish words and the blunt gravity of the expression on her face made me laugh. And laugh. In a way I'd thought I'd never laugh again.

"What!" she said. "It's true, Mom!"

"Okay."

"It's a long time! A whole year! That's—" She caught it too, her argument's silliness, and the laughter began to bubble in her as well. "Mom, that's a whole twelve months!"

We clutched at our stomachs. Our faces burned red. A tiny line of spittle spooled down Cheryl's lip. Minutes slid past. We couldn't stop laughing. When, finally, we regained control of ourselves, we were in an altered headspace.

Robert had said: "She wants to go back to before all this happened. Just like you, Julia. She just doesn't know how to do it." Well, now we'd both succeeded, or it appeared we had. As our laughter petered out, self-consciousness settled in and our awkward desire for normalcy hovered between us.

Her fingers rose to graze her cheek—so softly, like they were cradling a baby or feeling for a message imprinted there. A small twitter of charitable feeling worked its way out from under her skin.

Maybe I'm not the most organized person. Maybe I need help keeping the dust balls and dirty clothes from taking over our house. Maybe I overthink every last thing and see resonances other people can't in the tiniest, most mundane human interactions—I get pre-monitions; I dwell over implications other people choose not to notice. Maybe things that should be easy are hard for me. Sure. I'll admit it. I'm easily spooked and I'm always on the lookout for the next person who's going to label and dismiss me, but it doesn't matter. None of it matters when Cheryl smiles at me in that quiet way. This small gesture of recognition, this—I want to call it adoration—it's the spitting image of how Sarah used to look back when she would coax me out of my fear. When I get this look from Cheryl, I can bear myself for a little while.

We floated in a shallow silence, both of us conscious of the safety contained there. Though we weren't speaking, we were communicating. As long as we didn't say anything, neither of us would say anything wrong. We were timidly straining to let each other know how calm and peaceful—and normal—we could be.

The safety of home was reinforced everywhere. I could hear it in the house sparrows chattering at each other, in the chipmunk rummaging in the rain gutter. I could see it in the pine needles floating on top of the tarp on the pool, in the way the cedar stain Robert had slathered on the deck had already, in just two years, begun to fade. Every tiny detail reminded me that, though this place gave off the texture of great tranquillity, I couldn't let myself sink into it, not while the memory of that frigid day continued to hover like no-see-ums over the yard.

I wanted to say, "So, there it is, then. Now you know who I really am. I wish I could have told you in some other way," but I knew I couldn't bear to hear her say she wouldn't forgive me.

The thing I said instead was "I love you, Cheryl."

She shifted a tiny bit, pulling back like she was sliding out of a daydream. "Don't," she snapped.

"No, really, this is important. It's important that you hear me say this."

"I know you love me. Can't we not talk about it?"

Her words were clipped and sharp, but I was persistent. "I love you and I understand there are things about me that must be hard for you to understand."

She shook her head back and forth, as though unceasing movement could ward off everything she wished wasn't true.

"Cheryl—"

"Stop!"

"There are things, experiences—"

"Stop! Stop! You have to!"

"I've had experiences in my life that it wouldn't be right for me to tell you about."

"Then, don't, Mom! Stop! Stop it! I don't want to hear about things I shouldn't know! Why can't we just have a nice time? Why do you have to ruin everything?"

The way she was looking at me! Like I'd just told her I wasn't her mother.

"Okay," I said. "You're right. I'll stop."

We sat there, both of us wishing we could go back to the moment just before when everything had seemed like it was all right.

"Are you sure you don't want any Crystal Light?" I said.

"No."

"It's just right inside. I'll go get it for you."

"I said no, Mom. I don't want any Crystal Light. I want—" Right there. That was the moment when she made up her mind. "Forget it," she said. "I don't want anything."

Robert had told me, "She'll bounce back. She can't hold what happened against you forever."

He couldn't have been more wrong.

VII

In Dinkytown

One

On the morning of August twenty-first, I saw a short piece, just a paragraph, in the "Local News in Brief" section of the *Pioneer Press*, which fortified and confirmed the flecks of Cheryl's life I'd been receiving:

COFFEESHOP FIRE

Minneapolis firefighters responded to a two-alarm fire in Dinkytown last night. The fire, which blazed for nearly three hours, took place at the corner of Fourth Street and Fifteenth Avenue, in a converted warehouse that, most recently, housed the Sabotage Café, a coffeeshop owned by Mr. Richard Milton of St. Paul. In 1999, this establishment was shuttered by the Department of Health. Since that time, the building has remained vacant. Police are investigating the possibility of arson.

It threw me into a panic. I was nauseous, hyperventilating. Without thinking through what I was doing, I called Robert at work.

"Something's happened," I said. "Cheryl and her—they were—she's—it's—she's—Robert—she's—something bad's happened, I know it I know it—"

"Take a deep breath, Julia," he told me. "I can't understand you unless you calm down."

I screamed at him. "I can't calm down! Your daughter's in trouble!"

I could hear his fingers tapping at his computer keyboard.

"Okay?" he said after enough time had passed in silence for him to believe he'd quelled something in me. "Better now?"

"Did you see the paper?"

"Today? I glanced at it."

"You didn't see about the fire?"

"I guess not."

"In the café?"

"Nut-uh."

"There was a fire. The Sabotage Café. That's what the place was called. And Cheryl was staying there."

"Was she?" He perked up.

"She was there. She was living there. With her boyfriend."

"You know this."

"Yes, I know this. I wouldn't be telling you if I didn't know this."

"How? How do you know this?"

"Let me read you the article."

"I've got it right here. I just pulled it up online."

"So, you see what I mean, then."

"It doesn't say anything about Cheryl. It doesn't say anybody was living there at all."

"She was *there*!" I said.

"She could be anywhere, Julia." There was weariness in his voice, trepidation.

"She was staying there! She told me!"

"When?" His voice tightened and leapt in pitch. "When did she tell you?"

"She told me."

"Then, why didn't *you* tell *me*? Her case is still open. I could have had someone go—" The bottom fell out of his line of thought. "Richard Milton. Who's this Richard Milton?"

"That doesn't matter."

"He was in that band, wasn't he? He's that guy Cap. That guy you—" Something softened on his end of the line. "He was that guy," he said again, this time sadly, mournfully.

I couldn't remember what I'd hoped to achieve by calling him. I'd had a real reason, a practical reason, but now my desire for a comfort I couldn't bring myself to request garbled my mind.

"I'm going to ask you a question now," he said, "and it's probably going to make you angry, but—are you taking your pills? We agreed you'd take your pills. Are you taking them?"

"Do I seem like I'm not taking my pills?"

"I don't know," he said. "I really don't know."

"Maybe you don't understand what I've been saying. This is an emergency. All I need to know is if you're gonna help me."

"What are you planning to do?"

"Just—will you help me?"

I could hear him squeezing his eyes.

"Julia, I need something more than your intuition to go on before I drop everything and run over there. What if I make some calls and—"

"And nothing. Either you will or you won't."

"I can try to finish early. How's that?"

My mind was barging forward, searching for the questions that would lead to the right answers, narrowing in on the plausibilities, piecing out the story the paper had ignored. I headed down the hall toward the bedroom.

"Can you hold on till then?" he was saying. "And I'll call the precinct, okay? Maybe, six or so?"

"Fine," I said. Cradling the phone against my ear, I was pulling blouses out of the closet, holding them up to myself in the mirror, trying to find one Cheryl would appreciate.

"Hey," Robert said before hanging up the phone. "Julia? I'm sorry. Really. Hang in there, okay?"

I knew she'd be spooked by the cloak I'd made. I picked something else, a bright festive violet getup. Then, quickly, I dressed and grabbed my purse and drove off toward Dinkytown to find her.

Two

THERE HAD BEEN NO PASSING OUT, lit cigarette in hand, or kicking over candles in a drunken stupor. Intent had been involved in the setting of the fire.

Maybe they'd gone out in the late afternoon to sit by the river and escape the stifling tension of the squat. Cheryl and Trent and Devin, even Mike. It was chilly. The cold front that followed the rain of two nights ago had thrown down spikes and tethered itself to the plains.

Walking four abreast down the wide sidewalk, they played punching games, Trent's fist slamming hard into Devin's bicep.

"Don't hit me, dick."

"What?"

"Don't fucking hit me."

"Don't look at me, fucking Mike's the one who hit you."

This behavior no longer charmed Cheryl. Hidden behind it, she now saw a menace that wasn't rooted in any ideals. She was beginning to believe there was a difference between moral outrage and the impulse toward total self-negation, the blunt downward urge toward ruin.

"Mike didn't fucking hit me. Mike's way the fuck over there. Alright, dick?" Throwing a thumb over his shoulder, Devin glared at Trent. He didn't notice Mike crab-crawling up behind like a commando to flick his earlobe and spin away. "Leave me the fuck alone, Trent."

A shove in the chest, a leap, fist in the air, and Devin had Trent down on the sidewalk. The bottles they were carrying slid from their hands, somehow not breaking, though the brown paper bags were skinned off by the concrete. They rolled over each other, arms flailing, knees jabbing, across the curb and into the street. Then, when they were exhausted, they lay on their backs and stared at the traffic signs above their heads. The inevitable laughter came pouring from their mouths.

She knew her feelings were transparent. The best she could do to hide them was keep her mouth shut. Let Trent and the other guys think she was just pouting, asserting her prerogative as a girl. She felt dirty in her army jacket—not dirty-grimy but dirty-skanky, condemned. It itched. It smelled like all the things she'd once imagined she'd become with Trent. But she couldn't take it off in this wind. The shame she felt wearing it kept her sharp, suspicious, alone and alert.

And on they walked, over to the West Bank, heading up Riverside toward the St. Anthony Falls.

Their taunts had a harder edge to them tonight, and the silences lasted longer than usual. Cheryl wasn't the only one to feel the end nipping at her back.

Today was Mike's birthday; he'd given Chipotle his notice days ago and he'd already stopped down by the strip mall on Washington to work things out with the recruiter. His bluffs and boasts had turned out to be true, and tomorrow he'd be enlisting. As this sank in, Cheryl suspected, his contempt was lighting up Trent and Devin's minds like tiki torches; his words flaming there: derelict, dead-ender, small fry in a small town. Their anger was spiced through with the same futility they'd been trying to dodge when they first ran from the adults who'd loved and despised them. None of them had known what to do with it before, and none of them knew what to do with it now.

When Nineteenth merged and rose into the Tenth Avenue Bridge, they jumped the safety railing and slid single file, their arms spread like cranes, down the crushed-rock embankment that fanned toward the water's edge. First Mike and then Devin. Then Trent a second later.

They were just below the dam; the water in the deep center of the river churned chaotically, but behind the jetty angling in front of them, the water was still. As Mike and Devin each hit the lip of the retaining wall, their boots caught and bucked and they had to twist, leap, contort their spines, to veer under the iron girders of the bridge.

Cheryl skated in, recklessly, behind Trent. The slipping stones, the speed, the rush of lost control sent a pulse of adrenaline shooting up her system. Her ideals were gone now, but there was still fight in her—and resentment, because, even now, knowing how rancid Trent really was, she couldn't throw off her attachment to him. She suddenly loathed him, suddenly understood that, just like her, just like me, just like so many people, he was mostly lashing out at himself; the difference was he didn't care who he damaged along the way. She was stronger than me, though. Whereas my life in Dinkytown had eroded under me, dropping me into a place I couldn't escape, she had thrived in this subterranean world and she could choose to leave it on her own terms.

Lunging, she knocked Trent in the back with both hands. He fell forward, catching his foot on a loose pebble, and reeled toward the edge of the retaining wall and Cheryl suddenly wanted to take back what she'd done.

"Fuck-shit—Trent!"

His arms pinwheeled at his sides and he tumbled flailing into the river.

Floating slowly downstream, he grabbed at the sheer concrete, wrapped his fingers around streamers of algae that disintegrated at his touch. He was pulling away, slipping toward the rapids.

Cheryl calculated the geometry. She ran under the bridge and around onto the jetty, hoping to catch him as the waters merged, but when he hit the current, he was pushed toward the bank. She circled back the other way.

Devin and Mike, watching from under the bridge, did nothing to help. They didn't even bother to move out of her way.

"There's a fucking ladder, Trent, grab it! Fucking grab it!"

But the safety ladder slid out of his reach and he floated on downstream, past the edge of the concrete, trailing now along mudbanks. He lunged at ferns and saplings, pulling off handfuls of leaves.

Cheryl's boots stuck in the mud as she ran. She high-stepped through nettles, swiping the thorny branches away with her forearms. She tracked him, a hand here, a glint of t-shirt there.

When he caught a loop of root and hoisted himself out, she clung to him, babbling—"I was going too fast. I swear to God. I'm sorry. I couldn't stop. I'm so sorry, Trent"—knowing she was lying. And as he stood there refusing to forgive her, his waterlogged clothes sagging toward the ground, dripping, she cried.

He pushed her away. "You're a fucking bitch," he said. "And you're fucking going fucking first this time." With a shove, he started her marching toward his friends.

On the gravel, Cheryl picked up the six-pack she'd dropped. She cracked a beer and it sprayed all over her face. Mike stared at her from behind hooded eyes as she sat down, letting her know she couldn't hide from him. She gave him the finger.

For a long time, the four of them huddled under the bridge, dosing themselves with bourbon and beer and dourly celebrating the end of everything. When one of them did periodically say something, a wisp of sniping curled into the air.

"The Marines, man," Trent might say. "The fucking Marines."

"Yeah, be all you can be."

"That's the army, jackass."

Mike would clarify, talking mostly to himself. "Semper Fi, that's the Marines. It means Always Faithful. Fucking Always Fucking Faithful."

"The Marines are a bunch of fucking suckers. Fucking cannon fodder. They're the ones fucking who get blown up so the motherfuckers in charge don't have to."

Cheryl kept silent. She sipped her beer and dully watched the water flood past.

They were lost inside themselves. Each alone and angry, afraid of what would come next.

"That's why I'm kicking this shithole," Mike said a while later, like he was giving voice to some conversation entrenched inside his mind.

The look that passed across Trent's face was so close to sorrow that it made Cheryl sick. What's going to happen, she wondered, when I leave? Will he be as brokenhearted as he is over Mike? How many ways can I think of to hurt him? She yanked the bottle of Jim Beam from his hand, spilling a dollop of the brown liquor on her jeans.

"That's fucking mine, you prick."

"Yeah, good one," she said. Then she guzzled and as the alcohol hit her stomach, she bent forward like she was bowing before a god, rode out the warmth rising in the back of her throat, held her breath, spitting the saliva that gushed inside her mouth onto the concrete.

The big hurrah for later that night was to go see a band. Rancid. A bunch of screamers out of San Francisco, machine gunners who, like all bands of their ilk, pretended to yearn for total annihilation when what they really wanted was adulation and the money and women that came along with it.

Trent loathed them. Just looking at the listing in *City Pages* had thrown him into a fit that afternoon. "They're worse than fucking 'N Sync," he'd said. "At least the fucking boy bands know what they are. I mean, look at these motherfuckers. They think they're dangerous? They're not fucking dangerous. They're fucking . . . Look at that fucking mohawk! Green! He looks like a fucking clown. You know what they are? They're the fucking machine. They want us to think they're rebelling when they're really not."

A lot like you, Cheryl had thought. Then she'd said, "So don't go."

"We have to go. What the fuck else are we gonna do?"

"Hey, this would be cool." Devin's forehead strained as he tried to formulate a thought. "We could all shit in plastic baggies or something and smuggle it in in our pants, you know? And then when it got dark and the mosh pit got going, we could whip the baggies out and throw the shit at them."

Trent smirked. "We'd still have to listen to their crap-ass music, though."

On his way back from spanging, though, later that afternoon, he'd popped into Rainbow Foods and stolen a box of Glad Bags.

Now, under the bridge, as the bottles emptied and the beer cans piled up, he pulled them out and said, "So, should we do this? You guys got some shit in you?" He threw a bag at Devin, a bag at Mike. He didn't bother to give one to Cheryl.

Mike, with his usual cool, studied his bag with vague interest. Devin, though, was almost drooling with excitement—it was his idea; he didn't have them often.

What they're planning, she thought, it isn't bold. It's idiotic. Insipid. Was this what they thought a revolution looked like? "Don't I get a bag?" she asked.

"I figured you'd be chicken, Betty."

Devin's snickering needled at her back. He'd crawled off to a corner of the concrete platform, half hidden himself behind a girder. His ass was shoved into the air behind him and he was grunting, dramatically, groaning in ecstasy.

This wasn't the thing that repulsed her the most, though; what repulsed her was the effort they were making. Why couldn't they get it together like this to combat something like the corporate takeover of everything that had once belonged to human beings? Why couldn't they fight the downsizing of lives into lifestyles, the demonization of people who couldn't consume correctly? No new society would be built from their bile if this was all they knew how to do with it.

"Alright," she said. "See ya," and she stood up.

"Where you going, Betty? You can't just fucking go. We've got a plan here." Trent might have been shouting, but he wasn't standing up.

She spun on him. "Don't call me that. You think I'm stupid? I'm not your fucking Betty."

Then she was gone.

Later, she sat on the *City Pages* dispenser—down the block, across the street from the Boom Boom Tick—and watched the scene develop out front. The show didn't start until ten, which meant eleven, and the LCD on the credit union on the corner said it was only nine thirty-eight, but the crowd around the club had already begun to sprawl into the street. It was the usual skate rats and gutter punks, the all-ages kids who'd mostly linger outside through the whole show, hanging in the shadows around the corner, guzzling beers they'd slipped into their jacket sleeves, the vodka they'd hidden in Mountain Dew cans, smoking pot out of cigarette-shaped one-hitters. Among the ripped t-shirts and badly shaved heads, she saw a few people she knew. Benny. Tim. Flake. That kid who called himself Sal Paradise. A hippie guy she and Trent had gotten stoned with once; she hadn't bothered to learn his name. The crowd just kept getting bigger and bigger.

She wished for a moment that Trent was next to her so she could rub his face in how wrong he was about Rancid. They weren't sell-outs, they were fucking kickass. So, fuck him. Fuck you, Trent. She could like Rancid if she wanted to.

Her buzz had dissipated into a parched, bleary ache. She sat there, kicking the window of the plastic paper box, half wishing someone would wander over and talk to her, half wishing she could make herself invisible.

Little Tornado showed up with a couple of other greasy dirtbags who looked like they were about twelve years old. What do these people do with themselves? They're there and then they're gone and then they're there again. She hadn't seen Little Tornado since that one day at Jarod's house, and his appearance now almost shook her resolve, almost sent her skipping across the street—"Hey, Little T, whatcha up to? Somebody should teach you how to wash your glasses"—running toward him as though when she got there all the complicated and depressing shit she'd been through in the past two and a half months would be hosed away. She'd be back in the swoon of the first time she'd met Trent. She'd still be believing that he could turn her into someone capable of changing something.

But then she saw Mike leaning against the club's brick wall, his arms around the waist of a girl who looked like she must still be living with her parents, fuchsia highlights in her stringy black hair, eye-liner drawn out almost to her ears, a little too proud of being seen in the arms of the single black guy in this derelict scene. Pathetic. And way, way, way too familiar.

When it got to be almost showtime, a mob of thuggish University of Minnesota jocks arrived, guys with tousled hair and cowrie shells tied to leather strips around their necks, predatory looks on their faces, flaunting their pressed Golden Gophers t-shirts like gang colors. The whole football team. They marched through the skinny underfed kids out front, and behind them tromped a bunch of girly girls with belly-button rings and ludicrously high heels, their skin radiating a toxic orange from the fake tan and foundation and blush and cover-up slathered over it like finger paint. Cheryl could smell their bright perfume all the way down the block.

She knew how it went. There'd be a fight tonight.

The punk kids were drunk and daring. They bristled at the jocks pushing past them. Kids sitting on the curb accidentally—yeah, right—stretched their legs under the girls' feet. "Who invited the gorillas?" they muttered under their breath. "How many ways can you say asshole?" Just what the jocks wanted to hear. They muttered back. "Pound another nail in your forehead, dickwad." "Take a shower." They threw nickels and dimes at the backs of the kids' heads. Once everyone was inside and liquored up, Cheryl knew, the whispers would grow into shouts. The taunting would turn into shoving. Already, each side was dying to throw a fist. The spark would come in the stupidest of ways. Somebody'd bump into one of the jocks' girls and accidentally spill Pepsi over her top. Elbows would crash into jaws on the mosh pit. Somebody'd stage-dive and nobody'd catch him. The girly girls would whine about how bored they were—"This place is *gross*. They won't even make me a SoCo and Lime"—and their boyfriends would call them stupid bitches. Some gutter punk kid would defend the girls—not even strongly, just pointing out the obvious lack of respect—and a jock would swoop in and jab a finger in his face. "You only wish you could get ass like this," he'd say. And that would be that. The baggies Trent and Mike and Devin had filled would have found a worthwhile use after all.

Once the battle overtook the whole club, Cheryl wondered, which side would the band take? Was there any doubt? Trent was right. Why did Trent always have to be right? Rancid wasn't really punk rock. Rape music. That's what they were.

She was shrinking, shivering. She wished she had a golf ball or something small and hard to whip at the green scroll of information tracking across the credit union's LCD. Time and temperature. As if the world could be reduced to this.

Trent would say, "Resist or die." He'd say there were two options. Cower behind the social codes, the value systems set up by the fascists in charge, or go underground, live on the edges and fight.

Her problem wasn't with the idea; her problem was with the person spouting it. She'd seen what a flat, ordered existence had done to me. Beneath the gleaming floors of the malls and churches lurked a ruthless disregard for human beings. No matter how big the house you bought, there still wouldn't be room in it for the shaggier, hoarier, illogical and passionate parts of the human beings living within it. Believing you had to conform or die, you discovered, once you hit your thirties or forties—once you were my age—that the choice was false, that conformity *was* death, but it was all there was, and though your body was still able to make the trip to the grocery store, though you were still sometimes able to win the solitaire game on your computer and chuckle at *Everybody Loves Raymond,* you kept yourself going out of habit now.

The alternative was to end up like Trent, killing yourself quickly in a mad attempt to achieve some distant glory in a revolution that would never come.

There he was now, smoking a joint with Devin.

She needed to move before he saw her. She needed to propel herself away from the Boom Boom Tick. But where? Yet again, there was nowhere to go.

Later still, Cheryl stood alone on the second floor of the Sabotage Café, the fire already blazing inside her. The smell of the dog was everywhere now—it grew stronger the more she thought about it.

She flicked her lighter. It sparked but didn't catch.

She flicked again, held the flame in front of her and watched it wobble until her thumb began to burn.

She flicked again. The papers and 'zines piled on the shelf ignited.

Again, and the tapestry was aflame and the cardboard box it had been draped over.

And again. The entire Wreck Room lit up.

It pleased her to think Trent would know it was her. It pleased her even more that he wouldn't know why she'd done it.

Three

DINKYTOWN, WHEN I LIVED THERE in the 1980s, was the kind of place where, without much digging, you could procure a copy of Mao's Little Red Book, a slice of vegan whole wheat pizza, or a black-and-white-checkered Palestinian shawl. It was a dusty place, a corner of the city where cigarette butts accumulated and broken streetlights were rarely replaced. The Green Tea Smoke Shop, in its resinous, sandalwood glory, could deck you out with clove cigarettes, Nat Shermans in party colors, a bong called the Lobotomizer, shaped like Ronald Reagan's head, the bowl rising from his skull, right between the eyes. You could choose from a vast array of feather-tipped roach clips, devil's head rings and jelly bracelets. Outside the used-record store, Sonic Sounds, speakers had been mounted; during store hours, Lou Reed's *Metal Machine Music* could be heard from a block away. Ron's Tiny Diner would sell you a hangover cure and a shot of burnt coffee for under two bucks. Now all these places were gone.

As I drove through the neighborhood in search of Cheryl, I found very few of the landmarks I remembered. The cheap Korean joints had been replaced by Japanese restaurants with teak facades, crisp banners flapping above their entryways. Crazy Eights had a new neon feel to it. Instead of the bars where I'd once smoked opium, there were lounges on the corners—coyly named spots in which all the S's had been replaced by Z's. The Den was now the Rec Room, the Blue Room was Lunar. Where there'd once been abandoned factories and parking lots, there were retail stores—Borders, Cingular, Whole Foods. There was a new Eckerd Drugstore, a new Ben & Jerry's, a card shop called Satara with a giant wood carving of a Tibetan eye in the window. A Johnny Rockets was under construction. Caribou Coffee competed with the Starbucks across the street. Ragstock was now called Velvet and Lace. Banks had begun to show faith in the neighborhood, flashing their colors, plopping ATMs onto corners like pop machines.

Everything was new, even the old things. The streets of Dinky-town used to be known for their potholes and fault lines, but they'd been given a gleaming coat of asphalt. They were clean now, and blindingly black.

The sidewalks were crawling with people, but not the kind of people I was searching for. These new people's clothes were frayed, but only slightly, and too colorful—bright and buoyant transliterations of their wearers' ironic dispositions.

There was no sign of Cheryl or her ilk, but I refused to give up hope. They were probably hiding in the aftermath of the fire.

In the spot where the Nix Bar—site of so many of the horrors of my past—used to stand there was a restaurant with outdoor seating. It was going by the name Dinerrific, and though it was Saturday, the words *Sunday Brunch!* had been written in a cheerful flowery script on a chalkboard out front.

All the places where I'd caroused with oblivion, and where I'd thought Cheryl was doing the same, had been painted over and fumigated. The monuments to my unraveling were gone, utterly erased, except in my memory, and this made me oddly sad. I'd bat-tled so hard, and for so many years, to be able to live with my cruel experiences that to now return, apprehensively, timidly, to the places where they'd been thrust upon me and find them bulldozed, flippantly replaced, seemed like an injustice. A spiritual injustice. There was nothing left for me to point to and say, *See, this, here, this is where it all happened,* nothing to prove what I'd been through was real.

Or almost nothing. I hadn't gotten everything wrong. The Red Barn was still there, and Positively 4th Street. Dunkin' Donuts and Arby's and KFC were still kicking. The Boom Boom Tick Club was still around, but the marquee no longer advertised live shows; instead it reminded the neighborhood's youth that Thursday was karaoke night and Saturdays did the time warp back to the eighties.

And Sabotage was there—or the charred wreck of it.

I pulled over to examine the damage. The top floor was decimated and the windows downstairs blown out. The crude sign that had hung over its door was propped against a wall; its various grades of paint had burned at different speeds, leaving behind a cracked ghostly negative of what had been there before. One of the side walls had been burned completely through, and I could have stepped inside, but I was afraid. It was enough to see the metal cylinders that, the day before, had supported tabletops, the ribs of bent dowels that had been the backs of chairs. I didn't want to find any real bones— I didn't want to stumble onto the dog.

All I wanted was my daughter, and I didn't have to enter the ruins to ascertain that she wasn't there.

Four

AFTER SETTING THE FIRE, she ran aimlessly, changing direction on a whim, then changing direction again, headed everywhere, nowhere, until stomach cramps forced her to slow down and then she walked. She didn't see anything. She didn't know where she was trying to get, but when she arrived at Jarod's house, it seemed as though a subconscious plan of action had been propelling her forward the whole time.

Just being on the patchy lawn out front calmed her. Instead of knocking, she circled the perimeter, peeping through the windows. Neither Jarod nor his mother seemed to be home, or if they were, they were already asleep. Anyway, the junker wasn't in the driveway.

The front door was unlocked, so she stepped inside and a damp, synthetic, fruity smell wrapped itself around her like cellophane. Nothing had been dusted. Nothing had been washed. The stain from the spilled bong was still there on the carpet, crusty now like a scab, and the couch was still covered in dog hair. But the place had been tidied up—not pristine, but neat. Somebody had been making some small effort. The dirty dishes were now stacked in the sink instead of strewn across the flat surfaces of the house. The litter of junk mail and threats from collection agencies had disappeared from the TV stand and all that was left there were a few copies of *Entertainment Weekly* and a *TV Guide* or two.

The digital clock on the microwave said it was eleven forty-five. Early. Jarod's mother would be at work at this time, but what about Jarod? Could it be—was it possible—that he had gone to the Rancid show? Doubtful. Cheryl couldn't see him getting it together enough to even know the band was in town.

The house contained a darkness beyond lack of light, a fatalism stripped of the chaos and romance that made the Sabotage Café so lively. The tenderness and pity she'd felt for him came back as though it had been waiting for her. Here life was trapped in the tedium of time. There was nothing else. Nothing to strive for. No hope by which to measure achievement. On top of the VCR an egg-shaped pot of air freshener had been placed, the source of the syrupy, sickly smell. It reminded Cheryl of nursing homes.

She flicked on the TV, turning the volume down until she could barely hear it. There was nothing on, of course, but she kept tapping through the channels anyway. Eventually, she settled on Letterman—he was sometimes funny, if you could get past the show's smarmy vibe of entitlement. Dave was doing one of his audience quizzes—"Name the Cut of Beef," it was called—commending some old guy with a comb-over and a beer belly on the "service you've done for your country." It turned out the guy had been in the air force or something. If Trent were here with her, he'd be shouting right about now, "Bullshit propaganda . . . fucking fascists," and searching for an empty bottle to throw at the tube. Cheryl simply turned the channel. Howard Stern. A paid advertisement for Nautilus equipment. That idiotic born-again show with the preacher who sported a permed mullet. The least bad thing she could find was *MTV Road Rules*, and for a while she jumped back and forth on alternating commercial breaks between this and a travel thing about New Orleans.

An especially loud commercial for a local car dealership—"No money down! No money down! And did we mention, no money down?!"—shook her and she realized she'd been dozing. She turned the volume down another notch and sat up a little straighter. A chipper woman wearing a pink silk blouse was standing over a vat of boiling oil, talking to a bony middle-aged black guy—the deep furrows in his cheeks accentuating his every expression—about some sort of deep-fried New Orleans treat called a beignet.

"Jarod?" The voice quavered less than Cheryl remembered, but its needy whine was as grating as ever.

Afraid that if she did nothing the ho-bag would hobble into the room, Cheryl got up and poked her head around the door to the woman's bedroom. There she was, on the bed as always, but instead of being beached helplessly on her back, she was propped up on pillows against the headboard. Though all the lights were off, a sad little copy of *Soap Opera Digest* was splayed open on the mattress beside her and the television was tuned to the same stupid travel show Cheryl had been watching in the other room.

"Hi," Cheryl said, lifting her fingers in an embarrassed little wave.

"Oh, it's you." Jarod's mother gazed at her blankly.

Leaning against the wall, her hands clutched together behind her back, Cheryl waited for the woman's judgment to come snaking out toward her. The ho-bag. In the TV's ghost light, she was even spookier than Cheryl remembered. *Icky* was the word, like besides her evident physical ailments, she carried some secret disease around with her, a kind of mental deficiency that couldn't be cured—sadness beyond sadness, terminal hopelessness—and if Cheryl got too close, she'd catch it. She knew exactly how this disease worked. It crept out of your brain, down into your bloodstream and suddenly your body became heavy and useless, a trash bag filled with water that jiggled but wouldn't budge when you tried to lift it. She'd seen me come down with the very same thing, right before I'd exploded that night. Jarod's mom and I were similar people. We both knew the dark secrets for which there were no words. We'd both accidentally exposed these secrets to our children.

"What do you want?" The words shot from the woman's mouth like lugies.

Cheryl refused to say. She didn't have to answer to anyone.

"Where's Jarod?" the woman asked. "Did he bring me my aspirin?"

"He's not here."

Gazing off, the woman appeared almost wistful.

"You want me to get you some?"

The woman turned spiteful. "You can't really do that if he hasn't bought it yet, can you?"

A wounding confusion jittered through Cheryl. She might as well have been back in middle school, cornered again by that roly-poly busybody girl who wore too much perfume and trapped her in conversations about things she didn't know, things she couldn't have known and did not need to know—which Beanie Babies were worth the most money, that the Teletubbies were gay. Whenever Cheryl admitted her ignorance, the girl would shudder, aghast, and pat her shoulder. "That's okay," she'd say in a tone that made clear it was very much not okay. Oh, what was her name, I want to say Randi—it ended in an *i*, I remember that. Her mother was the leader of Cheryl's Brownies troop, and she was as bad as her daughter except she added "dear" to the end of every "That's okay."

I can't believe I'm forgetting these things. I shouldn't be forgetting these things. They're all I have.

Jarod's mother's eyes were full of distrust and, Cheryl thought, hate. "The ho-bag? Don't worry about her," Trent had said that first night while they'd been upstairs in Jarod's room. "She doesn't give a fuck what we do." But she did give a fuck. She cared immensely. Cheryl had heard her come home in the middle of it. And they'd left the dirty sheets for her to find later. She'd figured it out, or maybe

Jarod had collapsed in her room and spilled all the emotions he'd hoarded inside himself. Maybe he'd cried. She'd comforted him.

Cheryl wanted to bolt from the room. She could hear Jarod's mom's thoughts hissing through the silence, *I haven't forgotten. I might not be able to do anything about it, but that doesn't mean I have to like you.*

In self-defense, she said, "Jarod told me I could come by whenever I wanted."

There was no reaction. The dull contemptuous stare just continued, holding Cheryl in place like a searchlight. She swayed diffidently, waiting to be dismissed. When the woman released her and reached for her magazine, Cheryl fled back into the living room. She wasn't wanted here—but she couldn't bring herself to leave.

Sitting on the couch, her knees drawn up to her chest, she let herself sink into unhappy thoughts of me. This was where she always went when she was upset. The events of her life were arranged in a spiral, spinning faster than she could keep up with, and when she tried to stop their vertiginous movement, she found that the void at their center, the dark outline that was sucking them in, had the contours of my silhouette. Whatever kindness she'd felt toward me before was gone now. Ruined by the ho-bag's self-pity and scorn. The good me, the reasonable one who knew how to listen and was careful to preserve the balance between watching her passively and guiding her along, had been corrupted again, turned green and ghoulish by the associations she'd found between myself and this woman.

If only she could think of somewhere else to go, somewhere she wouldn't immediately want to flee. She could hop a train. It couldn't be that hard. Stupider, more strung-out kids than her did it all the time. But trains reminded her of that sad Tom Waits song Trent had played for her back when he'd still thought she was worth impressing. They'd been hopped up on some meth he'd picked up from she had no idea where, and he'd been doing his DJ thing, playing song after song after song after song, each one the greatest piece of music in the world. "It's the lyrics," he'd say. "They're fucking so fucking great. Listen." And then he'd talk through them. "No, wait, listen." He'd start the song over and proceed to talk through them again, explaining each line, shaking his head in rapture. "You hear it? Don't you think it's the fucking greatest thing ever?" Cheryl would nod, because regardless of how good the song actually was, she thought *he* was the greatest thing in the world. The one by Tom Waits really was pretty great, though, about a bunch of scraggly little kids protecting each other from a brutal society. She could only remember the last couple of lines: *something something all the way down the drain to New Orleans in the rain.*

And New Orleans was right there on the TV in front of her. This could be a sign, but she didn't believe in them. Signs and symbols and the resonances they contained, that was my arena. She refused to trust anything that wasn't real.

She zapped the TV off—its glimmer was only making her feel more hollow—and sat in the gray light that filtered in through the windows, picking dog hairs one by one off the couch, berating herself for still, unbelievably, being hung up on Trent.

In the kitchen, on top of the fridge, she found a carton of Pepperidge Farm goldfish, and under the sink, a bottle of Gordon's Gin. She poured a shot into a Burger King/*Lion King* giveaway glass and carried it and the goldfish back to her nest on the couch. There, she killed the time with handfuls of greasy, smiling crackers, washing them down with sips of piney liquor. Sip after sip. She didn't want to be falling-down drunk, she just wanted to be what she and her friends called happy, to occupy herself with something other than thought.

By the time Jarod finally got home, she'd gone through a third of the bottle, rationing it out in ever larger slugs. This'll be the last one, she'd told herself, screwing the cap back on after each pour until finally she'd just brought the bottle in with her so she could drink straight from the source.

"Jarod!" she said. "Have some gin!"

He was carrying a load of shopping bags, brown paper inside of white plastic. Food stuff—not junk food, not Pringles or Ding Dongs or anything she'd want to eat, but bread and eggs and cartons of juice and milk—bulged out of the pinched openings. Cocking his head and squinting for a second, he registered her presence, then wandered into the kitchen. The light came on. She heard rustlings and plops as he unloaded the bags, the refrigerator door opening and closing.

She took another gulp from the gin. Then, reminding herself not to act drunk, she hopped off the couch and headed after him with the glass in one hand and the bottle slung low in the other. "Have some gin!" she said again, leaping up to sit on the lip of the sink. She was suddenly, absurdly giddy. "What's with all the food?"

Ignoring her, he continued to unpack, organizing items by kitchen location and making space for them where they belonged. There was butter and clementines and baby carrots. He took a bottle of Advil from a bag and set it on the table apart from the food.

"It's like you're a suburban dad or something, I mean, not like mine, but like somebody else's."

He glanced at her and returned to the fridge with a block of American cheese slices. "Where'd you get that gin?" he said.

"It was here."

She picked the bottle up off the counter and studied its label, then poured a couple fingers into her glass. "Here, have some. It gets better the more you drink it."

"It's my mother's."

"So?"

"So, you shouldn't be drinking it." He was suddenly so proper.

The giddiness began to deflate inside of her. She gulped down a mouthful of the gin and stared into her glass. A small fleck of black floated there, but she didn't bother to fish it out. "Don't tell me you're pissed at me too," she said quietly.

"I'm not pissed. You just shouldn't be drinking it."

There was something strong about him today that she didn't remember being there before, like he'd figured out a way in which to be less lost. It made her jealous. The whole point of Jarod had been that he was one of the few people she knew who was weaker than her.

"Hi, Jarod," she said with theatrical sarcasm. "How are you? I'm cool, Cheryl, how about you? Oh, you know, I'm alright. Sort of shitty, but you know, whatever. Life sucks, then you die or whatever, right? Thanks for asking, though. It's nice to know at least one person cares about what's going on in my pathetic little life."

"If you drink all her liquor there won't be any left for her and then she won't be able to get to sleep." He knelt down and dug around in the back of the fridge. "Here," he said, pulling out a can of Busch. "Drink this."

Cheryl popped the tab and took a swig. It was cold and fizzy and it tasted like aluminum. She watched him clear cans of refried beans and tuna off the table and wondered if she should offer to help. "I talked to the ho-bag a little bit ago," she said. "She's pissed at me, isn't she?"

"Don't call her that."

"Why not? You do."

"Not anymore."

This news struck Cheryl as hilarious. Beer sloshed from the lip of the can as she laughed, dripped onto her wrist, her jeans, the floor. "Since when?"

He hedged. He withdrew. His face went flat.

She reached out and flicked at his shoulder, but missed. "Since when?" she said again, then teasing, "Don't tell me you've gone all goody-goody on me."

"Can you just not call her that?" He'd stopped what he was doing to stand in front of her, shoulders slumped, a jar of store-brand spaghetti sauce in his hand. He looked like he was pleading for mercy.

"Anyway," Cheryl said, "she hates me."

Jarod shrugged and went back to stacking things in the cupboard.

"She does, right? What did you say to her?"

He was doing his I'm-so-wounded-that-I-can't-speak thing again.

"I know you talked to her. What did you say?"

As he passed her on the way to the fridge, she punched his bicep. "What's the big fucking deal? Just tell me what you said."

She didn't think she'd hit him hard, but his response was to brace himself, legs wide, and shove back with all his might. The beer flew across the room and ricocheted off the lip of the counter. Cheryl went sprawling onto the wet floor.

"Jesus Christ, Cheryl, I didn't say anything!" He was shouting at her. "We talked about me and her, okay? And I don't want you to call her ho-bag. She's not a ho-bag. She's just . . . hurt."

She picked herself up and slumped into a chair, laid her head on the cold white Formica of the table.

"Everything isn't always about you," he said.

She tried not to move. When Jarod had arrived, she'd started having fun. She wasn't anymore.

"I know," she said. "Nothing's ever about me. I'm—" Something large and sharp was stuck in her throat. She tried to swallow, but it wouldn't go down. It hurt. *Insignificant. Nothing,* she'd been planning to say.

The table was empty except for the Advil.

She knew he didn't understand what he'd said. He was confused, afraid. He regretted having shoved her. But she knew she deserved it. She wondered how hard it would be to get him to hurt her—to really hurt her.

He plucked the Advil off of the table, and pausing on his way out of the room, placed a hand softly between her shoulder blades. She shuddered. She yanked at the ring in her lip with her teeth. Though he had very little will of his own, he was kind. He'd been sort of nice to his dog. He was devoted to his mother the ho-bag. That was worth something.

The gin buzz was gone. Now Cheryl was tired. Numb. The cool Formica was soothing on her forehead. She concentrated on that while Jarod was off in the other room with his mother.

Five

"WANNA GET STONED?" he said when he returned.

He led her out the back door and they sat on the mound of concrete that served as a stoop there. After double-checking that the door was shut tight, he sparked up the joint he had lodged behind his ear.

"Smoking outside. That's new," she said.

As he pulled on the joint, his neck stretched forward like he was straining to grab something just out of reach with his teeth. He was concentrating and gave no sign that he'd even heard Cheryl.

"Did the—" She stopped herself. "Your mother suddenly wig out on you or something?"

Jarod shrugged.

"Does Trent know you're here?" he asked, holding the joint out between his thumb and forefinger, pinched inside an okay sign.

"Can we just not talk about Trent?"

"I guess that's a no."

She took a deep pull off the joint and held her breath. "So what if he doesn't?" she said, the smoke leaking out around her words. "I don't belong to him. Really, though. Your mom's got something against me, doesn't she?"

"She's got something against everyone."

"Did she—" She dropped it, reminding herself not to fixate on her paranoia. "Did you guys hire a maid or something?"

"You think we have the money to hire a maid?"

"Everything's so clean."

"She's been getting up off her fat ass every once in a while and doing shit."

"Your mom?"

Jarod nodded. "Since she lost her job."

"Yeah, I heard about that."

He threw her a suspicious glance.

"Trent told me."

Taking a risk, she reached out and patted him on the shoulder, but when his muscles seized up under her touch, she pulled away again.

"The fuckers won't even let her get unemployment. You have to be fired for that."

"Trent said she *was* fired."

"That's because Trent doesn't pay attention. He'll sort of listen, but he's really just looking for something to be pissed about." He gauged her reaction. "Sorry . . . It's true, though."

The tight little smile frozen on her face hid her insecurity. She wasn't sure, but she sensed that she and Jarod were falling into a kind of intimacy. Edging ever closer to admitting that they'd abandoned something—she'd abandoned something—when she'd run off to Sabotage with Trent. "He's a dick," she said. "You can say anything you want to about him. What's this I heard about your mom's knee?"

"It got all swelled up again. What's it called. Gout. And for like a week, she couldn't walk at all."

"That's happened before, though, right? I mean—"

With another shrug, which both downplayed the importance of what he was saying and deflected any further questions from her, Jarod explained, "And they replaced her while she was out because she didn't call in sick. It's not the same as being fired because when they do the paperwork or whatever, they call it 'abandonment.' " He made little quotes with his fingers.

"That sucks."

"Yeah, well, they don't want to have to pay her unemployment."

So, this was why he was working at Rainbow Foods and why he hadn't come around the café much—it really hadn't been Cheryl's whatever with Trent. And this was the reason the dog had to die too. Jarod's whole life was centered around his mom. She understood that she was stretching, that the reasons Jarod had transformed from the lethargic adolescent she'd first met into the serious young man sitting next to her were too complex to be cracked this easily. For a moment, she felt an empathetic urge to raise herself up to his new sober demeanor, but this urge passed quickly, leaving a ghostly regret in its place.

Something rustled in the tree growing through the chain-link fence at the far edge of the yard. When she peered, all she could see were the dense leaves swaying slightly.

"She should go on disability," she said.

"She's not eligible."

"Just look at her! It's not like it's hard to tell she's fucked-up."

"You need insurance and paperwork and shit like that."

"She should sue."

"Cheryl, fuck! Can't you shut up about this for a while?"

Here, she now realized, was the essential difference between Jarod and Trent. Where Jarod sadly wondered at the injustice of it all, letting the world push him in one mystifying direction after another, Trent would know exactly how and why whatever was thwarting him had occurred. He'd know how disability worked. He'd have researched it on the Internet and written to the federal government or the city or the state or wherever for the official forms he needed to file his complaints and get what he wanted. He'd throw a tantrum, fight so long and hard that he no longer remembered who he was fighting against. Anger flared like a match in her. Trent might know how to shout and smash shit up, but Jarod knew how to endure.

The joint in her hand had gone out while they talked. She relit it and took another long drag. The dry leaves crackled. A seed hidden inside popped. She handed it back to Jarod. He was shrinking into himself in the same wounded way he had that afternoon at Sabotage, disappearing into the sweatshirt bulked up around his ears. Moist brown veins crawled up the thin paper as he pulled on the joint, causing it to canoe. Licking his fingers, he concentrated like a different kind of kid than he was, a kid more likely to hulk over model airplanes or die-cast figurines of dwarves and wizards. He delicately ministered to the joint in his hand, rolling it in his fingertips and rubbing spit like lotion into the quick-burning paper.

The world began to soften around the edges. The lights grew brighter and the shadows sank darker. Sounds Cheryl hadn't noticed before—cars roaming the streets, floorboards creaking in the house next door, crickets coming at her from all directions—now echoed like they were on reverb. The rustling she'd heard earlier started up again in the branches above her head. Something up there was restless. The sound faded away, then returned louder, closer, more frantic. There was a crack and a scampering and she saw a shadow fly toward the eaves of the house.

"The squirrels are all worked up about something, huh?" she said.

Jarod shrugged. "It's gonna rain."

"You learn that on the Discovery Channel?"

"Animal Planet. The Discovery Channel does, like, science shows and shit now."

Hilarious. She was definitely stoned. And not too far below his new surface the same gooey Jarod was still there.

The air was thick, but no thicker than usual for summer in the Midwest; it hung there, stagnant and heavy. The clouds floated high and wispy above them, long thick ripples, gray against the black night. What were they? Cheryl had learned their name in sixth grade, but this knowledge had floated away a long time ago. "It doesn't feel like it's gonna rain," she said.

Extending his neck like a turtle out of the cove of his sweatshirt, Jarod shot an arc of spit through the space between his two front teeth and then recoiled back into hiding.

For a while, Cheryl just watched him, contented, pleased to be here in the relatively safe and tranquil place that was his backyard. Then something changed and his mother's sour face began to hover over her, whispering, telling her, You're not wanted here. She reminded herself, it's just the pot. Her brain tingled as the drug's creepers slithered through her consciousness, curled around and strangled the good feelings she'd had.

She needed to move. To go somewhere and come back a different person.

"You want a beer?" she asked. She stood and stretched, her arms over her head, her t-shirt pulling up to expose her navel.

Jarod gave her that shrug of his.

In the kitchen, she spaced out on the refrigerator magnets. Jarod's mom was a fan of the plastic foods: a burger, a tangle of spaghetti, a Coke bottle out of which tumbled a flood of frozen brown liquid. There should have been a splat of fake vomit somewhere but Cheryl couldn't find one. The fluorescent light above the sink was freaking her out. This house was a dank place. The only thing that grew here was sadness.

When she returned to the backyard with the beer, it was drizzling, just as Jarod had predicted. She handed him his can and plopped down next to him. One sip from the beer, and she realized she didn't want it anymore. She set it by her foot. The rain was so soft and warm she could barely feel it.

She lay her head on Jarod's shoulder and stared off into the nothingness.

After a while, her senses sank back into her body. She could smell the clean, earthy fragrance of the mud. Water tapping on the roof. The rustle of leaves like a thumb flicking along a deck of cards.

"What are you gonna do?" she asked, not knowing quite what she meant by the question or why she'd felt the sudden urge to ask it.

He tipped his head and his cheek grazed against her forehead.

"I, uh . . . You've got a thing with Trent."

Holding herself still, she registered the slight upturn in his confidence. If there were a moment to admit the damage she'd done that night, this would have been it. Instead, she said, "I mean about your mother."

He shook her off his shoulder and sipped his beer.

"Mike thinks I should join the Marines with him," he said.

She couldn't tell how serious he was—the glum expression on his face didn't give anything away—but she'd never seen him display a sense of irony. He was gullible. He leaned toward the literal.

"That's a stupid idea." She wanted to say, You should come with me. We'll run away somewhere where the winters aren't twenty below like they are here. We'll go to New Orleans, just like in the song. But it was Trent who'd played the song for her.

"I heard they'll give you ten thousand bucks just for signing up," he said.

"Yeah, and then the next week they send you out to get your head blown off."

He shrugged. "My mom would like it. She could go to the doctor."

"Don't you have to be eighteen?"

"Technically. But what are they gonna do? They're desperate."

Cheryl took his hand and pulled it into her lap like a mother holding her child away from the flames. "It's a bad idea," she said.

The way he gazed at her, his eyes glassy with fear and longing, she was sure he'd do whatever she told him to, be whatever she asked him to be. But then she'd be responsible for what he turned into. He had no willpower of his own. She was going to have to make a decision now, it didn't matter if she was ready or not.

"Are you still stoned?" she asked.

Reluctantly separating his hand from hers, he dug in his pocket for the bag of pot.

She knew she should stop, allow whatever this new thing was with Jarod to remain hypothetical, unreal and deniable, but she didn't want to. She'd done so much damage already tonight that a little more wouldn't matter. You can't ruin something that's already ruined.

There was just one more thing she had to know. "Do you miss your dog?"

He shrugged and shrank back into his sweatshirt. She thought she saw his eyes well up, but he'd hidden his face and she couldn't be sure.

"Don't do that, Jarod . . . I mean—"

"What do you think?"

It was important not to prompt him, to hear it from him without giving him the answers.

"I mean, why didn't you stop them?"

"It was just a stupid dog," he said.

His hands shook as he crumbled dried leaves into the rolling paper cradled between his fingers and she decided this was proof enough.

They stood pressed up against the screen door, under the small aluminum awning that jutted out over the concrete step. The rain was still falling lightly. Neither of them said a word as they smoked, and when the joint was spent, Jarod packed the roach with the others at the bottom of his bag of pot.

And then she had her arm around his waist. She wasn't sure if she was destroying something or creating something, but whatever she was doing, it felt good. For the first time in she couldn't remember how long, she felt okay with herself in the world.

Pulling Jarod by the belt loops, she slipped her hand under his sweatshirt, then his t-shirt. She ran her fingers across his oily back, traced the contours of his ribs.

He was pliant, neither resisting nor reciprocating, and when she kissed him, he melted like water in her hands.

"Let's go inside," she said.

Then, for a long time, neither of them moved.

Six

LATE AT NIGHT, even now after all these years, I lie awake thinking about her. Rewinding and reviewing. Staring at the scattered details like they're cryptograms, like if I find the right piece of missing information, I'll suddenly know where she's gone and what she's doing and how to bring her back home. Everything I'm missing will be revealed.

I see Cheryl and Jarod moving sideways, stumbling over each other's feet, kissing. They rove around the dark mildewed room, two clumsy dancers, unable to synchronize their internal rhythms. One of them slips—it's Jarod, I think, his leg caught in a tangled pile of clothes—and then they're both sprawled out on the mattress, tongues still entwined, limbs curled around limbs.

They're upstairs. Back in the bedroom where she first gave herself to Trent. Jarod's mother is shut into her dark cell, directly below them, snoring, periodically moaning in pain.

Cheryl can hear her, which means it's possible she could hear them shuffling awkwardly on the oily sheet, could hear the shoes dropping to the floor, the groan of the mattress, the creaking wood of the bed frame as they roll onto their sides. When Cheryl unbuckles Jarod's belt, the steel jangles like a door knocker. How much noise would it take to wake the woman? How much would it take to rouse her from her bed and send her hobbling up the stairs?

"Shhh." Cheryl grins at Jarod. Then she whispers, "Have you ever done this before?"

He mumbles, "Sure," his lip trailing along her neck. But he doesn't know what he's doing. His hands are everywhere and nowhere all at once.

She doesn't care. She's not here for him. She's here to decimate her love for Trent, to plaster over the wounds before they fester, not because she thinks she can heal herself but because if she doesn't cover them with something, she'll pick herself bloody and return to him begging for more. Loving him was supposed to fix everything. It didn't. It just added another problem to the list. She's beginning to understand: love doesn't solve anything. Love distracts and disarms you, it whispers and lulls you into a false calm, leaves you unprepared for the next blow when it inevitably comes. She's courting numbness now. She's egging it on.

Outwardly, she's soft and tender, running her fingers through Jarod's short hair, touching the base of his neck, ever so lightly, watching as his body reacts.

He's in pain too. He too is an aching wound. He winces at her every touch. His mother's an unrelenting mess of needs. *Just like mine,* Cheryl thinks. *Just like mine except with mine there's no physical ailment, just an incessant attempt to suck me back in.* Jarod's mother can't do a single thing without his help. He constantly has to be ready, one ear cocked in case she starts bleating out his name. He has to work and cook and clean and he has to rub ointment into her knee. When she's out of Kools, he has to go get them, and if the Mobil station is out of the 100s and he returns with the king size, he has to listen to her berate him. But these aren't the demands that caused his abrasions. These things are easy. These things can be accomplished. What defeats him is the weight of the feelings she throws at him, the diamond-hard gallstones she's constantly flinging, too many to catch and too large to hold. There's no place to put them. They pile up in his arms and around his ankles. They're heavy. They're ugly. And though he knows he's supposed to take them away, he has no idea where to dump them. They chafe and burn and make his skin blister. She doesn't give him her joy—if it exists at all, she keeps it locked up, hidden behind her need. His joy goes there too, snatched away to carve room in him for another load of sadness. The sadness never ends. No matter how much of it he buries in the backyard, under spent marijuana leaves and empty beer cans, she's right there to heap another, even larger, pile into his arms.

Cheryl identifies. She recognizes herself in his behavior. *He is like me and I am like him except I ran away, one day I asserted my right to refuse, and he's still here taking it, he still believes, despite all the evidence, that there's some way for him to fix her,* is what she thinks. If, somehow, she can take some portion of his pain and hold it in the place where she used to tuck mine, her guilt might subside, she, maybe, just maybe, could live with herself.

Caressing his bony, pimply ass, running her fingers through his pubic hair, this is all part of her attempt at atonement.

And lying here in my bed, listening to her cries, I want to scream: *Cheryl, I understand. I'd say I forgive you, but there's nothing to forgive. I don't hold anything you've done against you. You were merely trying to save yourself.* But even if my voice could carry all the way to the place, wherever it is, she's gone, she'd just think I was trying to trick her.

They're naked now, except for the tattoos and piercings. It's almost impossible to stifle the animal sounds rising in them. "Shh," she says again, as much to herself as to him. "What would your mother say if she caught us?"

When she fucked Trent on this bed, they moaned and grunted, Cheryl screamed when he bit her shoulder. They didn't care. They were relenting to a chaos bigger than themselves. But this, here, with Jarod is different. She knows he won't save her or transform her life. He might think she can perform these feats for him, but that's because he's naive and confused by the new sensations flooding his nervous system. She's not even going to try.

He's discovered her breasts, and they enthrall him. He cups them, traces their shape with his palms. He squeezes. His fingernails are ragged and dirty. Then, lunging in, he begins to suck, all lips and no tongue.

"You better not give me a hickey," she says, and she believes for a second she'll return to Trent. If he were to discover what she's done with Jarod, he'd hit her. He'd hurt her. And she'd accept whatever he threw at her. She'd think it was exactly what she deserved.

Jarod's on top of her, slipping back and forth across her pelvic bone, stabbing at her abdomen, the fluid leaking from the tip of his penis, drying into a tacky glue in her pubic hair. He's digging for treasure in all the wrong places, mashing the folds of her vagina first one way, then the other. Things get caught down there. It stings. If she weren't so worried about his mother downstairs, she'd yelp. Instead, she bites her lip and tries to make her winces look like smiles. She balls the sheet up in her hands and squeezes.

The sensitive skin is pinched suddenly tightly, like Jarod's clamped a binder clip across her clit, and she lets out a muffled howl. He freezes, mortified, on top of her.

"Sorry," he says. "Sorry, sorry, sorry."

He holds himself on stiff arms, waiting for directions, hoping she won't demand he give up. His tongue is twisted against his top row of teeth.

"Shh," she says.

"Sorry."

She whispers. "Be careful. It's sensitive."

"I'm sorry."

When Trent asked, she told him, "Yes. It's yours. My pussy belongs to you." She hadn't been lying, but she'd been wrong. He'd just been visiting. Scrawling his name. Now, as she snakes her hand into the crevice between her legs and peels her labia apart, she relinquishes what's left of her belief in him. Even if he tries, he won't get her back.

For a moment, she feels the emptiness. Then, holding Jarod's penis steady with her free hand, she slips him inside herself. She peers up at him. A smile flashes briefly across her face but she can't hold it for long; it doesn't hide anything anyway.

His eyes are shut. He's concentrating. When he moves again, it's with extreme care. She's no longer there—she's an idea in his mind, and this makes things easier; all she has to do is relax and wait.

He slides back—a centimeter? Half an inch? An infinitesimal shifting inside her and she wraps her arms around his shoulders.

She thinks to tell him not to come inside her, but it's too late. He slams forward and collapses. It's over in seconds. He's whimpering now, like a puppy that can't find its mother.

Rubbing his back, holding him as he pants, she runs through the calculations in her head. She hopes she'll be okay, but she's not sure. She doesn't want to end up with Jarod's baby.

He curls around her, kissing her collarbone, already confusing her with the release she's just helped him achieve.

"Let me up," she says. "I have to go to the bathroom."

Quizzical, yearning not to let her go, he releases her and she tiptoes off to wash him out of her. She feels old suddenly, broken, almost like a grown-up. She's sick of being pissed. The sadness is hard enough without making it harder.

She's alone.

She can't give herself away.

Lying next to him later, spooning under the sheet, she feels tenderly toward him. His touch is a comfort, but this changes nothing.

She's still alone.

.   .   .

And when, the next morning, his mother's voice found its way up the stairs—"Jarod? Honey? Where'd you put my aspirin?"—jarring Cheryl out of an anxious sleep, she knew it was time to run away again.

She was too tired, though, and like me, she had nowhere left to go.

Seven

I DIDN'T KNOW exactly where Jarod's house was. It had to be less than half an hour's walk away, and I was sure it was west of the river, in a neighborhood that was flat and pallid and gray. Somewhere in the span just north of Cedar-Riverside. A place where the houses were crushed up together, in need of new paint jobs, where the lawns were choked with weeds and wrapped in chain-link fencing.

This was enough for me to go on. I'd head for the vicinity in my mind and troll systematically up and down each street. There'd be a sign—I knew there'd be a sign—and when I saw it, I'd stop. I'd call Cheryl's name and she'd come running.

What else I'd find there, I wasn't quite sure.

Maybe she was sunk in that harrowed place where the world loses its mass, where the void inside expands and causes hidden corrosion, that place where the people sitting next to you become translucent, half-beings, organisms as simple and motiveless as flagellum. She was curled on the battered couch in Jarod's living room, her head propped on the arm, staring sideways at the dead-bolted and barricaded front door. The TV was off. She was no longer an active agent in her life. She was waiting for the body slam of the future.

Earlier that morning, Jarod had told his mother everything, just like he always did, and she'd responded with an irritated wave. Rolling over in bed, she'd pulled a pillow across her head. Now, I was sure, he was far away, unpacking cartons of mixed vegetables in the frozen-foods aisle of Rainbow Foods. He was jittery, trying to forget that he'd betrayed Trent without tarnishing the glow of what he'd done with Cheryl, torn and reeling and confused by how this thing he'd wanted so terribly much could turn him into such a paranoid wreck.

And his mother sat guard, now, in a wobbly kitchen chair that she had dragged into the room with Cheryl, her bum leg thrust out straight in front of the door, her fingers prying the venetian blinds apart. She was searching the street, not for me, but for Trent. Trent with rocks in his hands, ready to smash the windows. Trent returned to claim what wasn't and had never been his.

Maybe he'd already pounded on the door, back when it had been just Cheryl and Jarod in the room. "Jay, I fucking know you're in there. Fucking let me in." And Jarod, terrified, had shouted back, "Go away, Trent. Just leave. I can't talk to you now." He'd opened the door a crack, pulled the chain taut and peered, one frightened eye framed by slabs of wood. Cheryl lay there limply as Trent's voice shot toward her—"Just let me fucking in, fucking what the fuck, Jay?"—piercing her, or not, she was too numb to tell. "What the fuck," he kept saying. "What the fuck, man. I can see my fucking girlfriend through the window, dick." Then he started slamming his shoulder into the door, rearing back and smashing and rearing back again. "Let me the fuck in! I'll fucking kill you, Jay!"

The house was cheap wood—it came from a box—and with each blow from Trent, it shook on its frame. Jarod tried his best, he shoved back, he braced himself, timing his motions in opposition to Trent's, pushing and pushing until the latch clicked. He slid lock after lock after lock into place.

That's when his mom finally pulled herself from bed. She slipped a rank t-shirt over her head and wedged herself into a pair of sweat-pants. Her hair all a jumble, she limped into the living room. It took her just a second to see what had happened: Jarod slumped by the door, head buried in his knees, Cheryl still splayed out, watching things that weren't there. Though Trent had stopped pummeling his fists into the house, he was still outside, squatting in the dirt. It was a typical scene, one she'd been through before how many hundreds of times with that nothing of a man, Jarod's father.

The ho-bag understood. She knew what to do.

Pulling herself past my daughter's shattered form, she hobbled to the door, nudged her son out of the way. She unlatched the locks and stepped out of the house. She stood over Trent. She watched him pick at the grass. She waited.

Trent might not have respected his elders, but he was scared of them; he was scared of what they represented.

"You done yet?" she asked him. "I can wait all day. Why don't you just let me know when you're done?"

He gazed at her, embarrassment eating at his will, and eventually, defeated, he stood up. His machismo had wilted. For a moment, he was just a gangly kid again. A bad attitude bottled in a dirty face. He slunk off to lick his wounds and she went back inside.

Now, she was ready for him, waiting for his return. As Jarod scurried around Rainbow Foods, unloading boxes of pears and zucchini, and Cheryl continued her numb vigil on the couch, she was doing the thing mothers are supposed to do, attending and enduring and keeping a close watch, preparing to sacrifice whatever it took to ensure that the child was safe.

But instead of Trent, it was me coming this time.

I'd have to thank her. I'd have to stand before her in my shame and allow her to revel in her pride and disgust. This was the price I'd pay to get my daughter back.

And what if Trent was still there, waiting down the street, sitting on the curb, hiding behind a bush? I'd have to be prepared for this possibility too. I imagined Cheryl huddled under my shoulder, her head buried like a perp walking past a camera. We'd race from the house to my open car door, slam ourselves in, hit the locks and roar off. Trent's rocks would fly past us. They'd zing off the bumper, the hatch, maybe shatter a brake light, but I'd get her away. Speeding, running STOP signs, I'd get her away.

Instead of going home, we'd head west toward St. Cloud. We'd stick to the back roads and as we shot through Willmar we'd flip it the bird. We'd keep going past all those monotonous fields of corn until we made our way into North Dakota. Then we'd veer up toward Canada. We'd cross the border, and still we'd keep going, through Manitoba, past Winnipeg, into Saskatchewan and north toward the Arctic. We'd get lost in the tundra, where nobody knew us, where the only wolves we'd hear howling in the night were the kind that walked on four legs.

I drove around for hours searching for Jarod's house. I refused to give up. If I did, I knew, all the things Cheryl believed about me would turn out to be true.

Running low on gas, I pulled into an Exxon station. A rusted-out station wagon with a handicapped sign hanging from its mirror was parked near the mini-mart's entrance. I kept my eye on it as I filled up. Not wanting to cause a scene, I paid at the pump and pulled across the street where I could be more discreet.

The station wagon's owner was a withered woman, maybe forty, but roughly aged so she looked much older. Her blond hair was in tangles and she'd wrapped herself in purple Vikings sweatpants and a windbreaker she'd earned with Marlboro Miles. She walked with a four-footed orthopedic cane, and in her free hand, she carried a bag full of junk food. Jarod's mother. It couldn't have been anyone else. Her left leg, not her right leg, was the one with problems, but still.

I trailed her around a corner, past a small playground and a Lutheran church, until she pulled into the driveway of a cramped Sears house with an enclosed porch. Unkempt hedges lined the perimeter, and broken flower boxes were mounted under the windows. The lawn had been strangled by crabgrass.

Parking, again some distance down the block, I watched Jarod's mother pull herself from the car.

It was all I could do not to jump out and accost her. I had to make sure she understood I was harmless, that I wasn't another maniac like Trent. She was going to be overprotective of Cheryl, and I'd have to show her I was capable, a levelheaded, reasonable adult. My thought was to wait until she was settled inside, then ring the doorbell like a normal person. We'd work things out calmly.

She rummaged in the back of her station wagon for a while, pushing cardboard boxes and water jugs around and pulling out giant, overstuffed Target bags. Given the pain her leg was causing her, she moved with remarkable agility. She favored her good leg, but she was self-sufficient, not once calling inside for Jarod's help.

After she slammed the hatch shut, she paused and glared at me. I waved at her. Then when she refused to stop glaring, I grabbed my purse in case she demanded ID and headed over to talk to her.

"Hi," I said, waving again, awkwardly. "I'm Julia." She was wary, unwilling to give me anything. "Cheryl's mom?" I said.

"I'll tell you right now," she said, "if you're a Jehovah or some kind of God thumper, you can turn around and get right back in that car. And I don't need any Tupperware, either. You can just go right on back where you came from."

"I'm Cheryl's mom," I said again. "I'm here to take her home."

"I don't give a flying shit what you are. I'm not blind. I know you've been following me." She pulled out a cell phone held together with electrical tape, and waving it in my face, she said, "I'll have you know I've got the cops on speed dial."

"I don't think you understand," I said. "I'm Cheryl's mother. Cheryl. Betty. Jarod's friends all call her Betty."

"I don't know any Cheryl Bettys."

"The girl you've got in there."

"There's no girl in there."

The severity of Jarod's mother's attitude made me feel tainted, like I deserved to be despised, and the urge to justify myself was overwhelming. "I handled things badly. I'm sorry. I'm more sorry than I've ever been in my life. I'm going to be better now. I'll do what it is I need to. I'll take the medication. Just let me have her, please. Then I'll leave you alone."

When I tried to touch her arm and reinforce my sincerity, she flailed away. "I don't know what you're talking about, lady, but you need to go now."

"I will. I promise. Just give me Cheryl back. Then we'll both be out of your hair forever."

"Look." She brandished the phone again. "I'm pushing the buttons. The cops are gonna come and they're gonna lock you up." But she didn't push the buttons. Instead, she grinned wickedly.

"I just want my daughter."

"There is no daughter here. I live alone."

"No, you don't! You're Jarod's mother. Trent's friend Jarod."

"I don't know any Jarod. Scoot along, now," she said, flapping her fingers. Her whole body was angled away from me. I repelled her. She was bitter, hateful. She'd given up on the possibility of goodness. "Go!" She was ruthless and I suddenly had to pee.

"Why are you lying to me?!" I screamed. "Why is everybody always lying to me?!" Then realizing what I must look like to her, I said, much more calmly, "Maybe his name's not Jarod, but you've got a son, right?"

A hesitation, and then she said, "Yes."

"And he's friends with my daughter. She ran away from home. Cheryl. She came here last night. She was scared. A short girl, with green or purple or some color in her hair. And she was drunk. She's got a pierced nose too. And lip. And a big ugly tattoo sort of right here on her forearm. I'm her mother. I really am. Here's my license to prove it. I want to take her home. That's all. Please." I sobbed. "Please."

"Listen to me, lady. I've got two sons. Roger's in Iraq with the Army Reserve and Karl lives out by Lacrosse, Wisconsin. You need to go find somebody else to bother."

"No! That's not true! That's completely not true!"

"Go on. Off my yard."

The cell phone still cocked in her fist, she looped her forearm through the handles of her bags and began leapfrogging them toward the house.

"Let me help you." I lunged for her bags, but she twisted them away and swung them haphazardly, like weapons, at me. They pulled her off balance and she fell backward. Her phone went skidding across the driveway. I tried to help her, but she jabbed her cane at me. "Don't you touch me," she said, kicking, dragging herself away.

There was terror on her face and I understood then that she hadn't been lying to me at all. And if she wasn't lying—if I was wrong—how much of the rest of what I knew was wrong too? Again, for the I-don't-know-how-many-thousandth time, I succumbed to the pressure. I couldn't trust myself. I couldn't trust my mind.

See, here's where my story begins to fall apart. The things I suspect and the things I believe and the things I try to tell myself must be true shatter against all the things I'm afraid of, the unspeakable things I refuse to imagine.

I backed away.

I left.

I did the only thing I knew how to do. I called Robert and asked him to save me again.

VIII

My People

One

SOMETIMES, WHEN CHERYL was a very small child, I'd wake in the night knowing she'd had a nightmare. I'd run to her room and arrive before she started screaming. By the time her tears came, I'd be holding her head, smoothing the thin hair along her temples. Her eyes would burst wide open and she'd see my face.

"It's you!" she'd say.

"It's me. I chased the monsters away."

During the three months I was in the hospital, before Cheryl ran off to wherever she went, Dr. Rahajafeeli had me on a cycle of Risperdal and Trazodone. The Trazodone turned my dreams into swirling epic sagas—dreams that cycled through multiple story lines where the ground would fall away or I'd open a door and I'd slip into new, unrelated, frightening scenarios. And Cheryl would be there, lingering just outside of my vision, watching me stumble through dungeon after dungeon. She held a mirror in her hand, and when I was in trouble, she'd raise it above her head, bending the light toward me. This time it was her chasing my monsters away.

Halfway through my stay, Robert brought her to visit me. He waited in a chair in the twelve-foot span of hallway on the other side of the ward's locked door so she could see me alone. I don't know what he told her to expect, but she looked stricken—brow furrowed with tension, arms clutched tight around herself—as she was being buzzed in.

People here didn't get visitors too often and some of the other patients in the ward were curious about her. They sat on the molded red and blue plastic chairs chained to the walls, or peered out from behind the doorways of their rooms: Raymond, who'd only recently been homeless—his hands shook and his face was nicked with cuts from when they'd shaved him. Trish, prim in her gleaming gold patent leather shoes, so ominous under her hospital gown. And Kim, and Pablo with the bandages on his wrists, and Terrance and Lewis and Sam. And Rachael, who thought she was Joan of Arc, and Dylan, not much older than Cheryl herself, who looked perfectly normal until you noticed the hundreds of small round scabs—crusty and angry—from where he'd pressed lit cigarettes into his skin attempting to kill the ants he'd seen crawling there. While I led Cheryl past them, she held her head stiff, like a dog with a cone latched around its neck.

Ward rules dictated that doors remain open throughout the day, and the more skittish patients had nowhere to hide. They cowered on their beds or at the small blond desks under their windows. They were as scared of her as she was of them.

We were almost at my room when Peter Langenfelt, tall and way too skinny, wandered toward us. He held his weight low and even, which made him look like he was gliding. Stopping in front of us, he leaned forward on stiff knees and scrutinized Cheryl. She flinched, catching herself before she recoiled, and strained her lips into a tight smile.

"Blessed," said Peter. "Walk in peace." His hair was dirty, feathered down the middle. It hung in his eyes and tumbled over his shoulders.

"Cheryl," I said, "this is Peter." I held her elbow and eased her back a step. She was spooked, I could tell, and I worried that if I tried to comfort her, I'd trigger an outburst in Peter. "My daughter, Cheryl," I told him in warning. "She's come to visit."

"We've been waiting for you. We knew you would come," he said. Instead of the standard pale-blue hospital gown, he wore a stained floor-length bathrobe tied shut with a sash around the waist. "So blessed and beatific. So pure and sweet," he said.

Cheryl let him cup her hand between his palms. When he leaned in to kiss it, his sash slipped and his robe fell open. He was naked beneath it, his penis jutting out half erect, and he had her tight by the wrist.

She twisted and pulled, still trying to stay calm.

"Peter," I said. I'd seen Dr. Rahajafeeli mollify him with this tone of voice, level and stern, somehow fixed, unquestionable. "Let us past now. We need to go to my room."

But he held on, squeezed tighter, and Cheryl yelped in fear and suddenly two orderlies were running toward us, grabbing Peter's arms and twisting them behind his back, towing him off to lock him in his room. As the door slammed shut, he shouted, "See what you've done?!"

I wondered how she was comprehending all this, if her compassion was large enough to recognize these people—my people—as something more than other. To see them as I did. They were human beings at the edge of the dream, too wise for their own good, no longer able to fake conformity. These were the people who came to me in the night, whose voices I couldn't push out of my head. They were brave and they deserved to be treated with dignity. The thing that hurts most is other people's fear.

"Okay?" I said.

She nodded. She didn't look at me.

Placing a palm lightly on the small of her back, I tried to make a joke. "Welcome to my world," I said. It didn't get a smile.

When we reached my room, I sank onto the bed. "This is a hard place."

"I know," she said.

"The people here—"

"I know, Mom."

Finally, she looked at me. She wouldn't sit. She stood in front of me, scrutinizing the room, an empty box with a barred window at one end. Decorating the walls were the pictures I'd drawn, five, ten a day, with the crayons they'd given me, each one a crude portrait of her.

All the things I'd been hoping to tell her seemed stupid and obvious, trite in comparison with the broken fact of my confinement.

"I should go, Mom," she said after a while. "Dad's out there waiting for me."

I panicked. It seemed like something should have changed, something should have been released before her visit with me ended.

"Can—" I said. "Do you think maybe—there's a candy machine in the TV room and—but I—they don't let me have any money. You don't think, could you maybe give me a dollar? I've wanted a candy bar since the day I got here."

All I knew how to do was take from her. And this one last time, she gave me what I'd asked for. She slid a finger into the pocket of her jeans, pulled a crumpled bill out and laid it in my hand. Then she ducked away.

She didn't visit again.

Where is she now? She might be huddled on a sidewalk somewhere, in some distant downtown, alone, covered in soot, trying to scare up enough change for one more stab at oblivion.

It doesn't matter.

I try not to wonder.

Sometimes I think maybe she'll show up in Plymouth and knock at my door. She'll say, "Mom, I'm not afraid. I know who I am now. I can care for you."

I know that's not true, though. I understand what happened. Searching for a way not to become me, she followed her black flag over the edge of the earth. She's never coming back.

Acknowledgments

Thanks are due to the MacDowell Colony, Ledig House/Art Omi, and the Joanne Frank Home for Impoverished Writers, where much of this novel was written and rewritten.

To Lisa Dierbeck, Gordon Haber, Mike Heppner and Jeremy Mullem, who read drafts of this book with much-needed critical insight; to Elizabeth Senja Spackman, whose memory of the Minneapolis streets proved essential; and especially to Ben Schrank and Elizabeth Weinstein, who indulgently allowed me to show them every, sometimes unreadable, version of the work in progress.

To Richard Abate, who protects me.

And to Gary Fisketjon and Liz Van Hoose, as well as the rest of the staff at Knopf; a writer couldn't ask for a more supportive team.

"*A near-magical collection. . . . This is a book that will stay with you for a long, long time.*"
—The Miami Herald

SHORT PEOPLE

In this acclaimed debut collection, James Michener Fellowship winner Joshua Furst explores the perils and paradoxes of childhood in ten harrowing, moving, and surprising stories, offering a rare and unsentimental depiction of the lives of American youth. In "The Age of Exploration," two boys experience the world so differently—Billy through science; Jason with fantastical powers of imagination—that they sense their lives will stray irrevocably away from each other. In "Red Lobster," which won the Nelson Algren Award, a gaggle of children try to please the father who has rounded them up from their various homes to take them to a fateful dinner. And in the collection's climactic story, "Failure to Thrive," a maternity ward nurse takes compassion too far. Emotionally astute, brilliantly written, these stories mark the arrival of a powerful new voice in American literature.

Fiction/Short Stories/978-0-375-71407-8